SHIABA

By
Willie Orr

ISBN: 978-1-914399-32-9

Printed and bound by Ingram Spark
Cover Design © 2023 Mercat Design, images courtesy of
Dreamstime. All Rights Reserved

SPARSILE
BOOKS

To Jan with love

Prologue

There is no road to Shiaba. A grass track serves the isolated, island settlement. Twelve houses, not quite in a row, their dry stone walls a yard thick and no higher than a man, corners rounded to spill the storms, base stones bigger than a bullock, squat on a remote hillside defiantly facing the sea and the twin peaks of Jura.

The men who built them with their bare hands chose well, settling on a stretch of kind, fertile land. Behind them, the heather slopes of Cruachan Min gave summer grazing for their black cattle, the beasts which were their living and paid the rent. In front, a steep drop down to the rocky shore and, to the east, the wild cliffs of Carsaig. Two small windows, facing the sea, gave some light to the dim interior where the beasts shared space with the people.

No English was heard round the hearthstones or out on the peat banks. There was the sweet scent of peat smoke and butter milk, the groans of hand-mills and thud of churns, the taste of ewe cheese and bere bannocks. They built a school for their children and then a mill for their corn. More than twenty families lived here until the winter of 1846.

Now there are none. Only the stout walls of the houses stand as a monument to the Gaels who built them. Nothing remains of the roofs and grass grows over the hearthstones. An air of melancholy pervades the ruins as if the people, when departing, had left their sorrow in the stones. This is their story.

1

Catherine knelt by the hearthstone in the middle of the floor, idly stirring the stew over the peat fire and waiting for Calum to bring in potatoes for the pot. She was looking forward to that—potatoes straight from the beds, still smelling of earth. Smoke from the fire curled round the pot and floated up towards a gap in the thatch above her. She thought of Calum out in the cold dusk, bent over the beds, his fingers smeared with freezing soil, while she was warm, sheltered from the frost by yard-thick stone walls. She glanced at the children, Mary absorbed in combing wool for spinning, Archie making circles with a stick in the ashes. They were precious to her, having seen so many perish after birth.

She was startled when Calum flung open the door and stood frowning at his hands as if there was blood on his fingers, as if he sought an explanation. Bewildered, she thought, like a child. That's what she liked about him, his innocence, his tendency to be amazed by simple things—a butterfly wing or an agate polished by the sea. Yet his frown betrayed more than bewilderment. Shock perhaps, fear even.

'They're all gone,' he said.

She stopped stirring the stew and watched him.

'What are you talking about?'

He rubbed his fingers together, trying to remove some filth.

'The potatoes. Every one, Catherine. Just a mass of grey slime.'

'Nonsense, Calum. Some of them maybe. Not the lot.'

A ripple of worry troubled her thoughts, a brief disturbance of her calm temperament. She was sure the flame of the tallow light flickered. She glanced at the two children on either side of her to see if they had noticed. Mary still absorbed in combing, Archie with his stick in the ashes. In the rafters above her a hen shook itself and a fine feather fell into the peat embers, flaring momentarily and lighting their faces.

She heard footsteps outside and Robert, their neighbour, burst in, breathless and barely able to speak, his eyes wide and his lips flecked with foam. The children leapt to their feet and ran over to Calum.

'It's the plague!' he wheezed. 'God save us all!'

'What? What is it? Calm yourself, Robert,' said Calum

'The plague that hit Ireland. Dying in droves they are, the poor people. I've heard the stories, Calum. The potatoes rotting in the ground. The poor with nothing to eat. Bodies by the roadside, their mouths full of nettles and grass. Whole families dying in their cabins, their skin clinging to their bones like parchment. Dying in thousands. Terrible, terrible scenes.'

'Enough, Robert! We have heard the stories.'

'The same. The same pestilence. Famine and fever following. In the name of God, Calum, what are we to do? What is to become of us?'

'We will be all right. We will. Go home now. We will talk later.'

Catherine watched the two men, Calum with his arms round the children, Robert with his hands clutched in prayer as if his end were imminent. She was glad that she had chosen the steady one. Robert turned and scuttled out of the house, forgetting to shut the door. Catherine rose and, limping slightly after kneeling for so long, walked over and shut it. The layer of peat smoke in the roof space under the thatch swung in the draught. The beasts in the far end of the house stirred and grunted behind the sack-cloth partition.

'Sit, Calum and tell me what is happening.'

She reached up above the table, turned up the wick of the lantern and sat down, waiting. He led the children to the fireside and joined her.

'Robert is right. Every one turned to slime, grey stinking slime.'

He looked down to examine his hands again as if to confirm that the putrid remains of the tubers were still there.

'Not all of them surely,' she said. 'Some must be free of it.'

'Hardly any. It's the Irish pestilence right enough.'

'But how can it cross the sea? '

'God knows. Maybe the Islay men going to Ballycastle for horses. Maybe the gulls carry it. Maybe it comes with the rain. I don't know.'

She stared into the lantern, thinking of what Robert had said and imagining the bodies of the poor rotting in their houses. It could not happen here, surely. She turned to look at the children and thought of them starving, crying for meal when there was none.

'How much corn is left, Catherine?'

She rose and lifted the lid of the kist.

'Not enough. Not without potatoes anyway. A few weeks. No more. If you had planted more corn last spring, there would be more.'

'How was I to know the potatoes would fail? It was a grand crop in the summer. Better than ever. If it had not been wasted, there would be more than enough.'

'Will we starve, mother?' Mary asked from the fireside.

'No,' Calum answered. 'We will find a way.'

Catherine closed the kist.

'What way, Calum?'

'I don't know. We could sell the cow.'

'And what would the children do for milk? At least they have milk. No, not the cow.'

Mary stood and hurried over to her father.

'And not the calf either. You' re not to sell the calf. My calf. You won't, will you?

'No, Mary. Not yet anyway.'

Catherine was touched by the worry in her face, the way her eyes pleaded with her father, searching for the soft spot in his nature. A clever girl, forthright and open. She was proud of her, particularly when she argued with her father. Her mind always seemed to be a step ahead of his, not that he was simple. She noticed her bare feet and thought she should get the cobbler to make her some shoes but then remembered the failure of the crop.

'There's the note from the drover,' Calum said, running his fingers through the girl's hair, 'promising to pay for the stirk when he comes back from the tryst. We could sell it for meal.'

'That's the rent. For God's sake, Calum. The Factor will have us evicted, if we don't pay.'

'I will go to the kelp.'

'The kelp is finished. They don't need our kelp in the south. They have new ways. And they don't need our cattle either. They have their own breeds for their navy. The big droves will never be seen again. All gone, Calum. The things that helped us in the past can't help us now. We should have gone to Canada with John MacGillivray like I said.'

She was quite breathless when she finished and surprised by her own vehemence,

Calum slapped the table, the sudden reaction startling Mary who stepped back.

'I will not leave Shiaba! I've told you before. This is my home. The people built this house for my father when he was married. He broke this ground and cleared the stones from the rigs with his bare hands. He lifted stones that no other man in the township could move. He carried white sand from Kilvickeon and seaweed from the shore for the potato beds. He could have fed three families with his crops. He is buried here and his father too and my mother. I will never leave, Catherine. I have tilled this soil since I could lift a spade. It is under my nails, in my skin, part of me and I am part of it. The only way I will leave is in a coffin.'

'And that, Calum, is precisely the way you may go. But not you alone remember.'

A silence, like a shroud, settled between them. Catherine found her hand shaking. He was so stubborn at times yet she admired him, the way he could snatch words out of his head to express his passion. Infuriating, though, his clinging to the land when there was so much more promise in Canada. He would stay. She knew that. Even if she and the children grew weak with hunger and the hunger sickness, even if the pains of starvation twisted his face like a gargoyle. A worrying thought struck her—what if she had to choose between staying with him and leaving with the children to save their lives? She imagined him standing outside the door as she walked away with the children, Mary barely able to walk and weeping for her father and Archie sick with the fever. It would not come to that, surely.

§

A solitary figure in the amber dawn, he stood staring down at the freshly turned earth. Faint plumes of peat smoke rose from the scattered row of houses set on an escarpment high above the sea. Every house, built of stone and fashioned with rounded corners, defiantly faced the south-west gales that ripped up the firth from Jura. In the east, the sun stained the cliffs and the wings of the gulls on the shore. Behind him the slopes of the summer grazings glistened with webs in the heather. He bent down and lifted what seemed to be a healthy tuber but the outer skin cracked in his fingers and grey slime oozed between them. Flinging the scum away and shaking the dregs off his hand, he stooped again and found a small tuber which was unaffected. He smiled, placed it in his pocket and searched for another. There was hope. Then he remembered the small tubers were next year's seed. If they ate them, there would be no crop at all.

As he bent over the beds, sweat moistened his thin beard and mucus gathered on the peak of his pointed nose. As he moved his feet, his boots clung to the wet soil, making him stagger. A sturdy man with features carved by his years of battling with the weather and skin creased by the wind yet, in spite of the rugged jaw, there was a softness in his eyes, a dreaminess that Catherine, when they met in Uisken, had found irresistible.

Determined to prove her wrong, that they could survive the failure of the crop, he scraped in the soil for healthy tubers with his frozen fingers. They had coped with famine before, the people of Shiaba, and they would cope again, sharing their grain and what they saved from the summer. Yet he remembered the letters from the men who had sailed for Canada. He had read them carefully.

> *Lott 22, Lloydtown P.O., King, UC*
> *Dear Calum, I have seen John*
> *MacGillivray who left Shiaba you may*
> *remember in 1845 going to Owen Sound where*
> *he has now bought 200 acres of land—all*
> *paid down cash— 2 cows, 8 sheep, a yoke of*

oxen and a new waggan—the waggan which
would cost about £20—and bought since
another 100 acre. Archy his son has told me
he saved himself £100 besides clothes and
other expenses. Tell Rachel that I have seen
her brothers and sisters and all are well. I was
this day thrashing to Malcolm and he has as
much wheat as would feed all the inhabitants
of Kilvickeon parish. I do not rue anything
but the scarcity of Gaelic preachers. My
compliments to all my old neighbours and I
hope that I shall see a good number of them
inhabiting Canada yet for there is no Factor,
Ground Officer nor Donald Drover here to
meddle with you—beanachd uile uchdo Donal
Drover.

   Yours faithfully, Archie MacGillivray.

He had been tempted. Canada seemed to be a country of freedom, opportunity, promise. He had imagined himself felling tall pine trees, clearing the land and ploughing with a pair of oxen. Yet he had chosen to stay to prove that it could be done, to prove that he was better than the men who had left. He turned and stared out over the sea. This was different, a new threat, inexplicable, mysterious like the aurora, but also perilous. He had known hardship when the corn crop failed but there had always been potatoes. Without them his wife and children would starve. He had to do something.

He thought of Catherine, remembering her expression as she nursed their first child, the love and enchantment in her blue eyes, the tenderness with which she offered her breast, the way the fine down on her cheek glistened in the lamplight. He had never seen anything as beautiful as her that night. A lock of her long, fair hair, hanging over one brow as she looked down at the child. The hint of a smile on her lips. He had wanted to kiss them, but, feeling that any movement would shatter the perfection of that moment, he had remained where he was, seated in front of her, mesmerised.

He remembered when they met on the shore at Uisken, their shoes sinking into the shell sand, he had noticed her bare ankles above shoes in need of a cobbler. He had wanted to buy her some warm stockings. He had seen her before sometimes, digging the heavy land of her potato beds in Ardtun or bent under a creel of seaweed. She never seemed to cover her hair, even in the rain, but let it blow in the wind. Vanity, her neighbours said. They regarded her with sympathy and suspicion— sympathy because she had been left to care for her blind mother, suspicion because she didn't attend the kirk.

'I hate that voice of hers,' one of them had said. 'So loud and the way she says every word so carefully as if we were from another country.'

But he knew her reason. He had heard her explain to the teacher when her first-born went to school and the pupils were startled by her voice.

'It's a habit,' she said. 'When my father was drowned and I was left with my mother. I became her eyes, telling her what I saw, what I was doing, what I heard, everything. I was only eight then and thought that she might be deaf as well as blind. I couldn't think of the difference.'

He had not been deterred by her strangeness. As they walked up the shore, he had tried to memorise the features that pleased him—the eyes the colour of cornflowers, the insolent tilt of her nose, the glistening of the fine rain on her hair. He had noticed her hands as they gripped her shawl—a mother's hands, strong and nurturing.

There were three other women at the high tide mark, but they had turned away to avoid her.

'They have no time for me,' she told him. 'I don't walk with them to the kirk. Not since my father's funeral. The minister had blamed us for his drowning. A punishment for our sins. Our grief a test of our faith. I never went back.'

He remembered the flush of anger in her cheeks as she spoke and her strident tone. He had decided then that he would ask her to marry him.

Now he would have to find a way of protecting her, her and the children.

2

Charles Trevelyan stood at window of his spacious office in the Treasury, gazing out at the wet London streets and remembering India, particularly the steep, wooded hills of Simla and the snow-capped mountains beyond. He watched a horse-drawn carriage in the street below crash against a wagon loaded with bales, their wheels grinding against each other. The driver of the wagon leapt down, his drenched hair clinging to his cheeks, and tried to haul the liveried horseman of the coach off his perch. The latter raised his whip, lashed his attacker across the face and drove on. Charles saw a stream of blood slide down the man's face. Just desserts, he thought, as he slid his pocket watch out of his waistcoat pocket. George late again.

Trevelyan was still young for his position as Assistant Secretary at the age of thirty-two, but his diligence and zeal, his sense of propriety and justice and his precocious ability had earned him a reputation as an outstanding Civil Servant. He was aware, however, that his new position might not have been secured without the help of his wife's brother, Thomas MacAulay. The possibility irked him somewhat as he would have preferred to have won it entirely on merit. Still, the thought of his wife warmed him and he smiled, the corners of his drooping mouth almost causing a dimple. He was always sorry to leave the house in Clapham, although he enjoyed the brisk walk to Whitehall. An athletic figure with the stride of a countryman, he cultivated an air of superiority so that labourers in the street would recognise immediately that he was a man of importance. His handsome face nestling in his auburn whiskers and long, but carefully groomed hair, would have attracted attention anyway.

At last there was a knock at the door.

'Come,' he said, once again producing his watch so that George would notice.

'Sorry I'm late, sir. I had to call at the House.'

'Punctuality, George, is next to Godliness. I was writing letters here till three o'clock this morning and could still be here on time.'

His secretary, a short, stout man with a doleful face, bowed his apology.

'Of course, sir. There is disturbing news from Scotland which I think you should hear.'

'The potato crop has failed?'

'How did you know, sir?'

'It was obvious. The blight was so infectious in Ireland it was bound to reach Scotland.'

'It's a mystery the way it spreads—like a plague.'

'The ways of the Lord are mysterious, George. It might well be a punishment for the indolence and superstitious nature of the Irish natives and their rebellious priests. It is certainly an opportunity, an opportunity to reform the whole system of agriculture and land holding in that infernal country. The Celts in Scotland are different, however, inferior like the Irish but not as bloodthirsty or rebellious, though just as idle.'

'It is a wealthier nation, sir, with a professional class, men of business and substance.'

'Indeed. Indeed. But the natives in the Highlands and islands are as dependent upon the potato as the Irish. We can't let the Highlandmen starve, George. They make good soldiers and besides Her Majesty has a special affection for them. We will not have a repetition of the chaos in Ireland last year. I suspect the Treasury will once again have to carry the burden, but again the people must not be allowed to become parasites, relying entirely on our generosity. They must learn to work. We must use the famine to educate them in habits of industry and self-reliance. Do the reports from Scotland indicate the extent of the infection?'

'Almost widespread, sir.'

'And the grain harvest?'

'Seems reasonably successful.'

'That is a blessing. I want full reports from Scotland on the state of industry, the harvest, the potato failure. Use the ministers of the church, they are always a good source of information.'

'I have a report of a Parochial Board meeting in the Ross of Mull sent by the Duke of Argyll. It makes worrying reading. Written in August, it refers to "the calamitous state of the parish from the total failure of the potato crop". They estimate that they are going to have to place a tax of three hundred pounds on the parish by October. They asked the Duke's ground officer to procure five or six bolls of meal for the "famishing population" but he refused.'

'Did he indeed? I hope the Scotch proprietors are not going to be as mean as the landed class in Ireland. I may have to embarrass them into playing their part.'

'The local Board did authorise the Inspector of the Poor to issue letters for those in absolute want.'

'I must have a comprehensive report on the situation, George, as soon as possible.'

'Yes, sir. This split in the Church of Scotland. I understand it was over patronage. Is that correct? The new church rejects the influence of the proprietors.'

'Yes. Rebellious priests again. No wonder the Lord has visited the plague upon them. The people in the pews seem to have followed the rebels.'

'In large numbers, particularly in the Highlands.'

'More difficulties. Get the Church to write to the ministers who remain then, and the Poor Boards. I must have all the information. Any other sources you can think of. Even a list of the rebel priests.'

'Yes, sir. I'll see to that.'

'Thank you, George. You may go.'

Charles stood in thought for a moment. When he had accepted the position, he had not anticipated famine in his jurisdiction. Rebellion he had predicted in Ireland but not starvation.

And now Scotland. Still, he would face up to the challenge. With God's help he would overcome the catastrophe in Ireland and the crisis looming in the far north. Somehow he would use God's affliction to improve the lot of these primitive natives by leading them out of their squalor into a better way of life, a life of industry and dignity. It would be an immense task and he would have to sacrifice his time with Hannah and their children.

The famine in Ireland last year had not been handled well. It had been a mistake to buy Indian corn from America. The hordes of Irish poor descended on the grain stores like locusts, relieving the more prosperous ratepayers of their responsibilities. He imagined the skeletal mobs, their clothes filthy and tattered, their eyes wild with rage and hunger swarming round the depots, screaming abuse at the soldiers guarding the doors. He crossed to his desk and, flicking up his coat tails in a business-like manner, sat on the hard, upright chair that he had chosen in place of the comfortable leather armchair which he had found there. Lifting his pen, he addressed a letter to Sir Randolph Routh, chairman of the Relief Commission in Ireland, ordering the cessation of all public works and issue of meal.

These things should be stopped now or you run the risk of paralyzing all private enterprise and having this country on you for an indefinite number of years.

He was determined to avoid the chaos of last year when Peel had been in charge. He arranged that all correspondence on the Irish famine arrived unopened on his desk. He was the best person to take the necessary—and sometimes unpopular—decisions. He had been frustrated by the incompetence and failure of officials in Ireland and by the primitive state of the country. When the Indian corn arrived from America, there were not enough mills to convert it to meal. When he arranged for Admiralty ships to deliver meal to the West, the harbours were unnavigable. The Irish landlords were largely insolvent. The Poor Law guardians refused to help the starving people, claiming that they were bound by law to provide assistance only within the workhouses. When he ordered that landlords refusing to subscribe to relief funds should be identified and have to account for their failure to the Lord Lieutenant, local relief committees were unwilling to help.

It was a great relief to him when Peel resigned and had been replaced by Sir John Russell, a man whose views on political economy were closer to his own. The free market should be left to operate independently with no interference by the state. His plan for Ireland reflected this incontestable creed. His new plan decreed that no meal was to be provided by government, except perhaps to the most destitute districts. Irish arable farmers and corn dealers could provide for the hungry masses. Local relief committees were to provide work for the starving masses, the government providing a ten-year loan which the ratepayers would have repay.

He was pleased with his plan and dismissed the letters of dismay arriving on his desk from Ireland, even brushing aside an article in The Times which wondered why "the authorities cut off supplies with the undisputed fact of an extensive failure of this year's potato crops staring them in the face."

The reports of corn harvest failure were exaggerated to frustrate his plan.

Clearly these people did not understand the position. The Irish had created their own crisis with the sloth of the peasantry, the avarice and irresponsibility of the landlords, the incompetence of the administration and the troublesome priests—so the Lord had seen fit to test them. They must find their own solution. Now he had to deal with Scotland.

3

Catherine opened the meal kist and tried to calculate how much grain it contained and how little she could use every day to make it last the three months before Christmas. She dipped her hands together into the corn and lifted them, cupping them tightly to avoid spillage. At three handfuls a day, not counting herself, they might last until then with some milk and shellfish from the shore. She carried the last handful over to the hand mill, spilled it into the hollow and knelt to grind it. She could have used the clack mill up the hill, but the burn that drove its blades was always dry when she needed it. She preferred her own quern. As she spun the granite stone she thought of the letters from Canada.

She imagined the family living on their own farm, Calum striding behind a yoke of oxen as he ploughed new land for maize, Mary leaving for school with books under her arm, Archie teasing a squirrel and herself … yes, herself. What would she be doing in the new country? Not grinding her own corn but sending a cart to the mill. Not counting every handful of grain but watching a pile grow in the store after the harvest. But thinking of Canada brought another vision—Archie crying with hunger pains, Mary's face emaciated and pale as death, Calum gaunt and fearful and herself … would she die of starvation or the famine flux? Her hand stopped turning the stone. It might happen. The whole family could die, their flesh rotting like the potatoes, their bones scraped clean by rats. She shivered and spun the stone furiously to wipe out the image.

She would have to speak to Calum again, try to persuade him to consider leaving Shiaba. Calum. Adorable at times, infuriating at others. She remembered meeting him on the shore at Uisken when one of the emigrant ships was anchored in the bay. He had been standing with his hands in his pockets, watching the last skiff pull away from the sand and shaking his head, his brow creased in what she thought might be bewilderment. There had been a glint of sorrow in the corner of his eye.

'Your neighbours?' she said, nodding towards the skiff as it headed for the tall ship anchored in the bay.

He did not answer immediately but turned slowly to look at her.

She was shocked by the expression of anger in his eyes, just a glimpse, a momentary flash of fury, which softened immediately he saw her.

'No. Friends. From Saorphin.'

'Sad to see them leave.'

'They have nothing. They sold everything to pay the passage.'

'Brave. Must take courage to leave everything behind and sail to a new life.'

'Brave or foolish. They could have stayed. Just because they were in arrears. A bad harvest, a bit in arrears and he takes fright. One bad harvest. I don't understand it.'

She turned as she heard the mainsail of the ship drop and flap in the breeze.

'Perhaps they believe they will find a better life in Canada.'

'In the freezing wastes? Felling trees with trunks as thick as a house and hauling out roots to clear the land? Building a cabin with freezing rain running down your back and your fingers so cold you can't feel them. The rigs so thick with ice you can't sew seed.'

She remembered that vision of his—so very different from hers—but also his passion, the way he could find words so easily, the way his beard shook as he spoke. The speed with which his green eyes changed from fury to kindness as he finished his tirade took her by surprise, as though he suddenly emerged from himself to find her in front of him and to admire what he found. He did not try to hide his appreciation, so much so that she had blushed.

She finished grinding the grain and brushed the meal into a bowl. Not much meal for all her effort.

Walking out into the sunlight to check on the children, she looked down at the shore where Calum had gone to fish. He was not a fisherman, at least not a successful one. She found Mary behind the house in the potato beds, struggling with a fork and searching in the rigs.

'What are you doing, Mary?'

'Look! I've found some, some good ones, but they're very small.'

She came down and held out her hands, which were black with earth. In her palms were four small tubers.

'Next year's seed, child. We can't eat them. Not yet anyway.'

As she spoke, she saw Robert hurrying down the hill. Clearly, he had been to the village in Bunessan. He was quite breathless when he arrived.

'Good news, Catherine. They're giving out meal, meal in exchange for work.'

'Is this the Factor?'

'No, no. The board. Half a pound of meal a day and a half crown a week for cheese.'

'Not much, but better than nothing. I'll tell Calum.'

'Yes, yes. And I must tell Janet. Great news.'

He scuttled away. Always busy, always bent forward as if there was someone behind him threatening his life. Calum walked upright with a rolling gait like a seaman, although he hated the sea.

'We're going to get meal, mother?'

She had forgotten about Mary.

'So he says, Mary. We'll see.'

She looked along the row of houses to see if any other women were out, but she could only see Cath Boyle and Mary Beaton at the far end and she did not feel like walking down there. It was a warm autumn day and the sea below glittered in the sun. She sat by the doorway, her back against the stone wall. The green bracken near the shore was already stained the deep russet of winter. It was good news about the work. Perhaps they could survive after all. She looked towards Ireland and wondered how the disease could have crossed the sea. A mystery. Maybe it was a punishment from God. She never went to church now, except for festivals and funerals. Neither did Calum. Perhaps they should go. Yet she knew that Calum would scoff at the suggestion. She was still sitting there when Calum sauntered up the slope.

'Well, well. Her ladyship has time to sit in the sun.'

'I was waiting for you to bring back a string of saithe.'

'It's too bright for fishing.'

She laughed. Always an excuse.

'Robert says there is to be work in Bunessan. Work in return for meal.'

'Work for the Factor?'

'He says it is for the board.'

'You wait. The Factor will take it over. He takes over everything.'

'We need the meal. There is not enough to see us to Christmas.'

He said nothing but walked past her into the house. She did not rise to her feet but sat and watched a ship in full sail on the western horizon, imagining herself leaning over the rails as she and Calum sailed to Canada with the children. The

Canada described in the letters was not the one Calum had in mind. There seemed to be hope there and freedom. She had just made up her mind to speak to him again when the schoolmaster arrived. A tall, gaunt man with lank, silver hair and an infectious smile. There was no smile there today. In her hurry to stand she staggered, and he reached for her arm to steady her. She was annoyed with herself, thinking he might see her as weak and lazy.

'Ah Mrs MacGillivray, I'm glad I found you. I needed to speak with you.'

'I'm sorry, Mr MacInnes. I was dreaming.'

'I hope it was a pleasant one. Not like mine at the minute. Nightmares too often. Anyway I have come to tell you that I will be closing the school.'

She was shocked.

'Why? You're not ill, I hope.'

'No. I'm well, thank you. I can't continue. I cannot accept payment from people on the edge of catastrophe. There are no potatoes, the harvest was poor, stirk prices dire. The people will need every scrap of food this winter and they have their rents to pay. A bleak, bleak outlook. I cannot add to the hardship.'

'This is dreadful, Mr MacInnes. What are we to do?'

'Mary is a bright girl. It would be a tragedy if her schooling was neglected.'

'It is a long walk to Bunessan, specially in the winter.'

'It will be worth it, I assure you. I'm truly sorry, but my conscience will not allow me to continue.'

'What will you do?'

'I'll go to Glasgow. I should be able to find a position there, even as a tutor to an opulent merchant's child.'

'I'm so sorry. It's a terrible loss to us all.'

'There's a fearful time ahead, mistress. You should think of Canada or Australia. This land could become another Ireland with famine, disease, death.'

'Calum will never leave.'

'Think of the children. There is no future for them here. There is opportunity in the new world.'

'I know. I will speak to Calum again.'

'Now I must go and tell the others. God be with you, Mrs MacGillivray.'

'And you.'

She watched him walk away, leaving her shaken and rigid with fear. The full horror of the famine ahead became a reality. She stood with her arms clasped across her breast, staring blankly at the sea, seeing only the scenes that Robert had described.

4

John Campbell, the Factor for the Duke of Argyll, sat at his desk, twirling the feather of his quill in his fingers, his heavy brows so weighted with concentration that they almost obscured his eyes. Composing a letter in which he wanted to describe the destitution in the districts under his supervision without revealing that he might be responsible for it, involved a careful choice of words. Known locally as the 'Factor Mor', he was indeed a tall man with long lugubrious face and a beard and moustache which, like a muffler, combined to hide his mouth. He knew that his loyalty to the Duke and his determination to improve the estate on Mull, Iona and Tiree made him unpopular with the lower class of tenant, but he dismissed their distaste with contempt. His farm at Ardfenaig was sufficiently removed from the village to allow him privacy.

He gazed out of the window, watching his cows tossing hay off the frozen ground. They were in good condition and it was half way through winter. Christmas Eve in fact. He lifted the letter which he had penned to the Duke and read it through.

I am sorry to say the destitution here and Tyree is much greater than you can possibly imagine, several have fallen victim to famine. I was necessitated to reserve a large amount of our drainage money for Tyree to save the lives of the inhabitants. From there the various accounts I have received are beyond description. Unless something definite be entered into in taking a loan under the Drainage Act or otherwise I much fear the consequences. I shall in the meantime do everything to induce the people there and in the Ross to emigrate, although I fear it will be the best off who will go.

Seed corn and seed potatoes they will not have for a great portion of both is consumed already. I have given instructions to all and sundrae to prepare the ground for sewing carrots and turnips in spring. I have taken all the cottars and some of the small crofters on to our lists for draining work and have ordered tools and implements. In the meantime they are supplied with meal but to pay it up when working. There are eighty four men at work

which is all we can employ till a supply of
tools come to hand.

He nodded with satisfaction and shook sand over the letter.

He decided that he would have to make an attempt to visit as many of the holdings as he could on the Ross. He wanted to establish the exact extent of the destitution and see if anything could be done to solve the problem in the long term. The Ross was dangerously over-populated; there was excessive sub-division of holdings with too many landless cottars. The famine provided an opportunity. If the poorest and most worthless could be persuaded to leave, the land could be divided into viable farms, some of which could be turned over to sheep grazings and bring in a proper rent. Shiaba, for example, would make an excellent sheep farm.

The following morning, being Christmas, he ordered his servant to saddle up his pony as he and his wife, Flora, planned to attend the church in Bunessan. It was a crisp morning with frost crystals on the windows, so he made sure that she was happed up in a heavy overcoat with a rug over her knee in the trap. At the last minute her sister Anne ran out with a fur muff to keep her hands warm.

When they reached the village he saw that the sea was partly frozen. Pancakes of ice floated at the tide-edge like lily pads. The road skirted the sea and, as they drove along, he could hear the plates of ice crackling as they rubbed against each other. When they reached the village it was deserted, apart from a few people at the church door, one of whom stepped forward to take the reins of his pony. Nodding his thanks, he handed Flora down from the trap and they walked towards the door. The group stood aside to let them in.

The pews were far from full. Since the formation of the Free Church, the congregation had diminished year by year. The minor gentry like Captain MacLean of Scoor and their families still attended, but many of the less affluent members had deserted. He led Flora down the aisle to the pew reserved for him, second from the front. The front, he had decided, should be kept for visiting dignitaries such as one of the Argylls.

He was glad that Flora had brought her muff. There seemed to be little difference between the freezing air outside and the temperature within. Any warmth, presumably, was to come from the zeal of the spirit in one's bosom. He was a godly man, praying every night for guidance in his quest to make the world a better place, but he had reservations about public display of his faith. He was aware of the eyes of the congregation behind him, watching for faults, and the veiled hostility of the poorer class.

He sang the usual Christmas hymns with gusto and listened with a display of wrapt attention to the sermon while his mind was actually elsewhere, planning his next letter to the Duke and mulling over his plan for emigrating the least productive tenants and improving the land by enlargement of holdings and leguminous crops. He was so involved with his plans that Flora had to nudge him to stand for the last hymn.

He worried about the number of people attracted to the new Free Church, many of them the better class of tenant, actually holding a lease, and considered offering a piece of land to their minister as a glebe, perhaps a piece of his two hundred acres at Tormore. That might be politic. His Grace might not approve but, perhaps if he explained the wisdom of such a gesture, the old man might understand. He glanced up at Campbell's mournful face and decided to advance the idea, relieved to hear him pronounce the blessing.

As he left the church the Rev. Campbell ordered one of the Session to fetch the pony and trap.

'Thank you for coming, Mister Campbell, and Mrs Campbell. Hope you have a joyful Christmas.'

'Thank you, Reverend. I wish you the same.'

He handed Flora on to the trap and drove off.

'After lunch, my dear, I intend to take the horse and ride round more of the townships, the ones which I have not visited so far.'

'It is the Christmas day, John. Surely you deserve some rest. Besides, the day is so short you would have little time.'

'I cannot rest while these people are starving. Some have died, mainly from the fever. I will visit as many as I can and turn back when the light fades.'

'I wish you would rest.'

That night he wrote to the Duke.

> *It would be impossible for me to express in adequate terms the extreme state of destitution here. I have visited every farm on the Ross with the exception of Shiaba and in many instances was informed that death had occurred from actual starvation, indeed I have witnessed scenes not to be described ...'*

The following day he rode to Shiaba. It was one of the most remote townships in the Ross but he had always admired the excellent grazing, facing south and well drained. As he rode over the hill above Scoor and descended into the cluster of houses, he met one of the women, clearly suffering from starvation. Her blue eyes were sunk in their sockets, the bones of her arms protruded from the skin, her lips were blue, but she nevertheless exuded an air of defiance as she looked at him. Were it not for the ravages of starvation, she would have been beautiful. She brushed her hair from her face and waited for him to speak, to explain his presence. The child beside her was sick, her thin legs barely able to keep her upright. She was shivering and clutching her thin frock to her chest.

'Good day, mistress. Is your husband at home?'

'No. He's trying to gather whelks on the shore.'

'Whelks? You are eating shellfish? You have no meal?'

'A handful. I try to make it last.'

'There is work in Bunessan, work in exchange for meal.'

'He has not been paid yet.'

'What is his name? I will see to that.'

'Calum MacGillivray.'

'His Grace, the Duke, does not wish to see his people starve. The schoolmaster in the village is collecting names for a ship to Canada. His Grace will provide generous assistance.'

'Assistance providing we sell all we have. I have heard.'

'You would be wise to consider it, nevertheless. I intend to let this land to a sheep farmer.'

'You will have to remove us first.'

'You will get land elsewhere in the Ross, but you would be better to think of Canada. Has anyone died in the township?'

'No, but several have the flux and are very sick.'

'I will see that they get some laudanum. Your little girl is in need of it I think.'

'We do not want charity.'

'I will see to it nonetheless. Tell your husband the Factor called and what I said.'

'I know who you are, Mr Campbell. John Campbell of Ardmore, Factor to His Grace the Duke of Argyll. I will not forget.'

'And tell the others too. Good day, mistress.'

He tugged the reins and turned the horse's head away. Insolent woman, he thought, yet he admired her spirit, her strength in the face of such hardship, a strength that showed in her bearing, upright and defiant. When he looked back at the top of the hill, she was bent over the potato beds, scraping the earth with her fingers.

5

Calum shook the whelks into the pot of boiling water over the fire. Catherine and Archie were kneeling beside it, watching. Mary was sitting curled against the wall, her head on her knees and her arms locked around her shins. They could barely see each other in the gloom of the single tallow lamp.

'What did the Factor want?' Calum asked, sitting across from Catherine.

'He is letting the grazing to a sheep farmer.'

'He will have to remove us first. He will not find that as easy as he thinks.'

She looked up at his face, the jaw set, the eyes carefully avoiding hers. Had he been well, she would have seen anger there but she saw only lethargy and resignation. Starvation was affecting them all. Because he seemed so subdued, she decided to raise the other matter.

'He said that we should go to Canada. The Duke would help us with the fare. He said the schoolmaster MacDonald has thirty-three families on a list for Canada.'

He looked at her and shook his head. The familiar passion was missing but the determination was still there, muted but firm. For a moment she felt sorry for him. She had never seen him so lifeless. But then she remembered the children.

'We can't continue like this. Mary is sick. Look at her.'

'There will be meal tomorrow from the road work.'

'You said that yesterday. There's not enough anyway.'

She heard footsteps at the door and a voice calling.

'Are you there, Calum.?'

'Come in, Robert,' he replied. She could see that he welcomed the interruption.

Robert stooped under the lintel.

'It's dark in here. I can barely see.'

'No oil. The last lump of tallow is all.'

'I came to tell you that we have signed for Canada.'

'You're a brave man,' she said quickly.

A silence edged into the group.

'I'm sorry, Robert. Truly,' Calum said finally. 'We will be sorry to see you go. It is a bad time to be selling your beasts but they will make something at least. You will have a little money for the new life.'

'The money goes to the Duke. We are given the fare.'

'I might have known. When do you sail?'

'I don't know. We will be told. You should sign too, Calum. There is nothing here for the likes of us. The Factor Mor is set on starving us out and sweeping us away in favour of sheep. There is no Factor in Canada.'

Catherine waited for the usual tirade but saw only sorrow in Calum's eyes.

'We will stay,' he said quietly, 'May God go with you, a charaid. I hope you thrive in the new country.'

'I hope so too. Anyway, I wanted you to know. I must go back to feed the beasts. I'll leave you in peace. Goodnight to you.'

She watched him leave. Not bent forward, but more erect than usual with his shoulders back as though a burden had been lifted from them. She could not help envying him. It was the right thing to do. She was sure of that.

She emptied the water from the pot into another, thinking that it might make a weak soup, and spilled the cooked whelks into a bowl. Taking her only needle, she started to prize the whelks from their shells.

The next day the Free Church minister called. Catherine tried to sweep the feathers from the door when she saw him coming. She had killed the last hen and had laid it aside for plucking.

'Good morning, reverend. You have come a long way.'

'Good morning, Catherine. The Factor asked me to deliver this to you. A little laudanum for Mary. He said to mix it with castor oil, though I don't suppose you have any of that. How is the child?'

'Weak. She has the flux. From the shellfish no doubt.'

'I'm sorry. So many are sick. I buried four of my flock last week. Starvation and sickness everywhere. I hear that my colleagues in the south are raising funds to help but it may be too late. You were not at the meeting in Bunessan the other night?'

'No. I have not the strength to walk that far.'

'No. Of course. I'm sorry. I read out a letter from a Doctor Laing in Australia. He is offering free passage to people who want to go. A generous offer. I have twenty-seven names on my list for Australia, six heads of families and three young men. You should consider it, Catherine. There is work there and a better life for the children.'

'Calum is determined to stay. Besides Mary is scarcely fit for such a journey and we have no relatives in Australia.'

Mary had arrived in the doorway, leaning on the wall.

'Please can we go, Mother? I don't want to stay here any more. We will all die here.'

'Out of the mouths of babes …' he said. 'Advise Calum to think carefully. There are many in the district on the lists already. Robert, I believe, has signed.'

'Yes, he told us.'

'I will be sorry to see them leave. I'm losing half my flock it seems. Perhaps I will lose them all, if the famine persists. I do hope our friends in the cities will be generous. In the meantime we must pray and thank the Lord for small mercies. I must go now. I have others to see. God bless you both. I will pray for you, Mary. Your mother has some medicine which might help the flux. May the Lord have mercy on us all.'

He hurried away towards Robert's house.

She was about to lead Mary back inside when she saw Calum returning.

'Why are you home so early?'

'We are on strike.'

'What? What are you saying?'

Horrified, she pulled Mary against her.

'We are refusing to work for the pittance that they are offering.'

She struggled to absorb the words, to imagine the implications, to find a response. No work, no meal was the first and most obvious consequence.

'Why are you doing this? They will give you meal. The Factor said so.'

'A pittance. Enough to feed a mouse.'

'Better than none, Calum. In the name of God think of the children.'

'It is not right. They are using our hunger to force down the pay.'

'This is madness, Calum. Has the hunger stolen your wits?'

'If we all stand together, they must listen.'

'Nonsense. They have nothing to lose. They don't care if the work is not done. Madness. Madness.'

She turned and walked into the house, leaving him standing outside with his head down.

That evening she sat at the table in the faint glow of the tallow lamp. Mary had been crying with pain but, having sipped some of the laudanum, was now asleep on the bed beside her brother. Calum had left to attend a meeting of the men on strike in Bunessan. She was trying to think clearly, to find a solution. There must be a way out of the morass. If they stayed with Calum on strike, they would certainly die of starvation, become weaker and weaker until the hunger pains tore through their bellies. She could not allow that to happen to her children. There must be an answer. She thought of her cousin in Govan. Her man was a weaver with a good wage and her cousin worked in a Factory. They would not starve. She could go there. Yet she could not leave Calum. Foolish, stubborn, he was still a man of principle with an inflated sense of justice. That was a side of him that she adored—his integrity, his adherence to truth. He was suffering too. Starvation had weakened him, eroding his fibre and his resilience and he was painfully thin. She wanted to take him in her arms and soothe the suffering, hold him until the storm passed, until the sun shone through the darkness. She saw him mowing the corn in the sunlight, his scythe swinging easily, his strong arms rippling, the sweat glistening on his forehead and staining his shirt. She saw him lifting Mary above his head and laughing as she screamed. Her Calum, the man she loved. How could she leave him? How could she live in the city and leave him to starve to death? She imagined his emaciated figure dying alone in the house and herself buying shoes for the children. Yet he would never leave Shiaba and he would never win his battle with the Factor. She knew now that she was going to be forced to choose between him and the children. She felt tears warm on her cheeks.

§

John Campbell wrote to His Grace.

Relief has been afforded to the most destitute and those unable to work by the parochial board and to the able-bodied. Some were dissatisfied at the rates allowed for their work as being inadequate for their support, although I allowed them one fourth more than I ever paid for any kind of labour. They struck work and assembled in a body after nightfall in the village asking for meal. I desired the ground officer to inform them that, if they did not go quietly home and exert themselves more, they must starve. A number of them staid at home for a day or two, when craving of hunger forced them out, some of them scarcely able to walk. When I ordered them some meal they were very submissive indeed. I fear a few of the more troublesome are still on strike. I intend to issue a goodly number of summonses

of removal. Nothing but harshness and dread I
find will do, they are so naturally slothful and
indolent …

6

Dr Aldcorn, a popular practitioner from Oban renowned for his compassion for the poor, stood in Parliament Square, amazed by the elegance and grandeur of the Houses of Parliament where he was to meet the Marquis. He had already visited St Paul's cathedral, almost losing his balance as he stared up into the vast space beneath the dome hundreds of feet above him and overwhelmed by the sheer magnitude of the interior. It was magnificent and a monument not only to the architect and thousands of tradesmen who built it but also to the power of the nation whose wealth and confidence had financed it. The Houses of Parliament spoke of the same imperial might, especially the great hall where he remembered Thomas More had been tried. He felt its antiquity as he climbed the worn stone steps on his way the central lobby.

Trevelyan rose from his desk to meet the delegation from Scotland. He knew already the nature of their plea but felt that he should see them nevertheless.

'Good afternoon, gentlemen. Please come in.'

George, his secretary, introduced them.

'I think you may already know the Marquis of Breadalbane, sir, and Mr Fox Maule. This is Mr Campbell of Monzie, Mr Tod Chiene the Factor for Mr Campbell of Islay, Dr Candlish of the

Free Church of Scotland and Dr Aldcorn from Oban who is familiar with the destitution on the Island of Mull.'

A motley crew, he thought, but not to be dismissed. The Prime Minister had spoken favourably of the Marquis, which indicated that he was heading for a prominent position in the government. One of the few proprietors to join the Free Church, he was obviously a man of principle and strong faith. He was taller than the others and crossed the room with an air of confidence and authority. He was certainly more handsome and elegant than his companions.

'Please be seated, gentlemen.'

Campbell of Monzie he knew from the House as Member for Argyll, an able speaker and founder member of the Free Church. The minister, Candlish, a squat, morose little man with a forehead which seemed to stretch to his crown above his mane of unruly hair, sat and glowered at him. He did not relish the prospect of debate with him.

'You have come a long way. I trust you have found suitable accommodation.'

'Yes indeed,' the Oban doctor replied. 'Superior to most of the hostels I have had to endure on my tours of the affected districts.'

'So how can I help?'

'I think that you will already know, sir,' the doctor continued, 'of the crisis facing us in Scotland and the alarming extent of destitution in the western highlands and islands.'

Trevelyan wondered why the doctor had chosen to speak first. He could see that he was passionate and anxious to press his case, but he should have shown the Marquis some respect.

'Through the local committees of the Free Church and its ministers, we have collected details of the dreadful conditions throughout the area,' the doctor was not to be interrupted, 'and we calculate that there are sixty thousand families urgently in need of help to keep them alive till next harvest. We estimate that six hundred thousand bolls of meal will be required at a cost of almost a million pounds.'

'The government will do all it can, Doctor Alcorn, but I must remind you that we have accumulated the enormous debt of twenty million pounds as a means of abolishing slavery.'

That was a sensitive subject which he should not have mentioned, realising that Breadalbane had received compensation under the scheme, but then he recalled that his own mother had been granted nearly seventy thousand for loss of slaves in the Caribbean. He wondered if the Marquis knew that.

'I can assure you, gentlemen, that the Prime Minister is aware and deeply concerned about the crisis. The Chancellor announced the other day that no fewer than seventy ships were on their way to America for supplies of wheat, rice and maize. Her Majesty's appeal has raised £170,000 and the British Association £263,000 for Ireland and Scotland, and Scotland will receive a sixth of this. The Government is also committed to help directly. There are loans available for the proprietors to provide work under the Drainage Act. The Admiralty has ordered a frigate to be based in Oban or Fort William as a depot for distribution of meal and corn under my friend Sir Edward Pine Coffin. Several of the steam ships employed in surveying have been sent to the West of Scotland and two other frigates— the *Aeolus* and the *Blonde*—are joining them.'

'I appreciate that,' the Marquis said, 'but the meal from these depots has to be purchased and the starving people have no means to buy food.'

'The proprietors and the Poor Law Commissioners and local committees will buy the meal and distribute it in return for work. The proprietors have a duty to give their small tenants the necessary assistance. The party receiving the rent or surplus produce of the soil should be prepared to return a portion of that to the tenant when the produce or harvest fails. I must say I'm delighted with the response of the Scottish proprietors compared with those in Ireland—the Duke of Sutherland, Matheson on Lewis, MacLeod of Macleod and of course, your employer, Mister Tod Chiene, Campbell of Islay.'

'There is still fearful hunger and disease,' Doctor Alcorn intervened. 'The people suffering put their children to bed and go to bed themselves immediately after dark to try and drown in sleep the cravings of hunger. In the Ross of Mull and Iona there is more sickness than other places. Let me quote a letter from the merchant in Bunessan—"there are several families in this district actually in a dying state from starvation and sickness and the number of deaths some days is between two to five. Sickness is on the increase particularly British cholera and dysentery."'

'Yes, I know the situation is critical and, as I say, the government is striving to help the afflicted. I understand, however, that there is a surplus of grain in Easter Ross. Surely that can be purchased for those in need.'

'The poorest have not the means to pay for it.'

Dr Candlish leaned forward and growled.

'It is well known, sir, that our church—the Free Church—was the first to move on this issue. Having appealed to our membership in December last, we raised more than £3,000 in Edinburgh. Throughout the land the church had raised more than £11,000 by January, and we have made available our ship *Breadalbane* to carry meal to the stricken districts. We hope that the government will show an equal level of generosity.'

'The government, Dr Candlish, is making every effort to see that the proprietors and rate-payers shoulder their responsibilities and is providing loans under the Drainage Act to provide work. The Inspectors of the Poor have been given more discretion to provide casual relief to those in great distress. We do not want people to die of hunger and disease. On the other hand, I do not want to give corn or meal away and have hordes of people descending on the depots and becoming a permanent burden on the state.'

'It seems, then,' the Marquis said, 'that the government is not prepared to help directly but will assist with loans those bodies and individuals who will take on the task.'

'That is our view. We must not interfere with the free market.'

'Well, thank you for your time, Mr Trevelyan.'

The Marquis rose, indicating that the others should follow.

'I have noticed many members of the press in the Highlands—the *Times*, the *Guardian* and the *Morning Chronicle*—let us hope that the situation does not deteriorate, bringing a multitude of deaths from starvation and the government a dreadful reputation. Good day to you, sir, I'm sure we will meet in the corridors.'

With that, the deputation departed, leaving Trevelyan standing at his desk and George shutting the heavy door behind them.

'They expect the government to solve the problem for them,' Trevelyan said, sliding into his chair again.

'The Free Church has led the way, sir. Considering its congregations can't be the most affluent in the country, many of them without a church and paying ministers from their own pockets, it's a remarkable achievement.'

'Indeed, indeed, but they need watching and we have the means to do that. The two destitution committees—Glasgow and Edinburgh—have formed one board. William Skene has been appointed secretary and I know he is happy to co-operate with us. He is an able man and shares my views on relief. He is to keep me informed of the strategy of the new board and I will check and vet everyone. As far as the usual Poor Relief is concerned, Sir John McNeill is a staunch ally. Effectively, George, every relief initiative will come through this office.'

'The risk attached to that, sir, is that, in the event of failure, we will take the blame.'

'No, George, the control is entirely informal, invisible. There will be no trail to follow. Now I'm going to finish my correspondence and then take a cab home to see Hannah and the children. Alice is such a joy at that age. Perhaps you could check the afternoon mail and see if there is word from Edward.'

He spread paper on the desk and lifted his pen as George left the room.

He wrote to James Baird of the Glasgow Committee:

> *Next to allowing the people to die of hunger, the greatest evil that could happen would be they are habituated to depend on public charity. The object to be arrived at therefore is to prevent the assistance given of being productive in idleness and, if possible, to make it conducive increased exertion.*

7

The old man looked up as Catherine came. His silver hair shone in the lamplight and his pen, ink and paper were ready on the table.

'Come. Sit Catherine.'

'Thank you, Alexander. This is good of you.'

'How is little Mary?'

'Poorly. Very poorly.'

'I wish I could help.'

'Perhaps you can. Writing a letter for me may help her.'

'Of course. I have everything ready.'

She watched the tendons move under the blue veins on his hand as he lifted the pen and dipped it in the ink. His fingers, twisted with rheumatism, could barely hold the feather.

'Who is this for?'

'My cousin in Glasgow.'

'You know where she lives?'

'No, but I will send it to the minister and he will know.'

'You will need to speak slowly, Catherine. I can't write quickly. What is it you want to say?'

She dictated carefully,

> *Dear Margaret, There is terrible hunger in the Ross now and the flux. You will have heard of the failure of the potatoes and we have nothing to see us through to the spring. I do not know what will become of us. Mary is very sick.*
>
> *We have no corn left and we will have to sell all the cattle to pay the rent. Could we come and stay with you till the worst has passed? I can surely get work there so that the children can eat. If we stay here, we will surely die.*
>
> *Your loving cousin, Catherine.*

'I have written your name, Catherine. You will need to make your mark here.'

He dipped the pen in the ink and handed it to her. She drew a cross beside her name.

'Does Calum know about this?'

'No, he does not and he is not to know. I may not go at all. It depends on him. If he continues to refuse work, I will have to go. I cannot watch the children suffer and die.'

'As you wish but I think it is a mistake—not to tell him, that is.'

'It is my wish.'

'Very well. I'll see that this reaches the minister but what about Mary? She is very sick is she not? Is she able to travel?'

'If she stays here, she will die. Can you not talk to Calum, persuade him to give in? He respects you.'

'He is doing what he thinks is right.'

'I know. I know. He is a man of principle. I have always admired that, but this is folly, a contest between him and the Factor, a contest that he will never win.'

'A contest between right and wrong. That is how he sees it. Right must prevail.'

'Please talk to him.'

'I'll see what I can do.'

'And if I go—and God knows I don't want to leave him—will you look after him for me? I do not want to lose him.'

'Of course. He is my neighbour. We will all help.'

'Thank you, Alexander. That is of some comfort.'

She rose and crossed to the door where she stopped and turned.

'Good night. Remember, he is not to know.'

Alexander smiled and nodded. She felt that she could trust him.

Catherine placed two peats on the fire, walked over to the bed, and lifted her shawl. The children lay asleep, Mary helped by the last drop of laudanum. She swung the shawl over her shoulders and moved towards the door.

'Where are you going?'

Calum raised his head from the table and frowned.

'I'm going to Bunessan.'

'Why?'

'I'm going to see if I can get some meal.'

'You're going to beg? Going on the parish?'

'No. I'm going to put our case to MacQuarrie. We can't continue like this. The others are back at work and earning meal for their families.'

'Not all of them. Some are more manly than others.'

'More stubborn and foolish. Three of you. For ten days now. While we starve. Can you not swallow your pride for the sake of the children?'

'And let the Factor win?'

'So it's a contest then? David and Goliath. Is that how you see it?'

'It's a matter of justice.'

'It's a matter of pride, foolish pride. At our expense. Mary will wake soon. There is no more laudanum so you will have to listen to her cry. You can give her some milk.'

She walked out quickly before he could retaliate.

A cold north wind met her at the top of the hill, piercing her shawl and thin frock, but she hurried on down to the track leading from Scoor to Bunessan. A flock of wild geese rose stridently from the rigs beside Loch Assapol and soared over the trees beside the manse. By the time she reached the road above the village, her heels were blistered and sore. She should not have worn her shoes but didn't like to appear in the village without them.

She was sure that MacQuarrie would be sympathetic. He was the leader of the Baptist congregation and an inspector for the Poor Board. However, she had another reason to speak with him. As she passed the mill she could hear the millstones grinding and smell the meal on the wind, a sweet, soft scent that she tasted on her tongue with relish.

When she reached his house she hesitated. Perhaps she was being foolish. Perhaps Calum would win his argument and return to work. Perhaps she was being impulsive and should wait. But then the sound of Mary crying in pain came back and she knocked on the door. He was a kindly man with a gentleness that set her at her ease immediately.

'Good morning, Mrs MacGillivray. That's a chill wind. Come inside.'

'I don't wish to disturb you.'

'Nonsense. Come in, do.'

The house was very different from her own, with a chimney and grate for a fire and plaster walls between the rooms. He issued her into the kitchen where his wife, Mary, was baking bannocks. She smiled a welcome to her.

'You've come a long way, mistress,' he said. 'You must have some tea. You look perished.'

'No thank you, Mr MacQuarrie. You are very kind but I have little time.'

'It is not a kindness. It is a rule in our house that every stranger will be offered hospitality. I know about your husband and his stand against the Factor and admire his courage, but I can imagine the hardship that must bring on his family.'

'A foolish man, foolish and stubborn. His children are going to die. Mary is sick already and so thin you can see every bone in her body. But I did not come to beg for help. I came to ask if you knew of a boat going to the Clyde.'

His wife stopped stirring the dough and Catherine could feel his eyes studying her. She looked out the window to avoid their scrutiny.

'There's a boat in the bay just now with men from Tiree heading for work on the railways. I understand that it is to leave in two days' time. Is Calum thinking of joining them? There is work available with good wages, I believe.'

'Yes. At last. He is hoping to go,' she said hurriedly, hoping that the deception would not be detected by these godly people. She was sure her discomfort must be apparent in her avoidance of their glances. In the end she was so shamed by their virtue and concern that she spoke the truth.

'No. I am telling a lie. Calum will never leave Shiaba. The boat is for myself and the children. If we stay here, they will die. I will get work in the city and earn enough to feed them and buy medicine for Mary. I have a cousin in Glasgow. I will go to her.'

'That is a shame, Catherine,' Mrs MacQuarrie said. 'I can't imagine how it must feel to be driven to that extreme.'

'It is a courageous decision, one to be admired,' her husband said. 'I am so impressed that I will see that your fare is paid, if you decide to go. The Board is assisting men to go south for work so there is no reason it should deny a brave female.'

'That is very kind but I have not decided yet. Please do not tell anyone of my intention.'

'Of course not. If Mary needs transport from Shiaba, I can arrange a pony. Now, you must have some tea.'

'I would feel guilty drinking tea while the others have none but thank you. I must leave now. Will you speak to the captain of the vessel and say that I may join them?'

'I will. May the Lord go with you.'

'And with you both.'

As she turned to leave, he thrust a bag of meal into her hand.

'Take it. Eat. This is my body which was broken for you.'

She noticed tears in his eyes.

'God bless you, sir.'

She felt like placing her arms around him just to feel his kindness next to her, to sense for a moment that there was a life not as harsh and cruel and cold as her own.

Her blisters were so painful on the way back that she tore a strip off the hem of her frock and wrapped it over her heels.

She stopped at the top of the hill above the township and looked down on the cluster of houses. A thin plume of peat smoke rose from the thatch of each one and was quickly snatched away by the wind. They seemed to cling to the land as if they were part of it, as if their stone walls had hauled themselves out of the earth. The massive stones, hanging on the ropes which weighed down their thatch, were surely going to crush them back where they came from. She wondered how many fires there would be in fifty years' time and imagined the roofless buildings, their thatch stripped away, their roof timbers rotting and pointing to the sky like fingers of dying men clutching at life, the lintels broken, moss covering the hearthstones. The people would be gone, scattered over the world in Canada, Australia, Liverpool, Glasgow. The graves of those who stayed would be in Kilvickeon among the ancient gravestones, so old that the names were worn away. One might be Calum's.

She walked down the slope and entered the house.

Calum was still sitting at the table but Mary was awake with her back against the wall, rocking with pain. Placing the bag of meal in front of him, she crossed to Mary and took her in her arms.

'I don't want charity,' Calum muttered.

'It's not charity. It is a gift from MacQuarrie. He is a good man. They are good people. If you will not have it, the children will.'

'And you too, no doubt.'

'That's unkind, Calum, unworthy of you.'

He turned away and picked the dirt from his nails.

'While you were away the sheriff's men were here with summonses of removal. Argyll has let the whole of Shiaba, summer grazing and all, to a sheep farmer.'

'You knew it would happen sooner or later.'

'That doesn't make it right: "to flit and remove themselves, their wives, bairns, families, servants, subtenants, cottars, dependents, goods, gear furth and from their respective occupations and possession of the land of and farm of Shiaba." I know the words off by heart.'

'Everyone?'

'Yes. Every family received a summons'

'So what are they going to do?'

'Alexander is to call a meeting.'

She was shocked and squeezed Mary tight against her. She had not anticipated the threat of eviction, not so soon anyway. Perhaps Calum would come with her now. Perhaps they could start a new life in the south. That's what she wanted. A new life. With Calum. She did not want to leave him behind. In spite of his folly, his obstinacy, his selfishness, she still loved him. Yet he had said plainly and many times that he would never leave Shiaba. She decided not to speak of her plan.

8

John Campbell was about to write to his master, choosing his words very carefully, when he was startled by a knock on his study door. Irritated because a drop of ink had fallen from his pen on to a clean sheet of paper, he shouted angrily, 'Come in, damn you.'

As the young man tentatively opened the door and peered round the corner, the Factor, seeing that it was one of his servants from Islay, apologised immediately.

'I'm sorry, Dugald, I was lost in thought. What can I do for you?'

'I have heard, sir—and it may not be true—that His Grace, the Duke, has died.'

'Yes, it may well be the case, I'm afraid. May God rest his soul. Lady Anne will be most distressed. Still, we had better wait for confirmation from Inveraray before we decide on the best means of showing our respects. I would hope to hear from the young Marquis himself. In the meantime, Dugald, we carry on as usual.'

'Of course, sir. I thought you should know.'

'Quite right. Quite right. Thank you. You may go. Are the heifers fed?'

'Yes, sir. We have plenty of oats left in the barn.'

'Excellent, young man. Tell Kirsty to bring me some cordial.'

Dugald left the room and Campbell crunched up the spoiled sheet of paper and tossed it in the basket

So, he thought, the young Marquis takes over, an educated young man with an understanding of political economy, an interest in science and a firm believer in emigration but, most of all, married to a Sutherland—two mighty families in the land coming together. Surely a good omen. Here was an opportunity to improve the lands and rid them of the mass of small tenants who were nothing more than parasites.

Once again he lifted his pen to compose a letter of condolence to the Marquis and his mother but this time was interrupted by the maid's voice in the hall and another knock on the door. It was Kirsty, but without the cordial.

'Sorry to trouble you, sir. There is a Dr Boyter to see you.'

'Clearly I am to have no peace today. Bring him in, Kirsty.'

He had heard of the naval surgeon, retired on half pay, and now working for the Destitution Committee. He was taken aback by the man's appearance, for he was expecting a younger man but instead found a frail, elderly gentleman, clearly exhausted by his travels round the suffering districts. He was displeased that Boyter had already visited some of the townships in his area.

'Good morning, Mr Campbell. Dr Boyter. I've been appointed to see to the distribution of relief.'

'Yes, Dr Boyter. Please sit down. Can I offer you a refreshment?'

'No thank you.'

Boyter remained standing

'I had heard you were in the district. It would have been courteous to call on me first as His Grace's representative on Mull.'

'I'm afraid such formalities have to be dispensed with in this crisis, Mr Campbell. I have to see that those who are starving are fed as quickly as possible.'

'You are not suggesting that we are neglecting our duty in that respect?'

'I'm sure that all those in a position to help will fulfil their responsibilities. I am here to see that the meal purchased for famine relief reaches all those who are in need.'

'And it is my responsibility to administer the Duke's affairs on his estates. I will see that the meal is distributed efficiently to those who are willing to work.'

'I have appointed Mr MacQuarrie to see to the distribution. He will be in charge and will report to me. I am confident that he will fulfil his duties admirably.'

'MacQuarrie the merchant? The Baptist?'

'Yes'

'This is outrageous. You are interfering in our affairs. His Grace will hear of this.'

'I have already spoken to the young Marquis and have authority to proceed. He is anxious to see that there are no deaths attributable to starvation. I trust you agree with his sentiments. Now, if you will excuse me, I have more townships to visit and have little time.

'Of course. You must do your duty. Thank you for calling, sir.'

'I would have called sooner but I decided to start at the eastern end of the parish. I will see myself out. Good day, Mr Campbell and thank you for your time.'

He left the room.

The Factor's fingers trembled as they lifted his paper knife and stabbed the desk. The impudence of the man, treating him like a lieutenant on one of his ships. Leaving time for Boyter to be clear of his farm, he marched out to the yard and ordered the stable boy to saddle his horse. He was going to confront MacQuarrie.

Riding towards Bunessan where he had been told Mac-Quarrie was often to be seen taking notes of the men employed there, he rehearsed what he was going to say. He did not want to offend the man in case the young Duke visited the district and his own discourtesy was reported. He would merely try to get evidence of malpractice. He was pleased to find the merchant by the shore.

'Good morning, MacQuarrie. You have a large squad of men here.'

'More every day, Mr Campbell. Between eighty and a hundred as a rule. They are building new landing places and improving the harbour, tasks to benefit the community.'

'Their wages?'

'Nine to ten shillings a week. There are also about sixty working at draining and receiving meal. I think we relieved about a hundred and thirty families last week.'

'All are working for the meal?'

'Some are not able to work, being old and infirm or sick with the fever. A great many pledge their cattle in return for meal. I doubt if the beasts will ever be redeemed. It is all that they have.'

'And the men on strike. Do they receive meal?'

'They were not employed by me but by your Ground Officer but, should they be starving and too weak to work, they would be given meal. They would not be allowed to die. In any case I believe they have all returned to work.'

'Not all and I will deal with the recalcitrants. I'm pleased to see that your men are improving the pier. My arable at Ardfenaig would benefit from draining.'

'I have been advised to ensure that the work does not benefit any single individual.'

'Of course. But an enhancement of my harvest would mean more meal in the parish.'

'To be sold, naturally—not given away.'

'I see you are something of a political economist, MacQuarrie.'

'I am a humble merchant and serve the Lord in any way I can.'

'Very noble. I will leave you to your task'

The Factor turned his horse and headed back for Ardfenaig.

He returned to his study and composed the letter to the young Duke that he had been contemplating before Boyter arrived.

Your Grace, Please accept my sincere condolences on the death of your beloved father. I am sure that all the tenants, sub-tenants and cottars on these lands of Mull, Iona and Tyree will mourn his departure and remember his generosity through times of scarcity and trouble. He will be sorely missed.

You will receive along with this a list of emigrants amounting to upwards of 900 souls. Only 6 families were able to pay in full, 32 families able to pay part and 11 able to pay a little. However 78 of the families were completely destitute.

With few exceptions these are the poorest and most worthless on the property and, whatever may be the cost of sending them, the money will be most advantageously laid out for, if they were to remain another year, it would cost more to keep them alive than the cost of sending them to Canada.

In the meantime I am doling out meal in as small quantities as possible and only in cases of urgent necessity to keep body and soul together and, with all that, the quantity given out is fearful.

I will, Your Grace, keep you informed of progress here. In the meantime, rest assured that I will look after your interests to the best of my ability.

Your humble servant, John Campbell.

9

Calum, unsteady and weak as he crossed the floor, left the house for the meeting. Catherine rose from the fire and hauled out the sack which she had concealed beneath the bed. Pulling on her shoes and wrapping her shawl round her shoulders, she placed two more peats on the fire and, lifting the blanket from the bed, she folded it round Mary.

'You look like a monk,' she said. A faint smile was the only response.

'MacQuarrie's pony is behind the school house. You will have to walk as far as that. Then you and Archie can ride all the way. You've never been on horseback before, have you? You have to hold on with your knees.'

'Where are we going?' Mary asked.

'Bunessan. To Mr MacQuarrie's house. For more meal.'

'Is father not coming?'

'He has to go to the meeting.'

Opening the door, she took the children's hands and stood for a moment, looking back at the room, the bare stone walls, the scrubbed table with its two chairs, the single bed and the hessian partition. Their home where the children were born, where Mary took her first steps across the earthen floor, where Calum had held her hand while she roared at Mary's birth, where Mary had read aloud the lines of a book lent by the schoolmaster. It was painful to leave it all, the memories, the evenings where they laughed at Calum's stories. Imagining him, an emaciated, helpless man alone by the fire almost made her turn back. Yet there was no other way. She had to save the children.

She lifted them on to the pony and headed for the village.

By the time she reached MacQuarrie's Mary had to hold on to the pony. Flux was running down her legs and she was shivering under the blanket.

When MacQuarrie came out he was clearly horrified.

'Catherine, she is very ill. She will never reach Glasgow.'

'I have to try.'

'There is a surgeon in the house. Dr Boyter, a naval man. I'm sure he will help.'

'He might try to stop me leaving.'

'He's a compassionate man. He will understand your plight. I will fetch him. Wait here.'

She was not inspired with confidence when the doctor appeared. Weariness and fatigue showing in his sagging shoulders and weeping eyes, he looked at Mary and shook his head.

'Mr MacQuarrie tells me you are trying to sail for Glasgow.'

'Yes but my daughter is ill and needs some help with the fever.'

'She's not just ill. She is almost starved to death. She needs washed, fed and rested.'

'The ship sails tonight.'

'If you take her on board, she may die.'

'Come, Mrs MacGillivray,' MacQuarrie intervened, 'Let's take her inside and wash her and try her with some broth.'

'A very little,' the doctor said, 'and I will give her some laudanum and castor oil.'

MacQuarrie lifted Mary from the pony and carried her inside, the doctor following him. Catherine tied the pony to a rail, lifted Archie and carried him into the house.

'What has she been eating?' the doctor asked.

'Shellfish and a little meal. We had milk till the cow was sold.'

'It is not surprising that she has the flux. The broth may help but she is very poorly.'

'I will swing on the broth. You sit down, Catherine, and I will wash her and, if you have no objection, dress her in clean clothes.'

Normally Catherine would have objected, but she was too weak to argue and collapsed into a chair.

That evening, fortified by some broth and bread, she felt stronger as she was lifted into a cart by MacQuarrie. Wrapped in a new blanket and dressed in warm clothes, Mary lay beside her, more at peace and with a hint of life in her eyes. Archie lay behind her, quite excited about the prospect of a sea journey.

'God be with you, Catherine,' Mrs MacQuarrie said as her husband drove off.

Good people, Catherine thought, if all Baptists are like them, it must be a remarkable church.

When they reached Fionnphort she saw the ship waiting in the sound. Seamen were already in the rigging preparing to sail and the ship's pinnace was waiting on the shore. MacQuarrie carried Mary down to the sand and waited while Catherine and Archie followed.

Dr Boyter, who had ridden behind them on his own horse, climbed down the slope after them.

When they reached the small boat, he spoke to one of the seamen.

'I'm Dr Boyter, bosun, formerly a naval surgeon. I want you to tell your captain that this lady and her daughter have to be offered every facility on board. The daughter, as you can see, is ill but I have given her some laudanum and she may sleep. I will see that she is met by a responsible person at the other end. Is that clear?'

'Perfectly, sir. Don't be concerned. I will see that the captain gets the message.'

He helped the trio into the boat and pushed off.

As the oars rattled in the rowlocks and dipped in the sea, the doctor turned to MacQuarrie.

'I doubt if the child will survive the journey. She should not be travelling. Yet I understand the mother's reason for leaving and I must admit I admire her courage and determination. A brave lady, MacQuarrie. I wish there were more like her.'

'Indeed. And little schooling. She looked after her mother who was blind till her brother came home. Her father was drowned at sea. A remarkable woman..'

§

Calum's meeting, debating over a suggestion that they should appeal to the Duke, lasted until the light faded in Alexander's house. Calum was outraged at the proposal.

'What will the Duke do? Provide us all with meal free of charge so that we can stay here? He has let the land to a sheep farmer so he wants to evict us all. Why would he want to help us now?'

'Our fathers and forefathers have paid rent to Argyll for generations,' answered Alexander, 'and always on time, though we have seen famine and crop failure many times before. The new sheep farmer is a stranger and has been known to default on his debts. The young Duke is an honest man. He will listen at least.'

'An honest Argyll? Never. It was an Argyll who evicted my grandfather because he would not join his regiment—his volunteers. They are all the same—Sutherland, MacDonald, Dunmore, Gordon. They want us off the land, swept away so that they can have sheep. Sheep before men, Gold before kinship. They do not lose sleep over the likes of us.'

Most of the men gathered there nodded agreement,

'You speak with great passion, Calum, and have a fine command of words but we must consider this carefully—'

He was interrupted by one of the children bursting open the door.

'Father! Father! They're here,' he gasped, looking at Donald MacKinnon. 'The sheep men and scores of sheep.'

Calum could hear dogs barking and the bleating of sheep. Then a sharp command and the dogs fell silent. The forty men assembled in the house looked at each other, shocked, bewildered. The knock on the door was forceful.

'Come in,' Alexander answered.

The tall man who stooped under the lintel showed no sign of being intimidated by the crowd. The plaid over his shoulder made him look heftier than he was but the crook in his hand, like a bishop's crozier, gave him an air of authority.

'I have come to value your livestock.'

'In the twilight?' Calum said.

'On whose authority?' asked Alexander, glancing at Calum with a frown.

'The Duke and his Factor. The land is let now and you have no right to have stock here. I will give you a fair price for your sheep. My herds have them gathered by the hill dyke.'

'We are here by right till the May term,' Alexander said, 'and our sheep can be here till then too.'

'They will be worthless by then. Sheep from all over the country will be selling then and your poor specimens won't stand a chance. I'm offering an early sale.'

'And how will you pay?' asked Calum.

'I will give you promissory notes now and cash when I return.'

'Chaff in the wind. We have heard of your notes. Worthless.'

'You are challenging my word? Who are you to do that? What is your name? I'll see that the Factor hears of your insolence.'

'I'm well enough known to the Factor. Others may fear you, drover, but I have no sheep nor cattle for you to steal.'

'We have no need of your notes,' Alexander intervened quietly. 'The people here are starving. They cannot eat promises. If you come with money, we might consider.'

'I will go then. You are foolish men. I will be in the inn till tomorrow if any of you change your minds. After that I will be heading for Dumbarton with the drove of cattle and sheep. When I come back you will be gone. All of you.'

'We will see,' said Calum, keen to have the last word.

The drover left without looking back.

'You should not annoy him, Calum,' Alexander said. 'We may need him yet.'

'How am I to sell my beasts?' Robert said. 'We will be leaving soon. Who will take them if he doesn't?'

'I will speak to the Factor.'

'He is off to Tiree.'

'I think this shows that there is a case for a petition. The Duke may not know of this.'

'I am going to the drover anyway,' Robert announced. 'I need to sell the beasts.'

'The Duke will take your beasts as part payment for your fare. You don't think he would pay your passage for you?'

Robert left the room quickly, followed by several others.

It was decided that the petition should be sent in the name of Neil MacDonald.

> *My Lord Duke,*
>
> *As one of the oldest tenants in the Ross having now verging on one hundred years of age, and having paid rent to your Grace's ancestors for upwards of fifty years. I beg to send you this petition by myself and the other tenants in Shiaba, trusting that your Grace will give us favourable reply to its prayer as it would be a great hardship and quite unprecedented to remove a man of my age who, as is natural to suppose, is drawing close to the house appointed for all living.*
>
> *Trusting that your Grace will order an answer soon—I have the honour to be with great respect, My Lord Duke,*
>
> *Your Grace's most and very humble servant,*
>
> *Neil MacDonald. His Mark X*

The petition was attached to his plea.

That the petitioners and their forefathers have been tenants in Shiaba about sixty years and on other parts of the estate of Ross from time immemorial –

That the Petitioners were lately warned to flit and remove from their respective possessions although they were not in arrears of rent but on the contrary have paid the same regularly though they had large families to support numbering including cottars upwards of one hundred persons none of whom received aid or were a burden on the parish –

That the farm has lately been let in one lot to one individual who is not a native of the Ross and neither he nor any of his ancestors ever possessed any lands under your Grace's noble ancestors –

That your Grace's Factor is presently in Tyree and the Petitioners are in a dilemma and in a state of uncertainty as to what is to be done with them all of whom, if they are to be removed, are expecting to be accommodated on other holdings on the estate but, as the Factor is not at home, they are in suspense as to what to do –

That this day the incoming tenant came with shepherds and men to value the sheep belonging to the petitioners without giving them previous intimation but, as he had not the money and could not find a cautioner for the payment and as he is not under good character—all the surrounding tenants and

others being afraid of him—they would not
deliver him the stock –
    May it please your grace to take
the Petitioners case into and to give in
consideration and to give instruction
whether they are to be removed under the
circumstances above stated and, if so, they
trust that they will be accommodated with land
elsewhere on the estate.
    Alexander MacGillivray; Archbd
MacGillivray; Duncan MacKinnon;
John Campbell; John MacKinnon; Allan
MacDougall; Duncan MacCormick..

Calum refused to sign as he had no intention of leaving Shiaba and did not like the begging tone of the petition.

10

'Why did you not tell me?' Calum leaned weakly against the door-post of Alexander's house and spoke into the gloom.

'I gave her my word—the word of any scribe.'

'But I have a right to know. In the name of God she is my wife.'

'It was her decision.'

'And the children. They are too weak to travel. Mary will die.'

'She might have died anyway. If you had returned to work, she might have had meal.'

'No! No! I could not do that. You know that, Alex.'

'Your decision, Calum. You will never win this battle. Campbell has the Duke and the power of the state behind him. You have only your stiff neck. That stubborn streak of yours has cost you your family and will be the death of you yet.'

Infuriated, Calum turned away and staggered towards his own house then turned back.

'Where has she gone? You can tell me that at least.'

'I wrote to her cousin in the South.'

'Glasgow then. She should have said. She had no right to leave like that. What kind of woman is she? Doesn't give a damn for the children and doesn't give a damn whether I live or die.'

'She cares for you more than you can ever imagine, Calum. I doubt if there is a woman in this township worships her man as much as Catherine. She had to choose between you and your children.'

Not wanting to hear any more, he walked away. As he reached the house a horse stopped and the rider dismounted. An elderly man who had difficulty releasing his foot from the stirrup almost fell.

'Good day to you. You are Calum MacGillivray?'

'And who are you?'

'Dr Boyter. I'm in charge of relief. I've been told that you are not receiving your allowance.'

'I've heard of you, I think. Ten years ago. In Tobermory. You were the agent for the *Brilliant*, the ship that sailed for Australia. It was your fine words that seduced the people and persuaded them to leave, was it not?'

'Indeed it was. They were given a free passage, meat, drink, bedclothes and a surgeon on board. Three hundred and twenty-two, if I remember correctly, were wise enough to sail, fifty-six from this district. None died on the voyage and they wrote to the captain to thank him for their treatment at sea.'

'You're here to persuade me to leave then?'

'I am here to see that all those in need are supplied with meal and I understand that, for some weeks now, you have had nothing. Are you able to work?'

'I was.'

'You have been ill?'

'I was working on the Factor's farm, improving his land at the Duke's expense, but what we were paid would not feed a hen let alone a family. "Starve them into habits of industry," he says. We refused to work till he paid us fairly.'

'You held him to ransom. That was not very wise. You are still in dispute?'

'I have not submitted.'

'And you have no meal. I will look into this matter. I am placing a man of my own choice to be in charge of relief and am anxious to recruit men for fishing, men of courage and resolve who will take instruction in the trade. If you sign for the scheme and, in the meantime, return to work, you will be properly rewarded.'

'You are holding me to ransom then?'

'I am a fair man, MacGillivray. Make your choice. If you had any sense, you would leave for Australia, a land of opportunity which has need of herdsmen and farm labourers. I have been there and was most impressed by its potential. I can see from your expression, however, that you are determined. If you insist on that course, you will have to work. I will see that you get meal enough to restore your strength.'

'I have little choice it seems.'

Boyter tried to mount the horse again but, having placed a foot in the stirrup, could not swing his leg high enough. Calum walked across and helped him to mount.

'Thank you, MacGillivray, you are a gentleman.'

Calum turned and went into the house.

He sat at the table and looked around the empty building; the bed where they had slept, the hearthstone where they had cooked, the empty chair opposite his. All gone. The beasts on the far side of the partition, the hens from the rafters, the meal from the kist. He remembered her hands turning dough, her fingers threading a needle, her feet on the flagstone floor but, most of all, her blue cornflower eyes and the smile that always melted his temper. Waking to see her face on the pillow beside him, he would reach out and touch her cheek in wonderment. How could such a beautiful creature be there with him? Remembering that, a tide of grief surged within him, swelling and thundering upwards in a torrent of sorrow, shaking his frame until it burst out in a wail that echoed round the empty room. She was gone, perhaps never to return.

When Robert came to see him in the early dawn next day he found him asleep with his head on the table.

'We've come to bid you farewell, Calum.'

'So soon Robert, I did not realise. I'll be sorry to see you go and your wife too. You have been good neighbours.'

'We wish you were coming too. You're becoming thinner day by day. There's nothing of you, Calum. I'm loth to leave you in this state.'

'That Dr Boyter has promised me meal.'

'That is a blessing. You must take it. It's not charity.'

'The Factor has nothing to do with it.'

'It's not tainted then. Take it. We must go now.'

He walked across the room and embraced him. Calum saw tears in his eyes.

'May God go with you, Robert. I hope you thrive in the new country. You are a brave man and I admire your courage. Please write to me.'

'I will with the help of God. '

He turned quickly and left.

11

Calum sat on the heather above the Uisken road, exhausted. He had walked from Shiaba past Kilvickeon graveyard, over the moss, past Saorphin and along the hillside until he could see the men working on the road. Some were breaking rock, others were barrowing it to the new track and others laying it as the foundation of what was to be a passable road to Uisken. He rested for a while, watching the crowd and trying to identify them, but they were too far away. He was reluctant to go down, suspecting that some would jeer at him as the leader of a failed strike. Yet he knew he had to join them as the first step on his plan to bring Catherine back. He would take up Boyter's suggestion of training for fishing and, if the pay was as generous as the doctor claimed, he would save enough to persuade her to return. If he had steady employment, it was possible. First, however, he must regain his strength.

He walked down the slope, searching for the foreman. The men breaking stone looked up as he approached. They did not sneer or laugh at him, but seemed glad to see him. Leaning on their sledgehammers or shovels, they welcomed him, asking after the Shiaba people. Clearly they knew about Catherine as they did not enquire about her. He told them of the drover's visit and they were outraged at the arrogance of the man. He noticed MacQuarrie down on the road so he left the men and joined him there.

'Well, Calum, it's good to see you. I'm glad you have come.'

'I had little choice.'

'The others here had no more than you. Like you, they have families to feed.'

Calum, knowing that he had helped Catherine to leave, was about to challenge him but managed to control his anger.

'What can I do here?'

'In the barrow over there you will find a cold chisel and a hammer. You can take the tools up with the men on the slope— the ones you passed—and chip off pieces of rock.'

'Like a convict on hard labour, my offence being hunger.'

'Only you are free to leave.'

Calum turned away, lifted the tools and walked up the slope. Looking around, he saw James Matheson from Scoor, an elderly man, kneeling with a heavy hammer in his hand, and walked over to him.

'You're too old to be kneeling there, James.'

'Yes, but I need the meal, a charaid. Margaret is frail and, if she gets much weaker, I will have a funeral on my hands.'

Calum knelt beside him, lifted his hammer and drove the cold chisel into a cleft in the rock. Metal on metal, the ring of the hammer joined the chorus of other hammers around them. Blow after blow, the chisel sank into the crack until the rock split. He heaved the loose stone aside. One of the young men hurried up with a barrow, lifted the stone into it, picked up several others and sprinted down the slope to the stone-breakers.

'He's in a hurry,' Calum said.

'They compete with each other, the boys. They're not right in the head. When that Dr Boyter was here he was delighted. I've no doubt it will get back to the big men in Glasgow and they'll say we don't need relief.'

'He told me I would get trained for fishing.'

'He told everyone that. If all his promises are kept, there will not be a fish left in the ocean.'

Calum frowned and drove his chisel into another split in the rock.

At the end of the day, Calum's hands, unused to that kind of work, were blistered. When he walked down the slope to return his tools, MacQuarrie had left but Hector Lamont from Ardtun handed him a bag of meal.

'MacQuarrie said you were to have this—in advance of your wages. He said to say that it is not charity.'

Calum nodded, took the meal and headed home, not looking forward to the long walk.

As he came to the rise above Shiaba, he saw hooded crows gathering over something in the heather and a black-backed gull perched on a boulder nearby. At first, he carried on, too tired to go out of his way, but then, his curiosity overcoming the fatigue, he turned back and walked up the hill. The crows scattered as he approached but the gull sat and defied him.

He found a ewe on its back, its lamb standing beside it and its belly swollen ready to burst. He knew that the gas, pressing on its lungs, would kill it, or that the birds would pick out its eyes, even while it lived, and open its belly to lay the entrails across the hill like white ribbon. He had seen it happen. These southern sheep with fleeces so heavy they could not rise when on their backs were prone to die in that way. The beast was still alive. He turned it over but it was too weak to stand. He was about to leave it to its fate when he saw the lamb. A lot of good meat, he thought. The ewe might well die and the lamb would be left motherless. A pity to waste the meat. He caught the lamb and carried it home.

He caught the blood in a bowl and cooked the liver over the fire. It was sweet and fulsome. He could feel it giving him strength. He would make black pudding with the blood and some meal and broth with the head. He cut up the rest of the small carcass and handed portions round his neighbours.

'Where did this come from?' Alexander asked.

'A carcass I found on the hill. It was dead.'

'You're a poor liar, Calum. It was one of the drover's lambs. You can be transported for such a crime. Hunger has dulled your wits. Folly, Calum, sheer folly.'

'The herds will never know. The mother was on its back. I righted her but she will likely die anyway and they will think the lamb wandered off.'

'The herds are not half-wits. They will search the whole hill for the lamb and then they will come here.'

'And they will find nothing. The skin and entrails buried. Never fear. Enjoy your meat. Mannah from heaven.'

'Temptation from the devil.'

Calum laughed and left, delighted with his good fortune.

12

'Her Majesty is minded to order the release of the Burghead rioters,' George said as he and Trevelyan entered the office in Whitehall.

'Good heavens! How did that happen?'

'You may remember the four men who were charged with rioting were sentenced to seven years transportation.'

'Yes and well deserved, I think. We cannot have mobs trying to prevent legitimate trade. Hunger does not give them the right to prevent the export of corn from their harbours. How has Her Majesty come to hear of the affair?'

'The men's wives, I believe, walked to Ardverikie on Loch Laggan where she was in residence in an attempt to appeal directly to her.'

'I hope they were stopped.'

'They were indeed—by Lord Grey who advised them to send a petition and he would see that it reached Her Majesty.'

'He never told me of this.'

'Perhaps he thought it of little consequence.'

Trevelyan sat at his desk, surveying a pile of reports with an expression of resignation.

'I rode into Kent at the weekend, George, and I must say the grain harvest looks very promising. Very encouraging. Saw a mechanical reaper working. What a splendid implement. I don't suppose we would see many of those in the wilderness north of Loch Lomond.'

'No, sir. But I have a report of the Glasgow Committee which is most optimistic about the harvest in the North. It mentions a letter from Dr Boyter. Let me find it. Here. It states that "there never was, in the memory of the present generation, so luxuriant and promising a crop as the year 1847".'

'Splendid, George. That is a relief. I did have some doubts when I ordered the supply of meal to be terminated and all our depot ships to be withdrawn. I hope Sir Edward made that clear to the Central Board.'

'Yes. They have sent out an order to all local committees that supplies are to cease by September, an intimation, they say, which was greeted without remonstrance—except from the Isle of Mull where destitution still prevails.'

'The Argyll islands seem to have suffered badly and yet the young Duke is doing all he can to relieve the distress. I'm impressed with him. He seems to be keen to improve his estate and cleanse it of the poorest and least productive tenants. I would like to have seen the relief funds used to encourage emigration, but I fear that the subscribers would be most unhappy. It was not possible.'

'Perhaps there will be a way round that?'

'I think not, George. I don't want to be associated with or involved in impropriety of any kind. As a matter of interest, what is the state of these funds?'

'The British Association in July had more than £420,000. And the Scottish Central Board has £45,000 and meal ships are still coming in from America with donations from Nova Scotia, Savannah, Indiana, Cincinatti, Ohio, Washington. Quite extraordinary.'

'Yes. We must make it clear that this grain is to be sold—not merely handed out to natives who are too slothful to work. I must give some thought as to how these funds are to be used, given the promising harvest.'

'There is a request for a Royal Commission to investigate the destitution in the Highland and Islands.'

'From the Central Board?'

'Yes. Apparently there was some argument about the request. It was raised first in July. Let me read you this section by a Mr Watson as minuted. Let me see.'

He rummaged through his papers.

'Do sit down, George. You make the office look untidy.'

'Thank you, sir. Here it is: "It was quite evident that, in the present state of the Highlands, there was an amount of destitution there which could only be alleviated by general measures to be adopted by Government. Unless some such measures were adopted they would just have a recurrence of famine and heart-rending destitution and misery and a recurrence of appeals to the public."'

'Not really making the case for a Commission.'

'No, sir, and the meeting thought it was wise to delay the request. That was in July. More recently they decided to withdraw it altogether, partly because they felt that the proprietors would be offended by it and partly because Sir John MacNeill opposed it.'

'Yes. Good man, MacNeill. I knew him in India. Local man too. Colonsay. Besides, Sir Edward will keep us informed. We can be guided by him. But I am resolutely opposed to any further intervention by government. We have a splendid team in Scotland with Sir Edward controlling relief, Sir John in charge of the Poor Law and Skene heading the Central Board. We have done well, George. Everything under control. We seem to have weathered the storm.

13

'You should not have done that, Calum. It was a generous gesture but we are all in it now. All of us who accepted it.'

'You were pleased to have it, Alexander, and it brought some colour to the pale cheeks of the children.'

'It was a terrible risk and they could catch you yet. Van Diemen's land. That's where they would send you. A whisper from one of these people and they will have you in chains.'

'That would please the Factor I think.'

'Oh yes. He is watching you, boy.'

'Maybe I'll steal a wedder so we can have a feast. I came to tell you what MacQuarrie said this morning They are stopping all the relief. Had you heard?'

Alexander's white brows lifted as he looked up in surprise and shook his head.

'Yes. All of it. MacQuarrie told me at work today and I saw the depot ship sail south. Orders from the South, he said, Trevelyan.'

'An evil one that. It was him who let the Irish starve. He hates us all, all the Gaels.'

'It will be a bleak winter, Alexander. I have no potatoes. Like everyone else I ate the seed, what little there was of it, and I sold the cow and calf and the rent's due at the term. I have nothing left. The little I earn on the road buys enough to keep me alive.'

'There was great talk of the fishing.'

'Fine words. I've heard nothing. They are building a good pier in Bunessan so maybe we will hear when its finished. I should never have agreed to learn. I have never been on the sea. When you hear it thundering on the reef out there and see the white spray shooting into the sky higher than the hill on Iona, you feel safer sitting by the hearthstone at home. Still, it's the only way I can earn some money and save to bring Catherine home.'

'You have had a letter from her?'

'You know she can't write. No. Nothing.'

'She will be fine down there. There is plenty of work in the city.'

'I hope so.'

The next day he was moved to the squad breaking stones. He felt stronger and was able to swing the sledge-hammer easily. The strength was returning to his arms and legs and he no longer had to rest above the road after the walk from Shiaba. It was a bright autumn day, with sun warm on his neck and the north wind tossing the stone dust into the heather. Over on the Ardalanish side of the strath, Duncan Bell was harvesting the last of the oats, tying the sheaves himself and propping them into stooks. What had been a promising crop of corn in the parish had been devastated by the recent storm, a dismal omen for the winter.

He was just about to swing his hammer when the foreman called him down. Calum could see the Factor waiting on his horse behind him.

'A word, MacGillivray.'

Keen to show that he was undisturbed, he looked the Factor in the eye and said nothing.

'One of the herds in Shiaba,' the Factor continued, 'is missing a lamb.'

Still Calum remained silent.

'Its mother is running around, bleating piteously and quite demented. The herd is convinced her lamb has been stolen.'

'That must be a great loss—to the flockmaster and the ewe. But then many poor mothers in this district mourn the loss of their little ones.'

'You were seen in the vicinity, MacGillivray, carrying something heavy.'

'A bag of meal, Mr Campbell. Nothing more.'

'Your guile will trip you up one day. I will ride to Shiaba and question the others and their children.'

Again Calum said nothing and watched him tug the reins viciously, swing his horse round and ride away.

'A dangerous one to cross,' the foreman remarked.

'The mighty can fall. Tell it not in Gath, publish it not in the streets of Askalon.'

'Take care, Calum.'

Some weeks later the foreman called him down again but this time it was not the Factor but a red-haired stranger waiting for him. He was not dressed like the others but wore an oilskin jacket and a knitted jersey.

'Are you Calum MacGillivray?'

He had a strange way of speaking, as if he was rolling the words around in his mouth

'There are many by that name in this parish.'

'Dr Boyter spoke of you. He said that you were keen to learn about fishing.'

'He said that the pay was better than the starvation wages I have here.'

'Do you want to learn or not?'

'I do.'

'Meet me at the new jetty in Bunessan tomorrow's morning.'

'I'll try to be there.'

He was at the jetty before it was properly light and before the fisherman. He looked down into a single-masted skiff, its sail still furled round the boom. Very small, he thought, yet solid with what looked like oak ribs, thick and strong. He did not relish the prospect of setting to sea, knowing that there were fathoms of dark water below the boat waiting to clutch a victim and haul him down into the depths. It must be terrible to drown, the pain in your chest as you try to hold your breath, the agony as you surrender and breathe salt water. Thinking about it, he nearly turned around and walked to the Uisken road but, at that moment, the fisherman arrived.

'You're early, Calum.'

'I had no pressing engagements.'

'Have you been in a boat before?'

'Never. I prefer solid ground under my feet.'

'You will be perfectly safe. We will not be going far. Climb down and sit in the stern—the back. I will go first.'

The fisherman scrambled nimbly down the stones and lifted a short ladder for Calum, who stepped down, feeling for each rung carefully. His feet slithered on the deck but he managed to reach the stern thwart.

He watched the fisherman unfurl the sail and, hauling on the halyard, hoist it to the masthead. It flapped in the breeze above Calum's head. Behind the mast were neat coils of line with scores of baited hooks. Must be a day's work there, he thought, baiting thousands of hooks; he hoped it wouldn't be his task.

'What's your name, fisherman?'

'Hugh.'

'Uisdean ruadh. Red Hugh, eh?'

'Just Hugh. Mind your head as I cast off.'

The boat tipped sideways as the wind caught the sail and Calum grabbed the gunwale.

'You're safe enough,' the fisherman said, sitting beside him, gripping the tiller with one hand and the main sheet in the other.

As the sail filled, the boat gathered pace and headed out towards open sea. Calum kept his grip on the gunwale and tried to look calm, not wanting Hugh to think he was nervous. He did not enjoy the rocking motion as the bow dipped through the swell.

'We'll not try the long lines this morning. There's some feathered hooks in the bow and we'll use them to begin with. We'll go round to the rocks off Kintra.'

'Is it deep there?'

Hugh took his eyes off the sail to look at him, clearly suspecting his anxiety.

'No. Not deep. Too shallow for big fish.'

When they reached the rocks, Hugh let the sail loose so that the boat drifted.

'Now go up to the bow and let out the line with the feathers. Let the end with the weight out first and uncoil it bit by bit into the water. Mind the hooks.'

Calum staggered forward, holding on to the mast, and knelt in the bow. The space smelt of fish and tar. As the boat swung in the swell, he could feel his stomach churning but he dropped the weight into the sea and fed out the line.

'That's enough,' Hugh said. 'Now hold on to it and jig it up and down.'

Calum obeyed, wondering why the movement was necessary.

'Were your family fisherfolk?' Calum asked.

'Aye. Four generations.'

'Where?'

'Cellardyke.'

Calum felt a tug on the line.

'There's one on.'

'Leave it out and keep jiggin'. There'll be more.'

His queasy gut forgotten, he looked over the side and saw the flashes of silver in the green water. It was exciting to feel the fish on the line. When Hugh told him to haul it in there were six fish flapping on the hooks. He watched Hugh unhook them and throw them into a creel.

'Pollock,' Hugh said. 'Just pollock. Feed out the line again,' he said.

After a few hours the creel was full and they turned back.

There were three men waiting at the jetty, crofters, men who had enough land and stock to survive the loss of the potato, James MacArthur among them. They had come to buy the fish. James had bought a stirk from Calum two years before and Calum felt the crofter had the better part of the bargain.

'So you're a fisherman now, Calum,' he smiled. Calum thought the smile might be a smirk.

'Yes. I can walk on the water too.'

Hugh climbed on to the jetty and Calum heaved the creel up to him, scrambling up himself.

After some haggling with Hugh, the men paid for the fish and walked away.

'Fishing will not bring your wife back,' James threw back over his shoulder.

Calum was tempted to pick a stone and fling at him.

'Here,' Hugh said, handing him two shillings. 'That's to tide you over. I'll pay you at the end of the week as I was told. Tomorrow, if the weather holds, we will use the long lines.'

'In deeper water?'

Hugh grinned and said nothing

Calum walked into the village to buy some meal but, as he turned the corner, he saw a crowd outside the store. Approaching them, he was shocked. When Catherine left, she was thin and pale and Mary was as near a skeleton as a living being could be, but to see a mass of emaciated people standing silently, their clothes in tatters, their barefoot children clinging listlessly to their skirts, their sunken eyes fixed on the meal-store door, was so horrifying that he stopped in the middle of the road. These people were not just starving, they were near death, many of them clearly sick. Some of the elderly were sitting on the road, holding their knees. Silence hung over them like a shroud. He did not want to walk past them, feeling ashamed of his strength and the money in his pocket, yet there was no alternative. The sea came right to the roadside and the other way by Uisken meant a long walk. Finally he moved forward, his head down, trying not to look into their faces, but they didn't notice him.

On the other side, as he climbed the hill out of the village, he realised that he had not bought meal.

14

John Campbell's face, blown up like a bladder above his collar, showed the extent of his fury. His wife, worried by his apoplectic rage, put down her book. He was sitting in his armchair by the fire but she reckoned that it was not the heat that caused the sweat on his brow.

'What is it, John?'

'This is outrageous!'

She saw the letter in his hand was trembling and assumed that was the cause.

'Sir Thomas Dick Lauder of the Fisheries Board has forwarded this to me for comment. A letter from Captain Stewart complaining that the men in Tiree have not been paid by me for seven weeks. Arrant nonsense. A lie. Listen to what it says,

> 'Indeed I must say that the Factor has
> acted from the commencement of the scheme
> in an indifferent and contemptuous manner
> not only in regard to the piers but also
> regarding the distribution of fishing gear etc
> I cannot help stating the contrast between
> Mr Campbell's conduct to us and the other
> gentlemen with whom we had to co-operate
> in other places, all of whom have been most
> agreeable is most marked.'

'Dreadful, John. Who is this Stewart?'

'A nonentity, an upstart with notions well above his station. Takes pleasure in causing discontent. I may have antagonised Munro, the fish dealer from Leith, last week on Tiree by pointing out that the price offered to the island fishermen was too little. I think he is friendly with Stewart.'

'What are you going to do?'

'I will have to reply to Sir Thomas.'

'I think you should have a cool glass of cordial.'

'Whisky would be better.'

She lifted her book again to indicate her disapproval.

'I find it irritating when we have spent so much on promoting fishing on Tiree. More than £1,000 fitting out boats and improving landing places, nearly £650 for labour on the pier and another £170 on gear and tackle. I think Munro has gained a great deal from our generosity.'

'Some people are never satisfied.'

'I saw that ruffian MacGillivray from Shiaba at Bunessan pier today. It seems that he has taken to the fishing.'

'Is that not a good thing? He may pay his rent that way and feed his family.'

'His family have left him. Sailed to Glasgow I'm told. That doesn't prevent him from stealing sheep.'

'You have the evidence to charge him? It's a serious crime.'

'I will find it, I promise you. I'll have him in the Duke's gaol yet. I'm sure he is behind the petition from the Shiaba men.'

'Did you send it to the Duke?'

'I'll send it in good time. There's no urgency.'

He rose from his chair and headed for the door.

'I'm going to take a walk.'

'Yes. That's a good idea.'

He felt easier when he was outside in the cool air. Colin MacLean was on a ladder securing the thatch on a corn stack. Campbell was pleased with the harvest, though it was not as abundant as the previous one, and stood for a while to admire the neat row of six stacks, their smooth sides, their evenly cut eaves, their perfect symmetry. Only Islay men could build stacks like that. They seemed to glow in the evening sun.

He walked towards the shore where the cattle were gathered around bundles of hay and leaned on the wall to watch them. Excellent stock, he thought, well worth the money he had paid. Good straight backs, broad haunches, sturdy forelegs. His selective breeding was paying off. An expensive bull, but his progeny would bring in more than enough to cover the cost. He compared them with the poor beasts of the crofters which he had taken in payment of rent. So thin and ill-bred that he couldn't sell them at the Bunessan market. He had been forced to find grazing for them at Tormore. He would have to explain his error of judgment to the Duke.

He stood for a while admiring the beasts, watching them toss the hay in the air as they shook it out, wisps of it getting caught on their horns. He liked the sound of them chewing, grinding the hay in their back teeth, and the movement of their soft lips. It was time to start them on turnips, he decided. He was the first to grow a field of turnips in the Ross and he was proud of the crop.

As he strolled back, he thought of the Shiaba petition and MacGillivray's sheep-stealing.

'I don't understand these people,' he said to his wife. 'They cling to their poor plots like limpets to a rock. They must see that they would be better in Canada or Australia. But they stay and grow thinner and more sickly every week. And their children—how can they do that to their children? Little ragged ghosts with blue lips and eyes sunk in their skulls. For their sake alone they should leave. It is the best who are going—that is the tragedy. The dross will remain. Without the aid they would have to go or starve to death, and when the aid runs out—and it will, believe me, Flora, it will—they will wait for the Duke or the people in the South to feed them. They will sit in their idleness and filth and howl for meal.'

'A fine speech, John. You should have been a politician.'

'I'm too straight a man for that. Prevarication and guile are essential skills for that profession. I'm sorry for the rant. I really despair of them and their folly. Now I must compose a letter to His Grace. I will not be long. Then perhaps some cocoa after prayers?'

'Yes. I'll ask Kirsty to see to it and Beth to place a hot pan in the bed.'

> *Your Grace,*
> *With this I enclose a petition from the*
> *people in Shiaba. They have no cause to*
> *complain as they were offered the farm at*
> *a cheaper rate than it is let for and they*
> *are accommodated (at least all who are in*
> *circumstances) in the vacant crofts elsewhere.*
> *The present tenant has given security for the*
> *stock and he pays £40 yearly more than they*
> *did.*
>
> *250 souls have set off from Mull and Iona*
> *for whom I have paid £1,600 in assistance and*
> *28 heads of families from Tyree on the "Eliza"*
> *bound for Montreal for I paid £480. Also 20*
> *heads of families from Tyree on the "Jamaica"*
> *for whom I paid £330—in the latter case the*

actual cost was £1,860 but by selling their
crops and stock we received £1,520.

  I have issued a goodly number of
summonses of removal, some for arrears
of rent and thieving and others for extreme
laziness and bad conduct as I feel it absolutely
necessary to make a few examples. The people
will not work till dire necessity confronts them
or they get an exorbitant rate of wages which I
am resolved they shall not get and, if it cannot
be otherwise accomplished, to starve them
into habits of industry for their own ultimate
benefit.

15

Catherine stood on the deck holding on to a piece of rigging. High above her a line of seamen, bent over a yardarm, were furling a sail. Hearing their voices, she looked up but the swinging of the masts made her giddy and she lowered her head to watch the gulls floating past the rail. She had come up for some air, finding the space below crowded and unpleasant. A crowd of Tiree men were heading south to work on the new railways and one of the wives, noticing Catherine's exhausted appearance, had offered to look after the children. She was glad of the few moments on her own, time to think of Calum and worry how he was going to survive if he persisted with his strike. She imagined him lying on the bed, his lips cracked and swollen, his eyes staring blankly at the rafters, the neighbours standing around as he passed away. Dreadful. She shook her head violently to disperse the image.

'Are you alright, ma'am?'

She was so startled by the voice that she almost fell over. The figure behind her was so bizarre that she raised her hands to protect herself. Dressed in knee breeches, a coat blazing with golden braid and a scarlet waistcoat, he bowed as she looked around. It was his black face that shocked her.

'Your little girl is very sick.'

She was surprised by his concern, wondering why he should be expressing it and why he should be talking to her at all.

'Yes. She has the bloody flux and is suffering from starvation.'

'I have a remedy for the flux down below. Please wait there till I fetch it. Will you wait?'

'Yes. Yes.'

He walked away, his buckled shoes clattering on the deck. She had never seen a black man before and had imagined them dressed in animal skins and carrying spears. Certainly not behaving with perfect manners and speaking so clearly. She was worried about his remedy, thinking it might be concocted by a witch doctor. When he returned, a little breathless from the climb, he handed her a bottle containing a slightly yellow liquid.

'Agrimony. Sticklewort. I made it into tea. The Indians in Virginia gave me this cure.'

'You were in America?'

'Yes, ma'am. As a slave. First in America and then Jamaica. I'm a free man now but still a servant to Mr Baillie. He has been good to me. He has been visiting his land in Glenelg. That's why I'm here. Give your little girl a spoonful of that each day. I know what you're thinking. That it's made by some witch doctor and it's a kind of poison.'

Catherine blushed and denied it.

'It's alright. I'm accustomed to such a view. Try it at least. It will do no harm, I assure you.'

'I'm sorry. I don't want to seem ungrateful. I have no money to pay you.'

'I don't want payment. It's a gift for the little girl.'

'Thank you. Thank you. I will try it.'

'My pleasure.'

He walked away and disappeared down a hatchway.

Still astonished, she stood by the rail and looked at the bottle, wondering if she should risk giving Mary some of the liquid. Such a strange man. Dressed like an aristocrat with the manners and speech of that class but black. She detected a kindness there, a genuine sympathy for Mary. What a contrast to her image of black men. She decided to try the mixture and went below.

She could smell Mary's affliction in the gloom as she stepped carefully down the companionway. She had managed to find a place for her near the stairs where there was some air. Mary was lying wrapped in the blanket with her head in the lap of the Tiree woman who was stroking her hair.

'She needs washed, Catherine. Poor child.'

'I know. I don't know what to do. I have some medicine for her but I have no spoon.'

'Take my place here and I'll see what I can do.'

Catherine looked around the long steerage deck, but there didn't seem to be a place she could wash Mary. The Tiree men were gathered further along the deck, one of them cursing the Factor Mor.

'Thank you, Mairead.'

She changed places with the woman and brought Archie under her arm beside her.

'Where's she going?' he asked.

'She gone to look for a place to wash.'

'I don't like the smell here.'

'I'll take you up after she comes back.'

'It's so sore,' Mary moaned.

Catherine looked down at her face, white and glistening with sweat, her dark hair sticking to her brow.

'My brave girl. I have some medicine for you. Mairead has gone for a spoon.'

Surely, she thought, this sickness will pass. Mary was melting away like wax, her strength flowing away in the flux. Perhaps she was wrong to take her from home. Perhaps she should have listened to Calum. Better to die in her own bed in Shiaba than on a ship at sea. If she died on board, they might bury her over the side. Roll the little body in a hammock and slip her into the sea. The thought horrified her. And it would be her fault.

'God forgive me,' she muttered.

'What did you say?' Mary asked.

'Nothing. Nothing. I was thinking.'

She saw Mairead hurrying back through the crowd of men.

'Here is a spoon and there is a gentleman back there who says that you can use his cabin. His servant has told her about Mary.'

'There are many sick on this ship. Why should he favour her?'

'You will have to ask him. I'll help you with Mary. I'll get my husband to carry her. You are not going to turn down the offer surely?'

'I can't, can I? First, I will give her this medicine.'

'I'll fetch, Duncan.'

When they reached the cabin at the stern of the ship, Mairead knocked and the gentleman opened the door.

'Ah yes. This is the sick girl Jacob spoke of. Please, lay her on the bunk.'

'She is not clean, sir.'

'No matter. I have seen plenty of flux in the Caribbean. You may clean her later.'

A sturdy man with a mane of whiskers and a face scarred by pox, he did not smile but his eyes, red-rimmed and bleary, were softened as he looked on Mary. Lifting his beaver hat off the bunk he threw aside the blankets.

'I lost a daughter of that age to fever in Grenada. Lay her down gently. I will leave you to wash her. My name is Baillie by the way. I should have introduced myself. Arthur Baillie.'

'This is most kind of you, sir,' Catherine said.

'You have Jacob to thank. He is a most compassionate person.'

'Is he the black gentleman?'

'He would be delighted to hear you call him a gentleman but yes he is an African. There is water in a jug there and a washing bowl . You may use my towel. Alas, I have no female attire but you may have my nightshirt. Comical perhaps but better than the filthy clothes. Right, I'll leave you.'

He left the cabin, followed by Mairead's husband.

'I can't imagine him as a slave master,' Catherine said.

'A pretty jug can be full of poison.'

'He seems kind, though.'

They washed Mary, bundled up her soiled clothes, and dressed her in the nightshirt.

'You have no man to help?' Mairead asked.

'No. He would not leave Shiaba. We would have died, had we stayed.'

'You were right then to leave. People are leaving Tiree in droves. I don't know what's to become of us. The men may not get work on the railway again. They left when they heard how bad things were at home and now they might not be taken back. God knows what will happen.'

Mary slept and Catherine noticed that she was sleeping more peacefully.

The women were wakened by a knock on the door. They had fallen asleep in the chairs and were horrified when they realised what they had done. Catherine, glancing at Mary who was still sleeping, hurried to the door.

'Sorry to disturb you ladies but we are in the Clyde and will soon be at the dock.'

Baillie stood, holding his hat, in front of Jacob.

'I'm very sorry, sir. We fell asleep.'

'I'm glad that you did. You deserved that. I have to pack my trunk or I would not have disturbed you. You may leave the child till we dock. Do not worry, she will be perfectly safe. Jacob is not a cannibal, nor a molester of children.'

Catherine hesitated, trying to hide her anxiety.

'That's kind of you, sir, but…'

'No buts, ma'am. I insist and, when we reach port, my carriage will take you to your destination.'

Catherine almost took his hand to thank him but stepped back to let him and Jacob into the cabin. Glancing at Mairead, she saw she was as stunned as she was. She didn't know what to say but gripped Mairead's sleeve and pulled her through the door.

'Do you think she'll be safe?' Mairead said as they made their way through the crowd of men.

'I am sure of it.'

Catherine was on deck as they sailed up the Clyde. The scene ahead was so alarming that she placed a hand over her mouth. Ribbons of black smoke, whipped by the wind, streamed from scores of chimneys. She could taste the sulphur and smell the burning coal. The whole sky seemed to be smouldering. An endless forest of masts, yard arms, rigging, ratlines, grew from the multitude of ships tied up at the quays. A small steamer sailed past, its paddles churning the dark water, and, as she leaned over the rail, she could see a stoker shovelling coal into its boiler. A cloud of its thick smoke enveloped her and made her choke. The fires of hell must be like this, she thought. How can people live here?

As they neared the quay, the noise and the activity on board became frantic, with officers shouting orders and seamen running, climbing, cursing, ropes squealing in their blocks, sails thundering in the wind. She felt the ship bump against the dock and lie still. The clamour below was just as loud, with dockers hauling gangways into place, carts rattling along the cobbles and men rolling barrels to the warehouses.

Mr Baillie emerged from the lower deck and came across to her.

'You have not to worry about the child. Jacob will carry her to the quay and I will hire a carriage to take you and your children to your destination.'

'I have no way of repaying your kindness, sir.'

'I am not expecting anything in return, ma'am. As I mentioned in the cabin, I lost a daughter from disease and would not wish to see such grief inflicted on any parent. I hope that she recovers.'

'Thank you, sir. May God bless you.'

He tipped his hat, bowed and walked away.

16

Trevelyan's dining room in Clapham was laid for dinner with silver cutlery, silver candle sticks, crystal glasses and decanters of wine. Crimson velvet curtains closed out any noise from the street outside and added warmth to the room. Trevelyan sat at the head of the table with his wife's brother, Thomas MacAulay, opposite him. On his right, his eldest daughter, Margaret, sat beside her mother's friend, Marianne Thornton. On his left, his wife, Hannah, and the Reverend Charles Bradley. The two younger children were in bed.

Trevelyan lifted his wine glass by the stem, rose from the table and raised the glass.

'Ladies—and I include you, Margaret, now that you are thirteen—and gentleman. I give you a toast. To the new *History of England* and its brilliant author Thomas MacAulay. To Tom.'

The minister stood and raised his glass. The two ladies and the girl remained seated but joined in the toast.

'*The History of England,*' they said together.

Thomas, at the far end of the table, looked embarrassed.

'It is not released yet, Charles.'

'Is it really finished, Uncle Tom?' Margaret asked.

'The first two volumes, Baba. I must remember to call you Margaret. If I don't take care, I will be calling you Baba till you are as old as your Mama and have Babas of your own. Yes, two volumes complete and I have plans for another three, perhaps four.'

'You are so clever.'

'Industrious, my dear.. Such a work involves hard work as well as intellect. When you are older, I'm certain that you will write wonderful novels which will be the rage of the century.'

The men sat down again.

'A great achievement, Tom,' Trevelyan said. 'It's a shame your father is not here to see it.'

'Indeed. But I am not the only one deserving of an accolade. I heard in cabinet today that you are being considered for a knighthood.'

'Really, Tom?' Hannah clasped her hands in pleasure and looked at her husband adoringly. 'How wonderful!'

'Will you meet the Queen, father?' Margaret asked.

'I would, if I were knighted, but remember the honour is only under consideration. Let us not be too hasty. There were many who saw our policy in Ireland as monstrous. It may never happen. Now, Tom, in memory of our wonderful days in India, I have ordered a special course. '

He clapped his hands and an Indian servant dressed in a turban and saffron suit carried in a large silver dish.

'A curry!' exclaimed Thomas. 'What a splendid idea!'

'I would like to have had frangipani flowers for the table, jasmine and sweet lilies and a cloud of incense, but we will have to make do with the scent of the curry.'

The Indian placed the dish on the table, its silver lid reflecting the candlelight and the glistening wine glasses. When he lifted it, steam rose into the air and the entire company seemed to take a deep breath to inhale the spiced aroma.

'Thank you, Sharbat Khan. It seems to be a popular choice.'

The servant bowed and left to bring in the rice.

'It brings it all back, doesn't it,' said Thomas. 'The majestic snow-covered mountains, the white church in Simla, that magnificent view across the valley.'

'More picturesque than Clapham certainly.'

'I've never been to India,' Marianne said, 'but Hannah has told me how beautiful it is.'

'Very beautiful, Marianne. I hope to return one day,' Trevelyan said. 'Certainly more inspiring than that infernal country across the Irish Sea. But let's not spoil the evening by discussing that issue.'

'Hear, hear,' said the Rev Bradley, using his pink hand as a gavel, 'Scotland is a much more civilised country. I believe Her Majesty is planning another visit to her subjects in the north..'

'Yes, she and the Prince Consort seem to have fallen in love with the Highlands.'

'Rather a romantic attachment I think.'

'Perhaps, but very useful to us at the moment. Her appeal raised £170,000, saving the government a great deal. We are not awash with funds after the Slave Compensation.'

'I hope she's not going to arrange another national fast day,' said Thomas. 'Gave me a dreadful headache.'

'Did raise funds, though, for the starving Highlanders,' said the Rev. Bradley. 'What is the situation there, Charles?'

'Worse than we expected, I'm afraid. Some reports suggest worse than last year.'

'What of Argyll? Wild Argyll where father was born?'

'Worse than others, Tom. The young Duke tells me that half of the emigrants last year died of fever and other illnesses in Canada. Apparently they survived the sea crossing but fell ill on the other side. Tragic really. The Duke makes every effort to encourage the surplus population to emigrate but with limited success. This news will not help his case nor mine.'

'I trust that he is not employing coercion,' said Bradley.

'Not at all. He assures me that the emigration is entirely voluntary.'

'Yes. He seems a good man.'

'A better manager than his father.'

'This curry is very hot, mother,' Margaret interrupted. 'My nose is running.'

'I hope it does not run far,' said Thomas. 'Its departure might mar your beauty.'

'Hot but delicious,' said Bradley, his brow shining with perspiration.

'Never mind, Margaret,' said Hannah. 'The dessert will cure the heat. Cook has made a syllabub and we have melon from Jamaica.'

'My favourite!'

'The news from France is very worrying, don't you think, Charles?' Bradley wiped his upper lip delicately with his serviette.

'I fear another Republic. The revolution shows every sign of succeeding. Our depression in trade was bad enough without that interruption. At least we don't have such violent insurrection here. The corn riots in the north-east were small beer compared to the streets in Paris—barricades, fires, trees torn down. I shiver when I read of the cry "Liberte, Egalite, Fraternite", reminding me of the guillotine.'

'It can't happen here, though, can it?' asked Hannah.

'I think our Reform Act has taken the sting out of the tail. I suspect their middle classes are jealous of it.'

'It didn't give women the vote, though,' Marianne said. 'We are clearly an inferior species.'

'You would just vote for the most handsome candidate,' said Thomas.

'And that would be you, Uncle Tom.'

They all laughed.

'Time for dessert,' said Hannah, clapping her hands.

"The Witness 9th February, 1848.

Meeting of the Glasgow Section of the Destitution Board Committee of Management.

After having carefully examined the Inspectors' Reports, your Committee states, with deep regret, that the mass of the population (until further details are got, the Committee refrain from specifying the proportion) in the different districts are in a very miserable condition. Indeed the remarks in Mr Sinclair's letter that the lower classes are no better off, if not worse off this season than last... from Tyree the Sub-Inspector writes, 'There are now so many applicants for the destitution meal that I do not know what to do with them—females in particular as there is no work for them.' Mr Gray of Arisaig writes, 'This district including South Morar is in very destitute state and has been more neglected than any other.' From Harris and Bernera: 'of the cottar class there are 225 male adults, 290 female adults and 149 children and, at the time the returns were got, these persons were altogether possessed of 16 bolls of meal.' The letter from Mr Sheriff Shaw states, 'I have seen enough to satisfy me that sheep stealing to an unusual extent is going on in Barra and that starvation is forcing the poor to such deplorable acts. I thought that the aspect of these Barra people about this time last year indicated a degree of destitution as could well be imagined but one of the parties brought here yesterday exceeds in the wretchedness of his appearance anything I have seen. He told me that, for several weeks, he and his family had subsisted entirely on fish with an occasional drink of gruel once a day made with meal obtained in charity.' Dr Boyter says that 'want and starvation must be expected ... the crofters have neither seed corn nor seed potatoes.'

Your committee have the satisfaction of laying before the Section a communication from Mr Trevelyan of the Treasury intimating that, as the Government steamer "Shearwater" could not be got ready in time, the "Zephyr" was ordered to the Clyde to communicate with the committee.

The Committee has decided to resume sending supplies.

17

Calum and Hugh scraped mussels off the rocks for bait. A bitter north wind pierced Calum's clothes and numbed his fingers as he plucked the black shells from the rough granite and dropped them into a sack. Behind him, the sea was tossed into a narrow, breaking swell all the way to Staffa. The freezing wind did not seem to trouble Hugh.

'How many of these do we need?' Calum asked.

'As many as there are hooks and some to spare.'

'In the name of God we'll be here all day.'

'We're nearly finished.'

'And then we go home.'

'And then we bait the long lines for tomorrow.'

'Slavery.'

'No. You are free to leave.'

When they had filled the sacks, they carried them back to the jetty where the lines were coiled.

It was a tedious task, breaking open the shells and pressing each mussel on to one of the scores of hooks and re-coiling the lines carefully. While he was working, Calum was thinking of Catherine and wondering what had happened to her and the children. Surely she could have employed a scribe to send him a letter. Perhaps she had ceased to care for him. Perhaps his stubborn refusal to end the strike had driven her away. He regretted it now. He had placed his obsession with justice above his devotion to her. He decided to write to her, expressing his regret, but maybe the regret would be too late. Maybe she had found another man. The sudden thought of her in another's arms made him lose concentration, a hook pierced his thumb and he winced with pain.

'Take care,' said Hugh. 'Get a hook through your finger and I'll have to cut it out.'

'I was thinking of fresh lamb's liver for dinner, with porcelain plates and silver forks and a bottle of wine.'

'That's more of a nightmare when you're hungry.'

'I enjoy tormenting myself.'

'You'll end up in an asylum.'

When the lines were baited, Calum turned to leave but Hugh called him back.

'Here,' he said. 'There's a string of ling in the boat. Take it home with you. Might not be lamb's liver but it is food.'

Calum hesitated.

'It's not charity. No-one came to buy them.'

As he walked home with the string of four fish, Calum passed through a flock of sheep and wondered if the Factor had managed to collect any scraps of evidence. He was sure that no-one in Shiaba would betray him. They were his people.

When he reached the house, he saw one of his neighbours standing outside his door. He looked so thin and ill that Calum walked down to speak to him.

'I have some fresh fish for you, Fergus.'

'They were not for us. I know that, Calum.'

'You have more need of them. You and your family and your old father.'

'To tell you the truth, they are all poorly. Janet has the fever and my father can't rise from the bed, and I can't leave the children to walk to work. Day by day we are shrinking, withering like leaves at the year's end. I can see every bone in my arms. Come in and speak to my father. He will be glad to see you.'

It was almost dark inside, the windows having been covered with sacking. There was no fire on the hearthstone and no beasts of any kind in the building, so the cold, damp air hung over the place like a fog. Calum crossed to the bed and looked down. He was horrified by what he saw. He did not recognise the emaciated figure at first, for there was nothing much more than a skeleton. The skull moved slowly in his direction, the lifeless eyes in their sockets following.

'Calum,' was all the old man could say.

Calum reached down and held his hand.

'Lachlan a laochain. You have a good grip yet.'

He remembered when Lachlan was younger how he would sing as they stacked peats and tease the girls until they blushed. How he would tell the story of Gorrie's Leap in the firelight and have the young men cringing as, in intimate detail, he told of the castration. He remembered his bright blue eyes and the creases in his cheeks left by laughter, the strong arms at the harvest, the silver hair in the wind. He bent down and took the old man in his arms as tears burnt his eyes.

'Fish tonight, my friend. Fish tonight.'

The old man could only nod.

Calum laid him back tenderly on the bed and walked over to the empty hearthstone.

Janet was sitting on a chair, staring at the ashes. She did not look up as he approached and he could see the bones of her shoulder through the thin dress.

'You have no peat?' he asked her.

'We have nothing. No peat, no meal, no milk, no potatoes, no beasts. Nothing.'

'I'll bring you peats. The fire should never go out, Janet. A cold hearthstone is next to a gravestone. I will see that the fire burns as long as you are in the house. You will have fire to cook the fish.'

'You're a kind man, Calum. We have not forgotten the lamb. The risk you took for us all.'

As he left, he saw the children cowering in the darkest corner and could imagine their famished bellies and hungry eyes.

My dearest Catherine,

I hope this letter reaches you safely and that it finds you and the children well and safe in the city.

I know now that I was foolish to continue my contest with the Factor and to risk the lives of the people I hold the dearest. I want you to know that I deeply regret my actions and that I understand why you took the children away.

You were right to do that and I was wrong
to drive you to that extreme. I should have
returned to work and provided for you and the
children. I wish I had shown my love for you
by doing that. I do love you, dearest Catherine,
you are more precious to me than all the land
in the Ross. Even as I write there are tears
in my eyes thinking of you and wishing that
I could hear your voice again and hold your
hand if only for a minute.

I am working with a fisherman and
learning about the trade so that I can save
enough to bring you back to me. If you come
back, I promise I will never let you go hungry
again. I will clean the Factor's stables or
scrub his floors rather than lose you again.
When I have saved enough I will come to
Glasgow to find you. In the meantime please
be patient and wait till I come. Please send
me a letter to let me know that you and the
children are well.

Your loving husband, Calum.

The following day Hugh sailed the boat to the deep water
south of Iona. A lone rock they called Bogha bhun a Choil was
said to be the place for cod. The wind had swung to the south,
nudging a long, gentle swell and a hint of warmth. Hugh lowered the sail and let the boat float some distance off the rock.
He showed Calum how to feed out the long line from the coil,
lowering hook by hook into the green depths. Then they waited.
The rocking of the boat and the lapping of the water against the

side was quite soporific and Calum found it difficult to keep his eyes open, having left Shiaba before dawn.

Suddenly the line was almost pulled from his hand.

'Leave it out,' Hugh said. 'But keep a good hold of it. Take a turn round the pin to be sure.'

Calum, completely alert and grinning with excitement, could feel the line becoming heavier. He looked over the side but could see nothing but a grey jellyfish. He itched to haul in the line.

Eventually Hugh gave the order and he wound it in.

'A bit at a time,' Hugh said. 'And coil the line as you take it in. As each fish comes in, unhook it and throw it in the creel.'

The first fish slithered in his hand and almost flipped back into the sea but he caught it in time. As they came up one after another he mastered the skill and saw the creel fill and overflow. He was astonished, having never seen so many cod in one batch.

'This would feed the whole of Shiaba.'

'They'll be sold to the dealer.'

'All of them?'

'We'll maybe slip the odd one aside.'

Hugh hauled on the halyard to hoist the sail and they headed for home.

'A good place that,' he said. 'We'll come back.'

Calum was thinking of Lachlan and John and wondering if he could persuade Hugh to give him a couple of fish for them.

'There's an old man at home dying for want of food. He's so thin you can see the bedsheet through him.'

'There are many starving in the Ross. If they worked for a living, there would not be so many.'

Calum, tempted to argue, contained the urge.

'His son can't leave the house because his wife is sick. He would work if he could.'

'You're asking for fish, is that it? Why not just ask?'

'I'm asking.'

'Then I'll see. I'm not supposed to give them away.'

'I know that, but even men from the east coast have hearts as well as purses.'

That night he carried two large cod home, cut the tail off one, and carried the other to Fergus. Remembering that he had failed to realise how much the family were suffering, he visited every house in Shiaba and was horrified by the state of the township. He felt guilty that he could buy meal, and that so many were starving. He had to do something—whether stealing lambs or fish or giving away his meal.

18

Catherine was tossed from side to side of the carriage as it clattered through the city streets. Mary lay on the seat opposite her wrapped in a blanket given to her by Mr Baillie. Still pale and drawn, but with her eyes open, she was watching the buildings flit past the window. Archie's head was buried in Catherine's shoulder.

'Where are we going?' Mary asked.

'To see cousin Sine.'

'How do you know where she lives?'

'She told me. Main Street Gorbals near a thatched house'

'Is it far? The swaying makes me feel sick.'

Catherine had not thought of that, and she wondered what she would do if Mary vomited over the seat.

'Not far. Do you think you could walk?'

'I tried on the ship and my legs were too weak. I will try again, though.'

'No, no. Duncan will be there to carry you in.'

She looked out the window as they passed a bridge over the river. Its roadway was so full of traffic there seemed to be no space to move—carts piled high with casks, carriages with liveried posterns, traps with hoods and hundreds of horses. She wondered how the bridge could carry such a load. She thought of Calum and how he would react to the scene, and imagined his face bright with excitement and wonder. He would try to hide it, try to seem unaffected by the extraordinary sights. Calum. Her Calum. He should be with her, sharing everything, enjoying the strangeness of it all.

When the carriage stopped, the horseman shouted, 'What number is it, missus?'

'Three-storey house beside a thatched house.'

'Wait there, well.'

The carriage jerked forward as the horseman snapped the reins. It moved a short distance and stopped again.

'This is it, I think,' he called out.

'Wait there, children,' she said, opening the door and climbing down.

'Can you wait a moment?'

'A moment. I can't wait all day.'

He made no attempt to leave his seat or to help her with the children. Had she been his mistress or master, he would have leapt down to hand her out of the carriage. She crossed the pavement and knocked on the first door. A complete stranger answered.

'Is Sine MacArthur not here?'

'Upstairs,' he said.

She climbed the stair and knocked again. This time it was a girl who seemed slightly familiar.

'Are you Sine MacArthur's daughter—Marion?' she asked.

'Yes and you must be Catherine. It is good to see you. Come in.'

'Can someone help me with Mary? She's too weak to manage. She's down there in a carriage.'

'A carriage? You should not have spent money on a carriage. Father would have come for you.'

Catherine did not want to explain, and was conscious of the horseman waiting below.

'We had no choice.'

'Mother and father are at work. There's just me. Would we manage her between us?'

Marion was tall and slender but Catherine noticed the strength in her arms and the confidence in her manner. Unmanageable red hair like her mother.

'We will try,' she said, and led the way down the stairs.

Determined to manage on her own, Mary struggled out of the carriage but found that she was not strong enough to walk. Catherine and Marion took an arm each and helped her up the stairs.

'I'll make some tea,' Marion said, as Mary lay down in the box bed. 'There's fresh bread and cheese on the table. You must be hungry after the journey. Have something to eat. Mother was not sure when you would come but she said to make sure you were fed.'

'I don't want to eat what little you have.'

'We have enough. Don't worry. We are all working,'

'All of you? Where do you work, Marion?'

'The new cotton mill—McBride's—round the corner. Mother works there too. They're cutting back, though, because of the poor trade. Lots of workers all over the city laid off or on shorter hours so we don't know if we're safe. Mary, there's a wee bit of broth in the pot. Would you take some?'

'Please. If there's enough. I would love some.'

Marion handed Catherine and Archie a pot of tea and a can of milk and swung a pot over the fire, a coal fire which blazed as Marion poked it. Catherine placed the back of her hand across her nose as the smoke drifted towards her. She knew that she had to get used to the smells of the city—the horse dung, the smoke, the breweries, the bakeries—and the filth in the gutters. She looked around the room, noticing the mould on the bare walls, the cardboard on the broken window pane, the wooden floorboards, the damp washing on a rope above the fire.

'And your father—does he work in the mill too?'

'No, no. He cannot bear to be inside now. He works on the new railway. Good wages. Works out about fourteen shillings a week, but they're cutting back there too.'

She ladled some broth into a bowl and carried it carefully over to Mary.

'Will you manage on your own, Mary, or will I help you?'

'I'll manage, thanks. It's kind of you.'

She struggled to sit up and took the bowl in her hands.

'Is Calum working?' Marion asked, sitting on the bed.

'He was on strike. He said that they weren't paid enough.'

'Did they win?'

'No. The others went back to work. For the sake of their families.'

'You have to stay together to win.'

'I doubt if anyone could win against the Factor. He rules in the Ross, a despot, a tyrant. Mothers scare their children by telling them "The Factor Mor" is coming. Like an ogre.'

'The higher they are, the further they fall.'

'Not him.'

They heard a woman coughing on the stairs, a hacking cough as if she had sand in her lungs.

'That'll be mother. It's the dust that does it. Cotton dust in the mill.'

Yet she did not look ill when she opened the door. Her red hair, usually wild and uncontrollable, was tied in a scarf which was white with dust. Catherine had forgotten her freckles and the infectious grin. A small woman, but wiry and afraid of no-one.

She came across and hugged Catherine. She smelt of sweat and what must have been cotton dust.

'Catherine, love, you're so thin. I can feel every rib. You used to be so sturdy. Have you had something to eat?'

'Yes, plenty. Marion has been looking after us.'

'And how is Mary?'

She crossed to the box bed and sat beside her.

'I feel better. Mother gives me medicine she got from a black man on the ship. I think it's helping.'

'A black man?' Sine looked round at Catherine for an explanation.

'I will tell you later.'

'Calum did not come?'

'I'll tell you about that too.'

'Fair enough, I bought a bit of mutton flank to make some stew but we'll need more milk. Could you go out, Marion? We have only two rooms, Catherine, but there is room upstairs for you and the children. Mary can stay where she is for tonight. I will show you later.'

Sine lit a lantern and led Catherine and Archie out of the room and up the stairs.

'I bought some blankets from the rag store next door. They're good and they're clean. I think they must have come from one of the big houses.'

'That's kind of you, Sine. What's the smell in here?'

'The middens out the back. You get used to it. I'll leave the lamp. Don't worry about Mary. We'll look after her.'

'Thank you. I can't thank you enough.'

'I'm glad you came. You were right to come. I'm sure Calum will survive. He was never one to give in. I'll leave you then. Good night.'

She took Catherine in her arms and left.

'Take off your shoes, Archie and get into bed.'

'Are you coming?'

'No. Not yet. I'm going to sit a while.'

She watched him climb into the box bed and sat on the only chair. Above her, black webs in the bare rafters swayed in the heat of the lamp. There was a pail in the middle of the floor to catch drips from a leak in the roof. A table and a chair. No other furniture. Yet she felt at home, relieved that she had accomplished her mission, pleased with herself. And she felt safe with Sine and her family below her. Although it was under the sarking, the room was not cold, perhaps gaining some heat from Sine's fire. She looked across and saw there was a grate and a sink. This would be her home for a while. Months? Years? She realised that she had no plan, no notion of how long she would stay. Maybe always. If she found a better life here and better for the children, perhaps she would never return to Shiaba.

But she missed Calum. She wanted him there, holding her, touching her face with that expression of wonder in his eyes. She longed to hear his voice, feel his beard on her cheek.

Perhaps she would never see him again. The thought struck her so forcibly that her breast heaved with a sob which she tried to suppress so that Archie would not hear it.

She woke having no idea where she was, but reassured to find Archie beside her. Struggling out of the box bed, she found a bag of meal on the table, part of a loaf and cheese, a can of milk and some tea. Clearly Sine had been in while she was asleep and had probably gone to work. She listened but heard nothing from the floor below.

'You don't need to get up, Archie. You'll be warmer in bed. I'm going to light the fire and make some gruel.'

She crossed to the window and looked down at the street. The glass was so thick with grime that it was difficult to see. Across from their house, there was a wine and spirit merchant's with a door set in the rounded corner of the building. A group of men were waiting for it to open. She wondered how they could have the money to buy drink, given their appearance. They seemed to be as impoverished as the people at home. She turned away and found that Sine had left kindling, coal and matches so she was able to light the fire in the grate and cook some meal.

When they had eaten, she took Archie downstairs where she was surprised to find Mary sitting at the table with Sine's other daughter, Sarah, who was about the same age as Mary. Unlike Marion, Sarah had long, lank dark hair and was far from robust. She had the pallor of someone who rarely saw the sun. Yet she seemed full of energy as she hurried to swing on the kettle for tea.

'You must be Sarah,' Catherine said. 'I see you're looking after Mary.'

'It's good to have someone of my own age in the house. Marion is older and thinks she's a young lady.'

'She's a very capable young lady.'

'She reminds me of that every day. She thinks she's the best piecer in McBride's.'

'At the mill?'

'Yes. I work there too. They use us in relays. That's how they get round the Ten Hours Bill. We end up with twelve or fourteen. The children too.'

'Are there many children there?'

'Many, some as young as Archie.'

'Could I get work there?'

'I don't think so. There are people at the gate every day desperate for work but they're all sent away. Poor souls, you can see the hunger in their faces.'

'I have to find work.'

'Try the big houses. House work. Folk in the big houses don't suffer. In fact, the owner of McBride's is looking for a domestic just now. I think he's in Abbotsford Place but I'll find out for sure.'

'That would be a great help, Sarah.'

She noticed that the colour had returned to Mary's cheeks.

'Mary, you look so much better. The medicine must be working.'

'It's lucky we met Jacob, isn't it?'

19

John Campbell to the Duke of Argyll 3rd September 1848:

> *From the state of the people here for want*
> *of food (the Relief Board having stopped all*
> *supplies) I am under the necessity of sending*
> *off a man express by this day's steamer to*
> *Glasgow with instructions to Mr Hill to*
> *Commission them to send off with the least*
> *possible delay by steamer a quantity of meal*
> *as there is not a grain in the district with the*
> *exception of a small quantity in the Parochial*
> *Board store. Yesterday they were at me in*
> *numbers begging for food, some of them*
> *actually in tears. I have caused the Inspector*
> *to write to the Board in the strongest terms*
> *representing the state of the people. In the*
> *meantime I shall give them a little to prevent*
> *any from starving from want and shall give*
> *work at drains to the really destitute able-*
> *bodied.*

The Factor rode out of Bunessan towards Scoor, the rain dripping off the rim of his hat. He could feel it seeping between his thighs and the flank of his horse. It was a soft rain with no wind but it seemed to penetrate every crevice. Having ridden through the miserable crowd at the meal store and explained to them that meal was on its way, the solitude of the ride past Loch Assapol was most welcome. The loch lay still and dark, and the silence, broken only by the clicking of his mount's shoes, hung over the land like a wet cloak.

As he turned east towards Shiaba, he passed through a herd of scrawny cattle which, he presumed, belonged to Captain

MacLean of Scoor. He knew that all the stock of Shiaba were in his possession or sold in his name to pay the rents. He stopped at the top of the hill and looked down into the township. The man MacGillivray would not be at home, although there was a faint wisp of peat smoke from his chimney. An insolent creature, he was nevertheless showing some signs of industry at the fishing and in a position to pay his rent. Yet he wanted to see Shiaba cleared of these small tenants so that the entire face of the hill all the way to Gorrie's Leap would be a profitable sheep farm, enhancing the Duke's rent and acting as an example of improvement.

He descended to the row of houses, passed MaGillivray's, and called at Campbell's, faintly embarrassed that the tenant bore the same name as himself. When he emerged from the house, the Factor was struck by his frailty, the transparent skin on his face and his lassitude.

'Are you not at work, Campbell?'

'How can I work? My wife has the fever, my father is dying and I must look after the children.'

'You will have to move anyway. Shiaba is let to one individual and I want the land here cleared for grazing. You will be better nearer Bunessan, in Ardtun. I have assigned a croft to you there and you will be near the meal store.'

Realising that the Factor was in the township, other people began to appear and soon a small crowd gathered outside Campbell's house.

'As you are all here—well, most of you at any rate—I want to make it clear that every house here will be receiving a further summons of removal in the near future. I have instructed the Sheriff's Office in Tobermory to set this in motion. You must leave this farm. It is let to a single tenant. You can prepare to leave for Canada where you will find a better life for yourselves and your children, or move to other holdings on this estate which I will find for you.'

He saw the antagonism and defiance in their eyes.

'You have no grounds to remove us from our homes,' Alexander said. 'We are not in arrears of rent and we have paid our rent regularly.'

'Your lease has been terminated and the farm let. That is the position. Besides, I'm certain that, by next May term, you will not have the means to pay the rent. In the meantime there is work for those of you who are able—and I can see several fit men here—and there is meal in the store. No-one need go hungry.'

'We will not be in a hurry to leave.' said John Campbell. 'If the Sheriff's men turn us out and board the doors, we will come in the night and break down the boards. If they set fire to the thatch, we will rebuild the roofs. Ourselves and forebears built these houses with our bare hands and we will not be removed easily.'

The crowd behind him nodded their approval

'If you commit a crime, you will be arrested. If you are arrested, you may be transported and that will save the Duke much expense. We will have the farm one way or another. Good day to you.'

Furious, he tugged the head of his horse round and left the crowd standing.

'These people in Shiaba are insufferable,' he said to Flora that evening. Sitting by the fire, he hauled off his boots and, curling his toes in his stockings, he warmed his feet in the glow.

'I wish you wouldn't do that,' she said. 'The odour is like a pig-sty. I thought you were not going there again, leaving it to the Sheriff's men.'

'I wanted to make the position clear to them.'

'Is that MacGillivray man among them still?'

'Oh yes. It may be difficult to remove him as he is now engaged in the fishing scheme of which His Grace approves. Still, I will find a way.'

He lifted his Bible from the table beside him and was about to read when he remembered the trouble on Islay.

'That is distressing news about Walter Campbell,' he said.

'Yes. Such a kind man and much loved on the island. Did all he could to ease the distress.'

'Too generous, Flora. That's what happens when a proprietor is too lenient. You have to be firm, ruthless even. If the small tenants can't pay their rents, they have to go, clear the land for sheep and let it for four times the rent. Walter unfortunately was not a good manager. The estate was already in debt before the potatoes failed. More than £180,000 I believe. The banks and his creditors had to step in.'

'Still, it's sad. He seemed to care about his people. A real gentleman.'

'Caring is not enough. MacLeod in Skye is heading the same way. Too generous also, importing shiploads of meal and advancing more than £5 each to four hundred families. Folly. And there will be more. Mark my words. More prominent families embarrassed. But not Argyll. We are safe here, Flora, thank the Lord.'

'I miss Islay, though. That view from the house out to sea, the fallow deer, the walk down to the point. A softer place than here.'

'I'm glad I'm not Factor there. We can't live on scenery, my dear.'

'It is hard for these families here, especially the mothers. I've been thinking I might organise a soup kitchen for them.'

'The problem with that sort of assistance is that it encourages idleness. We might have the whole of the Ross in a mob at our door.'

'We should do something for the women, John. I'm sure many of them would work if they could.'

'Some of them perhaps. I will think on it. The soup kitchen too. If we could limit it to the women. I have started a tile works on Tiree—fireclay tiles for drains—and that employs the women. Yes, you're right. Something for the Ross.'

He opened his Bible and started to read. She knew that the conversation was over for the evening.

The following day, the Factor arranged to meet Dr Boyter on the Uisken road. He resented his interference, but was well aware of the old man's contacts in Edinburgh and Westminster. He had mentioned Trevelyan's name on several occasions.

'The numbers are a little disappointing,' Boyter said. 'I had hoped there might be fifty or sixty able men but we have thirty-five, mainly old men and boys. The road will never be finished by the winter. It will be a godsend to the Bunessan fishermen, avoiding that dangerous sail round the Torran Rocks.'

'Yes. It's an excellent plan. It will also help the farms along the road.'

'I've had a meeting with the fishermen and have appointed Donald Shaw to be their agent here. They seemed to be agreeable to that.'

'Shaw the postmaster?'

'Yes. He seems to command some respect.'

'It would have been courteous of you to consult me.'

'I have made him inspector of the fishings,' Boyter continued, ignoring Campbell's comment, 'at twelve shillings a week instead of a commission on every creel caught. The fishermen will eventually have the use of the boats and tackle and half the profits, but I've made it clear that anyone who withdraws from the scheme will never again—either he or his family—receive aid under the Fund.'

'I approve of that.'

'The fishing is doing well. One boat in particularly landed a magnificent catch of cod last week. MacGillivray, I believe, was the local man.'

'Indeed. Most impressive, I'm sure.'

20

Catherine walked out into the street, leaving Mary to look after Archie. She tried to keep on the pavement to avoid the gutters but they were narrow and uneven and she felt she had to give way to other people. Walking on the road meant tottering on the cobbles. Abbotsford Place was some distance west of Main Street, but she was determined to find McBride's close. She had borrowed Sine's best shawl for the occasion and Marion's stockings to wear inside her shoes but she still felt shabby. She had never asked for work before and the prospect of pleading for it made her nervous. Not that she lacked confidence, but rather unfamiliarity with the normal procedure. Sine had rehearsed her introduction and how to negotiate wages but she had decided that she would follow her own course.

The streets were distinctly cleaner as she approached the tall houses of Abbotsford Place and there was gas street lighting. She found number 63 and turned into the doorway. She was amazed by the brightly coloured tiles in the close and stairway and the polished banister. She climbed the stairs, which had clearly been scrubbed that morning, and knocked on the door. The girl who answered was neatly dressed in a dark uniform with a starched white hat.

'Good morning,' Catherine said in English. 'Can I speak to Mrs McBride?'

'I will see if she's available. Is she expecting you?'

'No.'

'Can I ask your name?'

'Catherine MacGillivray.'

'Wait a moment please.'

The maid disappeared, almost closing the door.

'Mrs McBride wishes to know why you want to see her.'

'I am looking for employment.'

'Are you from Argyll?'

'The Ross of Mull.'

The maid's attitude changed immediately, almost ready to embrace her.

'I thought you were from the West by your accent and your name. I'm from Kilmartin. Wait a moment and I'll speak to Mrs McBride. Come into the lobby out of the cold.'

Catherine waited for some time and began to worry that the maid had forgotten. She looked around the lobby, taking in the signs of affluence—the ornate hatstand, the narrow polished table, the multi-coloured mat, the carved chair and the painting of a mansion house. She thought of Sine's home and that she and the girls worked in this man's mill, toiling so that he could live like this. When the maid returned, Catherine was shown to the sitting room. She was overwhelmed by the luxury in the room—the long velvet curtains, the intricate cornices, the ceiling rose with chandelier, the voluptuous armchairs, pictures on the walls and the fire blazing under the mantlepiece. She was startled when she caught sight of herself in the mirror above the mantlepiece, a pale, thin, frightened woman. In the middle of all this, Mrs McBride examined her from head to toe as if she was stripping her naked. Seated in a chair, she seemed to have grown like a delicate plant from a voluminous brocade dress, her little slippers peeping from the hem, her sleeves bulging like meal sacks. She was pinched at the waist by a tight bodice, and Catherine wondered how she could breathe.

'What can I do for you, young lady?' she said, arching her eyebrows.

'I'm looking for work, ma'am.'

'And why come to me?'

'I believe you need a maid?'

'Do you now? And what makes you believe that?'

'I was told that one of your maids has left.'

'Well, well. Rumour travels as fast as typhus in the rat-infested alleys beyond our mill. However, it is true that I need a housemaid. Where have you worked before? '

'I have never worked as a servant but I have spent many years looking after my mother who is blind.'

'At least you're honest, a rare quality in working-class women I find. Mary tells me you are from the island of Mull?'

'Yes, ma'am.'

'Island girls are usually reliable and work well. You look a little frail. Do you think that you can manage the tasks here? We have three children and a baby. You will do all the washing, ironing, cleaning, scrubbing floors.'

'I will do anything you ask of me '

The lady paused, placing her delicate fingers under her chin as if praying for guidance. Catherine waited patiently.

'Very well. I will give you a week's trial.'

'Thank you ma'am. That's kind of you. I promise you will not be disappointed.'

'What is your name? I should have your name.'

'Catherine. Catherine MacGillivray.'

'Well, Catherine, I'm afraid we have no spare room so you can either have the box bed in the kitchen or find your own accommodation.'

'If it's acceptable to you, ma'am I will live elsewhere. I have two children and can live with my cousin in Main Street.'

'Not a salubrious district and not exactly next door but it is in your hands. Be here at half-past six in the morning to see to the breakfast. You may go now.'

'Thank you ma'am.'

Catherine headed for the door but, as she turned the handle, Mrs McBride called her back.

'You did not ask about wages.'

'No ma'am. I will trust you to be fair.'

'Good answer, Catherine. I will trust you to do an honest day's work.'

On the way back Catherine did not know whether to be jubilant or apprehensive. The list of tasks mentioned by Mrs McBride was daunting, tasks with which she was not acquainted. Perhaps she would not manage. Perhaps the children would be unbearable. Perhaps Mr McBride would expect favours which she would refuse to offer. Yet it was work, and she felt that the woman would be fair and the wages would help her to feed the children and pay her rent.

As she passed the mill Marion was standing outside with some girls of the same age, all dressed alike with head-scarfs and coats covered in dust. She detached herself and came across to Catherine,

'Well? Did she take you on?'

'Yes but the list of tasks is a mile long.'

'You'll manage, Catherine. I'm really pleased for you. What's she like?'

'Dressed like a queen and speaks like one.'

'I've never seen her. She rarely goes out and, when she does, it's in a carriage into town. She likes to display her wealth, wealth milked from us.'

'It's a huge place you work in. Is it all McBride's?'

She was looking up towards the roof five storeys above.

'All his—with two hundred and fifty slaves inside, all busy making money for him. Come and see. The time-keeper's busy with one of the girls. He won't notice.'

Catherine followed her into the mill and was stunned. The thunder of machinery hit her so violently that she stepped back, placing her hands over her ears. With the whirring belts, the clattering jennies, the spinning shafts, and the white dust it was like a scene from hell, she thought. The vast floor with three rows of columns seemed to stretch into the invisible distance, the spaces between filled with vibrating machinery and identical human figures. Everything moving, spinning, shaking, swinging, heaving. It made her feel ill and she turned and walked out. Marion followed her, laughing.

'Too much for you, Catherine?'

'How can you work in there? It's a kind of hell. There's even children in there, crawling under the machines.'

'You get used to it. Even the dust. We have to work, Catherine. No choice. There's nothing else. We are slaves. Leave and we starve. That's it. The children get paid too, always a bit extra in the house. I'll need to get back now before I'm missed. There's broth in the kitchen for you. We'll meet later.'

Catherine stood with her back to the wall, recovering from the shock. She looked along the building. Its tall brick wall seemed to stretch right along the street. Massive, bigger than any building she had seen. All McBride's and she was to be part of his household. A kind of Duke with a mill for a castle and an army of women for his servants. She thought of the clean air of Shiaba, the silence of the dawn, the smell of the sea, the cry of the curlew and the peats smouldering on the hearthstone and wondered, for a moment, why she had left. She could feel thoughts of Calum emerging from the caverns of her memory, dismissed them quickly and hurried away, deciding to have a walk by the river.

When she returned to the house, the whole family was there—Sine, her girls and their father, Duncan, and her own children. There was an air of excitement in the room,

'Good to see you, Catherine,' Duncan said. 'It's been a long time.'

'Mary was a baby, I think, when you came to the Ross.'

'And now she's a beautiful young lady.'

He was a big man, his face creased with smiling, and his strength quite clear under his working clothes. His long dark hair was edged with grey and Catherine suspected that, were he not clean shaven, his beard would be white. His fingers were ingrained with black dirt from work on the railway.

'You should come with us, Catherine. It will be a great event.'

'Where? What event.?'

'A meeting on the Green. There'll be thousands there.'

'Yes. You must come, Catherine,' said Marion. 'Come and hear all about The Charter.'

'No. I have to see to the children.'

'Sarah will look after them. She's staying here anyway.'

'You should not miss it,' said Sine. 'There's a great atmosphere at these meetings and some exciting speakers, fiery and eloquent.'

'Oh, very well, I'll come, but not for long.'

When they reached Glasgow Green, there was a vast crowd milling around, clearly waiting for someone to take the lead. They were all working people, many of them clearly destitute. Eventually one of them climbed on to a heap of stones and called for attention.

'That's George Smith,' said Duncan. 'A great speaker. Let's move closer so that we can hear.'

Catherine, uneasy among such a mass of people, nevertheless followed.

'The Lord Provost and his motley crew,' she heard Smith say, 'have forced us off this Green in the past. That will not happen again.'

The crowd around cheered.

'They have offered us soup kitchens. We will have none of it. They have offered us pease meal. We will have none of it. It is bread that we need to feed our families. The Good Lord fed five thousand with five barley loaves and two small fishes. That was a miracle. We do not need a miracle. There is bread enough in the bakeries. Are we going to go home to our starving wives and children with nothing to offer?'

There was a deafening roar of 'No!'

'We will have our rights. Let us go together as a body and take our rights.'

Another man then joined him on the stones.

'This is not right,' he said. 'If we act as a mob, we will be charged with breach of the peace. The police will be called and maybe the military and—'

He was shouted down and he stepped aside.

Then another joined Smith.

'Give me three hundred good men and I will go up to the town and bring every man an eight-pound loaf or two four-pound loaves. Who will come with me?'

The crowd surged forward, shouting. She saw some young men, their eyes blazing with fury and excitement, wrenching out bars from the iron railings, others lifting stones from the pile. She heard a cry of 'Bread or Revolution!'

'This is not about the Charter,' Sine said.

'It's about hunger,' Duncan said. 'You must go home. This is going to get out of hand.'

'You should come too.'

'No. My workmate, Davie, is here. I saw him a moment ago. He's a right hothead. I'll need to find him before he gets into trouble.'

Sine turned, took Catherine's hand, and walked away.

21

Duncan followed the crowd as it left the Green and headed north into the town, a great moving mass of smouldering lava. He heard breaking glass and cries of 'Get the guns!' A group of the youths, armed with iron bars, had broken the windows of a gunsmiths and were passing out muskets to the crowd.

'In the name of God!' he said to the man beside him. 'This is madness.'

'This is Paris,' came the reply. 'Bread or Revolution.'

He turned away, trying to see if young Davie was with the group.

'They've no powder here,' one of them shouted. 'Get the other shop.'

The crowd followed them to the next street where they broke into another gunsmith's. He recognised Crossan as he staggered out through the broken door, carrying a musket. Several of the youths loaded their guns with powder and ball. Duncan was horrified, knowing that the baillies would call the military and that there would be bloodshed.

'Come home, father.'

Marion was beside him.

'In God's name, what are you doing here?'

'I was worried about you. Come on, come home.'

'I have to find Davie. He's stupid enough to be with that mob there.'

'You'll never find him in this crowd.'

'I have to try.' He pushed forward through the mass of bodies. Marion followed him.

He heard more breaking glass and saw another group break into a victualler's shop and hand out loaves and cheeses and puddings to the crowd. Soon the entire shop was cleared. That he could understand. That made sense, but anyone carrying arms could find themselves on a prison ship for Australia. He saw some break into a jeweller's and clear the shelves.

Then he heard it. The clattering of hooves above the din and the cavalry came round the corner, charging down the street. Their sabres were not drawn but the weight of the horses would drive the crowd back.

'Run, Marion!' he shouted. 'Run for God's sake!'

The whole crowd turned and fled back towards the river, carrying them both with it.

He could hear the cavalry close behind and tried to keep his feet as the men behind him pushed forward. Marion tripped and fell. He fell on top of her, but was pushed off. He looked up. The whole sky above him was filled with the massive body of a horse, and smelt of its sweat. Marion screamed. As the beasts passed he crawled over to find blood streaming from her leg.

Tearing off his jacket, he made a bandage from a strip of his shirt and wrapped it round the wound.

'Quick! 'he said. 'Before the police get us. Try to walk.'

He helped her to stand and they hobbled away towards the river.

As they crossed the bridge to the Gorbals, they met the cavalry returning. Duncan saw that their sabres were drawn and hurried on with eyes on the ground, worried that Sine or Catherine might be hurt. The further they walked, the more Marion leaned on him. By the time he reached home he was virtually carrying her.

'In God's name what happened?' Sine said.

'The cavalry. A hoof caught her leg.'

'Lay her on the bed. What did you go back for, Marion? I thought you were behind us.'

She didn't answer.

Catherine swung the kettle over the fire and quietly organised Kirsty to take Mary and Archie upstairs.

'Does she need stitches?'

'I don't know till we take the cloth off,' Sine replied.

'Let me see.'

Catherine knelt beside the bed and carefully removed the blood-soaked cloth. She had no idea where the confidence came from—perhaps from tending her mother's burns—but she took charge. She found a long wound where the horseshoe had sliced down the outer thigh.

'It needs stitches.'

'We can't afford a surgeon,' Sine said.

'I don't want a surgeon,' said Marion.

'Let's clean it first,' Catherine said. 'Pour some boiling water into a bowl and pass me the clean simmet off the line. Is there a druggist near here?'

'Adelphi Street up at the river.'

'We need sulphur and archangel tar.'

'I'll send Sarah'

Catherine cleaned the skin round the wound, dipping a strip if the simmet in the boiled water.

'It needs stitched,' she repeated. 'It's still bleeding badly.'

'There's Buchanan down the street,' Marion said. 'He's a kind man. I cleaned for his wife. Maybe he would give us time to pay.'

'It's worth asking, surely.'

She looked at Sine, daring her to refuse.

'Very well. I'll go.'

'No,' said Duncan, having been unusually quiet. 'I'll go. It's all my fault. I should have come away sooner.'

'You should,' said Sine.

He hurried out of the room, avoiding Sine's glare.

'Stupid man,' she said, after he left. 'He should have come back with us. He always has to be there when there's trouble. Looking for Davie was just an excuse.'

She sat in the chair and watched as Catherine continued to wash the wound.

Duncan returned with an elderly man, so tall that he had to stoop in the doorway. She was shocked. The resemblance to the Factor was uncanny but, on closer inspection, she saw the difference and relaxed. Under the heavy silver brows, the eyes were kind and the smile came easily, clearly used to creasing his cheeks.

'So, Marion, your father tells me you were kicked by a horse.'

'Yes, sir.'

He bent down to examine the wound. Catherine, still kneeling by the bed, noticed his long fingers and manicured nails.

'Possibly one of those cavalry steeds which came charging down the street earlier. No consideration for innocent pedestrians going about their lawful business. That's quite a wound, young lady, gaping you might say, but clean. It will need a couple of stitches and the procedure will be slightly painful but absolutely necessary. Perhaps your mother here could help me.'

'I'm her cousin, sir. Catherine.'

'Well, Catherine. You seem to be a competent woman. You will do perfectly. Now, young lady, I'm going shake out a little of this liquid on to a piece of lint. You will hold it over your nose, breathe deeply, and you will feel a little giddy but no pain. No pain. This is a trick I learned recently.'

The liquid smelt repulsive, quite nauseating, but Catherine was astonished by the way he was able to stitch the wound without Marion showing any signs of distress, but rather lying with her eyes closed. She watched with admiration his nimble fingers tying the gut as she held the lips of the wound together.

'There we are. All finished. I'll leave you a little laudanum for her.'

'Did my husband explain that we can't pay immediately?' Sine asked.

'He did. Marion cleaned for my wife at one time and I know her to be an honest and intelligent girl and therefore, by implication, having an honest family. You can pay me when you can or by cleaning my surgery when you have time. Good day to you all and thank you, Catherine, for your assistance.'

He bowed to her and left.

'How did you do it, Catherine? I would have fainted.' Sine said.

That night as she lay in bed, she remembered the procedure and was proud of the way she managed the crisis. She wanted to tell Calum how well she had done and how the surgeon resembled the Factor. Thinking of him, she wondered whether he had overcome his pride and ended his strike or whether he was lying in the corner of the house like a skeleton. Surely she would have heard if he had died. Someone in Shiaba would have sent word, Alexander for instance, but then he could be dead too. She had a vision of Shiaba with the houses full of corpses and the birds picking out their eyes. She should not have left. She should have stayed with him, even if it meant holding each other in the final hour, telling him one last time that she loved him. She missed him so much. She turned away from Mary so that she would not be wakened by the grief that tore the tendrils off her heart.

22

The following morning, she knocked the McBride's door at half-past six. Effie answered in her night clothes and bare legs, her hair not yet combed.

'God, is that time already? Come in, come in.'

She led the way to the kitchen, shutting the door behind them.

Catherine had slid out of bed at five to wash in a basin and dress in clothes which she had borrowed from Sine and Marion, having arrived in the city with only the clothes she was wearing. She had rolled her hair back in a bun and felt quite presentable.

'The children are still in bed, thank God, but they'll probably stir when I go in to dress. I sleep in with them. You could rake out the ashes from the range and get the fire going. Coal is in the cupboard there. I steeped some oatmeal in the big pot to make porridge.so you could start on that. I won't be long.'

'Is the mistress stirring?'

'Good heavens no! Not before eleven. Mr McBride has his breakfast in the dining room—porridge, bacon and egg, coffee.'

She left the room and Catherine stood in front of the range, working out what to do.

Eventually she lifted the poker, raked out the ashes and emptied them into a bucket. Then fetched some coal and tipped it unto the embers. The coal took a long time to catch fire and she wondered if she had done something wrong. It was all new to her. She sighed with relief when a glimmer of flame appeared in the grate and lifted the heavy porridge pot on to the range, pleased with her achievement.

When Effie returned she was in her uniform and herding the children in front of her. They were still in their night clothes, the two boys, perhaps less than five years old, glaring at her.

'This is Catriona, children. She has come to help in the house.'

'I want Bella back,' said the oldest. 'I liked Bella.'

'Well, she won't be back. Now sit up at the table.'

Catherine looked at the children, comparing their plump cheeks and sturdy frames with those of her children and wondering if Mary would ever look as fit as them.

She ladled out the porridge and placed it in front of them.

'We have sugar on it,' said John.

'Do they?' she asked Effie.

'Yes. Everything has to be sweet, I'm told.'

Catherine found a bowl of sugar and sprinkled some over the porridge.

'You had better cook breakfast for his Highness. It has to be exactly on time.'

She followed Effie's instructions and carried it through to the dining room. Mr. McBride was already seated at the table unrolling his napkin from its silver ring. He was a small squat man, although it was hard to be sure when he was seated, with a shine on his bald head. Not finished dressing, he was in his shirt sleeves, revealing unusually hairy arms. Bit like an animal, she thought. Yet he had a pleasant face with a dimple on his chin. Attractive and repulsive at the same time

'Ah. You must be the new girl,' he said as she placed the tray in front of him. 'You lift everything off the tray, place it on the mat and take the tray away.'

'Sorry, sir. I have never done this before.'

'Perfectly alright—Catherine, isn't it?'

'Yes, sir.'

'I'm sure you will learn quickly. Girls from the islands usually do. There are several in my mill. Pleased to say, none of my hands were involved in that dreadful outrage yesterday.'

'What was that, sir?'

'The riot, of course. Have you not heard?'

'No, sir.'

Saint Peter and the cock crowed thrice, she thought.

'Thousands of the lowest class, scum of the earth, on the Green. Broke into gunsmiths, bakeries, jewellers. Had to call in the cavalry. They soon fled back to the slums then, cowards that they are. If that wasn't enough, they came back to the city at night and broke all the gas lighting in Bridgeton. Criminals. Flogged and sent to Australia. That would soon cure them.'

'Yes, sir. Is there anything else?'

'No. no. You may go. I take it that none of your family were at the Green?'

'All at work, sir, except the children.'

'Good, good.'

He waved her away and lifted his knife and fork.

Her hands were trembling as she carried the tray to the kitchen. Lying like that was new to her and she was shocked by the ease with which she accomplished it. At the same time she was sure that he would have dismissed her had she told the truth.

'Have some porridge,' Effie said. 'I'm sure you won't need sugar on it, will you?'

'No indeed.'

'Do you hear that, children? Grown-ups don't need sugar.'

'Mother does,' said John.

The two women looked at each other and raised their eyebrows.

After breakfast Mr McBride called from the lobby.

'Effie, I'm leaving now. See if the mistress needs anything.'

'Yes, sir.'

They heard the front door close.

'Can you clear his breakfast table, Catherine? His dishes are washed in hot water from the boiler. I'll dress the children.'

'What else is to be done?'

'Clean the ashes from the fire in the sitting room and re-light it. The ashes go in the ashpit out the back. Clean all round the fireplace, polish the fender and rub down the fire-irons with the oily rag. Take the hearth rug outside and beat it. Sweep the carpet. Then go over everything in the room with a duster. Everything, chairs, table, all her bloody ornaments, globe lamps, pictures. Room has to be spotless when she finally decides to rise from her bed. You'll find a box with all the cleaning stuff in the cupboard there.'

Effie left the room with her clutch of children.

All the new tasks in an alien environment. Yet she was determined to master them. She had to work for the sake of the children. There were times when she felt so exhausted that carrying on took all her strength, but she kept going by thinking of a sleep at the end of the day.

She followed Effie's instructions and cleaned the sitting room and was dusting when she returned.

'The children's nursemaid will be here shortly.' she said. 'Tell her to go through to the children's room. I hear her ladyship stirring so I'll have to help with her dressing. Could you set a place in the dining room—same as the master's—do you remember how it was?'

'I think so.'

'She's very fussy about her breakfast so I'll show you what she likes. We've no cook so, if you make breakfast and lunch, I'll do dinner.'

That day she learnt how to make sweet milk for the mistress with cornflour, cinnamon and sugar; how to make yeast bread; how to black the stove and shine the brasses; she made broth for lunch, washed and ironed the master's shirts, polished the silver and made jelly; she learnt how to set the dining room table for four, with crystal glasses and fresh candles. With Effie's help she served the evening meal, the magnitude and variety of which astonished her. She had never seen so much food on a table.

'This is our new maid,' Mr McBride announced as she was serving the broth to the couple who were his guests. 'She is from the Isle of Mull.'

'The Duke of Argyll's fiefdom,' the gentleman remarked. 'Splendid young fellow. I met him once, Willie, you know. Has great plans for his estates, I hear. Wants to clear out the landless, the unproductive, send them to Canada and make sensible farms. If all the lairds followed his example, we wouldn't have to raise funds in the city for the destitute Highlanders every time there's a crop failure.'

Catherine stood awkwardly behind his chair, wondering whether she was supposed to respond or leave the room. She looked down on him as he lifted the soup spoon, his fingers handling it delicately, his ring glittering in the candlelight. His shirt collar was far from clean. "Clear out the landless" echoed in her head and she had to suppress the urge to tell him what was really happening, to describe the suffering of her people, the hunger, the sickness, the misery. She wanted to tell him what it was like to watch your child dying, to be driven out of your home, to feel the pain of famine. Most of all she wanted to empty the broth over his head. Instead she gripped her fists and said nothing. Speak out and she would be dismissed.

'You may go, Catherine. Thank you,' Mrs McBride said.

She left the room and returned to the kitchen.

'What's the matter?' asked Effie. 'Your hands are trembling and your face is paler than ever.'

'They speak of people as if they were chaff, refuse to be swept up and cast aside.'

'You learn not to listen. If you get angry, you are the one that suffers. You won't change them. They have the power, the wealth, the influence. You learn just to take their money and keep quiet, Catherine. Nothing's going to change. That mob the other day shouting about revolution. Nonsense. Bridewell or Van Diemen's Land. That's where their revolution will get them. Have some broth and calm yourself.'

She served the next course, finding that the conversation had moved on to the depression in trade and the situation in France. When she cleared the final course and carried the dishes through to the kitchen, she was amazed by the food left over. Effie divided the remains between them and they had an excellent meal, There was so much roast mutton that she was able to take some home.

When she returned to the house, Marion was bathing a gash on her father's head.

'Good God! What happened Duncan?'

'Hit with a stone. I went to the Green to look for Davie.'

'Old fool that you are,' said Marion.

'Huge crowd there. Never seen so many. They were planning to attack the gas Company at Bridgeton and the mills round there. I couldn't see Davie anywhere so I followed them into the town but they didn't get far. Hundreds of constables, their batons drawn, and cavalry with their sabres behind them, beat the crowd back to the Green but they gathered again and there was a roar from them like an animal it was, like one great beast roaring at the police. I never heard anything like it and they started throwing stones.'

Catherine wondered if she was wise to remain but then felt it would be disloyal to leave.

'You should have come home,' Marion said.

'I was still looking for Davie.'

'Your curiosity got the better of you.'

'No, no. I was sure he'd be there. There was this wee boy who took aim and hit one of the magistrates and the bold magistrate gave chase and caught him. The crowd roared, "Rescue, rescue him. Kill the bastards! Murder them!" and they surged forward, throwing stones and yelling. That's when I got hit. Then the military opened fire and there was chaos, folk running all over the place. I ran when I heard the shots.'

'Mother will be furious. You should have been at work.'

'We've been paid off. I was afraid to tell her.'

Marion stepped back and stared at him.

'What are you going to do?'

'I'll find something.'

'Fifteen thousand unemployed and you'll find something.'

They both heard the cough on the stairs and glanced at each other.

'Have you heard?' Sine asked, peeling off her headscarf and shaking off the dust,

'Davie Carruthers has been killed, shot by the troops at the Green. Two others wounded and likely to die. I knew it would end in bloodshed.'

She stopped speaking and stared at Duncan.

'And what happened to you? Why are you not at work?'

23

Calum dropped a bag of meal on to Fergus's table, glancing over at Lachlan.

'Thank you, Calum. He would be dead but for you.'

'You would do the same for me.'

'The children are better already and Janet.'

'Tell me, Fergus, do you know of anyone with a gun?'

'In the name of God! What do you want with a gun?'

'To dig potatoes. You didn't answer me.'

'There is a gun in Duncan MacKinnon's thatch. He will not know it is there. Neil Black brought it back from the American War. It would be better left where it is.'

'I don't suppose he left powder and ball.'

'You have me worried, Calum MacGillivray. You should not be talking this way. It is a sin to kill another man, even the Factor.'

'The sky was blood red at darkening tonight. Did you see it? It will rain before light. Wait and see. Now I must go back and hang the pot over the fire. Good night to you all.'

He turned and left the house.

'You should not have told him about the gun,' Janet said.

'It will do no harm. He has neither powder nor ball for it.'

'You know how he hates the Factor. God knows what he will do, if he lays hands on it. You should go down to MacKinnon's and tell them to dispose of it.'

'I can't do that now. Calum would know what I had done. Maybe it is just an idea in his head, a track leading nowhere. Anyway, the gun could be rusted, the stock eaten with worm, useless.'

'You should go nevertheless.'

'No. Calum is good to us. Without his kindness you might be dead. And certainly Lachlan …' He nodded towards the old man to convey his meaning.

'We should leave this place, Fergus. The Factor will get us out one way or another. We should go to Canada, make a better life for the children.'

'God's sake, woman, you can barely walk to the burn for water.'

'I'm getting stronger every day and the children too.'

'Thanks to Calum. Many months yet before we can even think about it. And what of Lachlan?'

'Don't concern yourselves about me,' a voice came from the bed. 'I will soon be in the place appointed for all of us. Go to Canada. I will be in Kilvickeon graveyard before you leave.'

'Never. We will stay here as long as you live. Never fear. You have my word.'

'Tell Calum to speak to me about the gun.'

That night Calum sat by the fire, staring at the faint, pulsing glow of the peat. For the first time he felt truly alone. He remembered the way Catherine placed the peats on the hearthstone, always the same. He did not weep, the kind of weeping where tears slide silently down the cheek, the kind of quiet self-pity that clings to grief. He roared with pain, the pain that comes from the realisation that you may never see the person you love again, the pain so forceful that it cracks the shell of who you are. He howled her name time after time, his body shaken with sorrow. One more moment with her was all he asked, one instant to tell her how much he loved her, that he would do anything for her, that he would never part from her again. Just to hold her hand, touch her hair, hear her voice again. Just once, once more.

The next morning Calum met Hugh at the jetty as usual.

'You can take her today. I'm going back to Cellardyke.'

'For good?'

'Aye. I'll never come back here unless I'm driven to it. Flies in the summer and rain in the winter. What a place! Anyway, you can handle the boat now and the lines. You look after her, she's not yours mind, but you get half the profit.'

'That sounds good. How are you getting back?'

'Steamer in Iona sound today.'

'Good luck, my friend. You are a good teacher.'

'I'd sooner be a fisherman, my own man, not working for someone else. See and coil those lines right. Don't want to hear of a drowning in the Ross. God go with you, Calum.'

'And you.'

Hugh walked away up the road to Fionnphort, shouldering a kit bag.

'Uisdean Ruadh,' Calum muttered to himself, climbing down into the boat, thinking that the fisherman may have seemed gruff and unfriendly, but he had taught him well and tolerated his subtle removal of fish for Shiaba. A kind soul under that callous exterior.

He hoisted the sail and cast off, heading for Iona.

There was little wind so progress was slow but he did not mind. The blue sea, the colour of the sky, glittered in the early sun and was so clear as he passed through the Sound that he could see crabs on the seabed. The white sand on Iona was so bright that he had to narrow his eyes. There was a freedom out there which he did not feel on the land. He could sail to Glasgow. He could sail to America. With his hand on the tiller and the breeze behind him, he could sail anywhere but he was content to float slowly through the Sound, the sea lapping under the bow. He wondered why he had been afraid of the sea and then he remembered the great storms that swept in on the shore below Shiaba and the barque wrecked on the rocks, its mast snapped like straws, its sails mere ribbons in the gale, its hull shattered and rocking in the massive swell. The small figures in the foam, their hands clutching the sky before they disappeared. The sea could be like that, cruel, indomitable. He was right to be afraid. He would respect its power.

If the fishing continued to be good, he could save money and still help his neighbours.

He could travel to Glasgow to find Catherine and the children—if they were alive. The thought threatened to cloud the brightness of the day with that dark despondency that plagued his evenings and he shook it off. They were alive, he told himself, someone would have sent word if they had perished. Yet a hint of doubt swam around in the back of his mind, tormenting him like a horsefly.

As he rounded the point he saw the black smoke from the steamship which Hugh was joining streaming southwards as it prepared to leave. He searched for Hugh on the deck as he came abreast of it but saw no sign of him. Other people, though, leaned on the rails and watched him sail past. A boat from Iona was crossing ahead of him heading for the steamer, its four oars dipping rhythmically in the tide. He knew immediately that the passengers were leaving their island for the last time, bound for Canada or the distant shores of Australia. Emigrants. The melancholy sound of their singing, heavy with their grief, drifted over the water and touched his heart so deeply that he found tears in his eyes. Psalm 69 in his own tongue. "Save me O God; for the waters are come to my soul." He lowered the sail and joined them as their grief flooded over him. "I am come into deep waters, where the floods overflow me," he sang for them. Then he heard the passengers on the steamship join in and, in the distance, the people on Iona and their singing filled the Sound as if every rock, every bay, every hill mourned their departure. And he knew that many of them would be carrying a sod of their native soil so that, when their time came, they could be buried with it.

As their boat disappeared behind the steamer, he gripped the halyard and raised the sail but he did not head for the fishing ground. He turned about and headed back to Bunessan. It did not seem right to be fishing when the pain of the emigrants still lingered in the air. He would go back to Ardtun and speak to Catherine's mother and, in doing that, would feel closer to her.

'Well, Mima, How are you?' he said as he walked into the house. It was dark inside, the peat smoke so thick that he could barely see the old lady crouched over the fire with a ragged cat in her lap. There was a chaff mattress on the bench seat where her son slept. The cattle stalls at the end of the room were empty but hens scratched in the bracken bedding.

'Calum MacGillivray. You have been a long time in coming.'

He was astonished by the speed with which she recognised his voice. No fault in her hearing.

'I have been learning the fishing.'

'There was a time before that. We could have been dying of hunger or the fever for all you cared.'

'Yes. I am sorry.'

'Catherine was right to leave you. She had the children to think of.'

'Have you heard from her?'

'So that's why you came, is it? Yes, we have had a letter. John read it to me. He is a good son. I want for nothing while he is with me.'

'He is working then?'

'John Campbell Ardmore has given him work on his farm.'

'The Factor! He is working for the Factor!'

'He does not put his pride above his care for his mother. When the Factor heard that John had been a soldier, he gave him work feeding his cattle and he is well paid.'

'The Factor who turns people out of their homes, who increases the rents when people are starving, who steals their cattle to pay for their arrears, who takes our land, the land that we have worked for generations, and gives it over to sheep or takes it into his hands. A sly man and greedy, a man without a heart, callous and haughty. How can John work for him?'

'Because he cares for his old mother, MacGillivray, and his soul is not inflated with pride. Catherine told me of your strike. I said it was foolish but she admired the stand you made against the Factor, a stand against injustice she said. Yet she had to go. Her letter is on the table. You may read it. John has read to me so many times he is tired of it.'

Calum lifted the letter, written in elegant copper-plate script.

> *Dear Mother, We arrived safely in Glasgow and are staying with Duncan and Sine MacArthur in Main Street, Gorbals. We met a wealthy landowner on the ship and his servant, an African from America, gave us a remedy for Mary which has worked like a miracle. She is better already. Sine and her two daughters work in a cotton spinning mill and Duncan works on the new railways. I am hoping to find work as a servant with the owner of the mill. If I can, I will send you some money. I hope John is caring for you and that you are both keeping well. I am glad that he has found work and that you will not suffer from starvation.*
>
> *Your loving daughter, Catherine X (her mark)*

He folded the letter and laid it back on the table.
'She is doing well,' he said.
'She is an able woman, stronger than you might think.'

'I know but I don't know why she has not written to me. I have written to her.'

'She will in time. I would offer you a strupach but I have no tea till John returns.'

'No matter. If there is anything you need, send word to the pier. I have a boat of my own now.'

'I know. I hear news of you at the church. John takes me every Sabbath. Tell the people at Shiaba I pray for them. I have even chastised the Factor outside the church for his behaviour towards them.'

'I can see where Catherine gets her spirit. I will give the Shiaba people your message. I am going there now.'

'Thank you. May God go with you, Calum.'

'And you, Mima.'

He left and headed back up the hill towards Shiaba. He was relieved to read that Catherine and the children were well, but annoyed that she had written to her mother and not to him. He could think of no reason why she would do that except perhaps to punish him. The sooner he possessed the fare to Glasgow the better. The gun would help with that.

24

Calum hid behind a rock, loaded and primed the gun. The sun had not yet risen and a thin frost lay on the heather. He scanned the hillside for signs of the shepherds but all was still, most of the sheep lying beside their lambs. He was nervous and that annoyed him, knowing that an unsteady hand would spoil his aim. If he was caught, he knew the consequences.

Slowly he raised his head above the rock and, inch by inch, slid the gun into a firing position. Again, he looked round the hillside. Reassured, he took aim and fired. A perfect shot. The stag dropped where it stood. Racing forward with the gun in his hand, he bled the beast and dragged the carcass towards the cliff. There was less chance of being seen on the shore. He rolled it over and watched it tumble towards the rocks. Once it had landed he turned and searched the hillside again, hoping that no-one had heard the shot.

Scrambling down the cliff path, he opened the belly of the stag with his knife and hauled out the heart, lungs, liver, stomach and entrails, still warm and steaming in the cold air. His hands were trembling, partly with excitement but largely with anxiety. The crime could send him to Australia for the rest of his life. Severing the head, he carried it down to the tide edge and buried it with heavy stones in a slit in the rocks. He did the same with the entrails but kept the edible organs. Tearing heavy sods off the rock outcrops, he buried the carcass, making sure that no sign of it would be left. The gulls would spot any remnant and they, in turn, would be seen by the shepherds. Scattering dead bracken over the bloodstained ground, he headed back to Shiaba with the gun.

Fergus had just risen and was about to walk to the burn for water.

'I have something for you,' Calum said. 'Let's go inside.'

He placed the heart and liver on the table.

'Christ Jesus, Calum! What have you done?'

'A stag leapt like Gorrie over the cliff. It was a shame not to deprive the hart of its heart.'

'You're a poor liar, Calum. You'll be gaoled for this. And where's the gun?'

'It's safe.'

'So you got powder and ball.'

'I did. I must go to work now. Enjoy your meal, my friend. There is more to come.'

He walked to Bunessan, beginning to feel a little more at ease, in fact rather proud of himself. He was going to supply Shiaba with meat and could sell all his catch, allowing him to save for Catherine's return. There were four other boats now, longer than his own, each of them in the hands of East Coast fishermen employed to teach men of the Ross to fish. The others had left by the time he arrived, all heading north towards Staffa. Calum hoisted sail and turned his vessel south towards his fishing ground. He had spent the previous evening baiting the lines and coiling them into the flat line baskets. Now, glad to be on his own as he smelt of entrails and stag, he washed his face and hands in the sea.

It was another good day's fishing. Late in the afternoon he turned the boat east towards Uisken and along the south coast to Scoor so it was dusk when he passed the point below Shiaba and dark when he reached the cliffs. There was enough light to see the place where the stag was buried, so he lowered the sail and rowed the boat slowly toward the rocks. There was a small gravel beach just below the burial place where he landed safely. At that point, the moon slid out from the clouds, a yellow scythe-blade moon low in the sky and shimmering on the sea. Dragging the heavy carcass down to the boat in the ghostly light, he managed to heave it over the side, returning to clear all the evidence on the shore.

Hoisting the sail, he headed back towards Shiaba, landing easily on the white beach below the township, where he buried the carcass again. Satisfied, he smiled, leaning against the bow of the boat and thinking of Catherine. She would pretend to scold him for the offence but he would see the admiration in her eyes. He was in no hurry now. He could return to Bunessan well before dawn, unload his catch and later look as though he had just arrived.

That evening he walked down to the white beach and uncovered the carcass. Using his knife, he started to skin it, driving his fist between the flesh and the skin, peeling off the heavy brown hide. As he worked, he watched the hillside for shepherds or men from the farm at Scoor. When he had finished he severed the haunches, cutting through to the ball joints, then he wrapped the rest of the carcass in the skin and buried it again. The cold air of dusk cooled the sweat on his face as he carried the haunches up to the houses.

'Now, Fergus, I want you to divide this between the families. You know who needs it most. Do it quickly.'

'You're insane, Calum. Someone will tell. News will leak out. Some people can't contain themselves when it comes to gossip.'

'I'll risk that. I have more faith in our people than you have.'

'Calum,' Lachlan spoke from the shadows. 'Forgive my son. I'm ashamed of him, showing so little gratitude. The rest of us are grateful and know the risk you have taken.'

'My worry for Calum came first,' Fergus said. 'Of course I'm grateful. I will never forget this kindness.'

'We live to help each other. Enjoy your meal. Good night to you all.'

In spite of his declaration of faith in his people, he thought it wise to hide the gun in the thatch.

25

'This morning, my dear Sir Charles Trevelyan KCB,' said Hannah, 'you and I are going to take a cab to Regent's Park. Tom has taken the children to town for the day and we are having some time together. No argument. You are to be my knight in shining armour.'

He was sitting at the table and she stood over him with a hand on his shoulder. He took her fingers in his and pressed them to his lips.

'Your wish is my command. I will ride to the office later.'

She produced his high hat from behind her back.

'Come then, sir knight. We will sally forth.'

She unhooked her bonnet from the hall stand, tied it under her chin and lifted her parasol. Taking his arm in hers, they left the house.

Taking a cab across the Thames to Regent's Park, they walked at a leisurely pace through the trees.

'There is something I wish to show you. I don't think you have visited the Colosseum. Tom, on one of his adventures with the children, was enchanted by it.'

They climbed the steps of the building, passing between the massive Doric columns of the portico and into the Museum of Sculpture where, beneath a transparent domed roof, classical half-clothed figures posed provocatively or declaimed silently.

'This is not what I brought you to see,' she said. 'Come this way.'

She led him into a large lift.

'They call this the Ascending Room.'

It raised them in an enclosed column to the next level where, with several other visitors, they stepped out on to a gallery. There they were completely surrounded by an immense canvas painting, a panorama of London as seen from the dome of St Paul's cathedral.

'Astonishing!' he said. 'It is as if you are there, looking over the city.'

It pleased her to see him so enthralled.

'It makes me feel quite giddy.'

'You can see my office. Look there.'

'It is said to be the largest canvas in the world.'

'Extraordinary.'

'I thought you would be impressed. Margaret told me about it. Tom brought them here last week after they had visited the National Gallery.'

They descended and walked out into the park, crossing the road where several carriages had drawn up near the steps. It was a warm day with the sun glittering on the lake and the sheep grazing with their lambs under the trees, but she could see that he was already pre-occupied with another matter.

'I may have a knighthood in London,' he said, 'but I will be remembered as a villain in Ireland, seen in the same light as Cromwell, an evil, callous creature who starved millions to death. Yet I have done all I can to prevent a catastrophe.'

'You have done your best, Charles. No-one could have done more. I know the hours you have spent late at night in the office. There will be many Irish who appreciate your labours.'

'I doubt it. Anyway, let us enjoy the day. A walk down by the lake, listen to the birds.

A little peace in the turmoil.'

'Yes.' She squeezed his arm and they walked on.

When they reached home, the children and Tom were already romping round the sitting room, playing lions and tigers.

'We have been to the Chambers of Horrors, father,' Margaret said. 'It was gruesome. I was sure the figures were about to speak. Uncle Tom pretended to be one of them and then sprang to life.'

'And we had oysters and caviar and olives for lunch,' added George, not to be outdone.

'I'm glad you enjoyed the lunch, George,' Charles said. 'If I recall, you didn't express much appreciation of our visit, the trip to the National Gallery. Now I'm afraid that I must leave you all and return to my duties in the Treasury.'

'Can you not stay a little longer?' Hannah pleaded.

'Believe me, I would prefer to remain but the Chancellor is waiting to hear my plan for Scotland. Anyway, Tom will keep you all entertained. I will return in time for dinner.'

'Congratulations, Sir Charles,' George said as he entered the office.

'Thank you, George. It is some compensation for my labours.'

'Well deserved, sir.'

'Still, we must focus our attention on the task in hand. You have been scanning the press and pamphlets published in Scotland. What's your impression of public opinion? My brother-in-law, as you know, is well acquainted with Edinburgh but, since losing his seat there last year, has become absorbed in his academic work and is therefore not familiar with current opinion, so I rely on your perusal of the journals.'

'It seems to me, sir, that the critics of the Relief—those who regard the Highlanders as slothful and suffering from moral turpitude—are gaining the upper hand. There is an opinion that industrious Lowlanders should not be expected to raise funds to support indolent Highlanders.'

'Good, George. That is to our advantage. Here is the plan for Scotland. We will limit the amount of meal to a pound a day. In Ireland we found that one pound, properly cooked, was perfectly adequate for an able-bodied man. Indeed, we fed three million on it. We keep it to a bare minimum. One pound for eight hours labour. That way only the most destitute will be attracted to work. I'm sure there will be an outcry, particularly from the Glasgow Section which is far too easy on the poor.'

'I think you're right, sir. There will be objections.'

'We will see. The Edinburgh Section will be with us. I also want them to appoint salaried inspectors so that we can control the scheme, preferably half-pay officers from the Royal Navy. The Central Board can provide the funds and the proprietors can contribute, as their estates will benefit from the work. The Government can no longer help. There is no more money. We have just survived one of the worst financial crises since the War—the "week of terror" as they say. Eleven banks broke last year so we had to step in and support the banks. I don't think the Scots realise how perilous a crisis the country is facing.'

'It seems that the destitution in the Highlands is worse than ever. The reports from the inspectors to the Glasgow Section indicate that the destitution is already, to quote, "fearful" and that immediate relief is urgently needed. There seems to be some difficulty with the advances for Drainage money. Both sections it seems are presenting what they call "a respectful memorial" to you requesting that we "do away with any obstacles or difficulty in the way of the proprietors procuring the drainage money".'

'Nonsense. If the proprietors presented schemes which were less obviously designed to improve their property, they might receive more favourable responses. If they were all like Argyll or Sutherland or Matheson, there would not be any difficulty. See if you can get the minutes of the Glasgow Section's meeting.

I had better read them in full and I will write to the Navy to see if they have any steamers available to send to the Highlands.'

'Yes, sir.'

'I am determined to see that the Government is not drawn into this morass in the Highlands, except to ensure that the funds raised by the public are administered with propriety and that widespread mortality does not bring us into disrepute. We must use this crisis to improve the Highlands so that such destitution is never repeated. Our responsibility, George.'

'Indeed, sir'

26

'Do you remember, Angus MacNiven from Islay?' asked John Campbell of his wife.

'Of course. From Barr.'

'I am thinking of creating a farm for him here.'

'In Ardfenaig?'

'No, no. In Ardalanish.'

'Beautiful place. Fertile too. Reminds me of Ardmore.'

'I need to extend it, though, and that will entail removing some tenants and that might be difficult. The MacIntyres have been there for generations. Baptists. Educated men. Would not be easy but worth an attempt. I would like to bring Angus to the Ross.'

'Do you not miss Ardmore?'

'I don't look back, Flora. We will prosper here. The young Duke seems to respect my efforts on his behalf and is keen to see the estate improved. Besides, I have more than a thousand acres here already and two hundred of arable at Tormore.'

He looked at the sleet and thought of the young lambs standing drenched with their ears down beside their mothers. Poor weather for any beast, he thought, cold and wet. Still, the mothers were well fed with turnips and bruised oats. It was time the lea ploughing was finished. He would speak to Dugald Campbell about it and ensure that the land was ready for the new seed. It pleased him to think that he was a pioneer of the new methods and crops. He was planning a visit to his cattle when there was a knock on the back door.

'I'll answer it,' he said, noticing that Flora made no attempt to lay down her tapestry.

It was one of the shepherds from Shiaba.

'Well, Donald. What a dreadful day. Sore on young lambs. What brings you all the way from Shiaba?'

'There are poachers on the hill. Deer poachers. I found blood on the ground near the march. I thought you should know.'

'Indeed. You are sure that it's from a deer?'

'Oh yes. Too much blood for anything else. And there is hair off the skin.'

'On this side of the march? On His Grace's land?'

'Just. The beast likely came off Lochbuie.'

'And there's no gralloch? No head or skin?'

'No sign. Maybe they came in from the sea. At night so they would not be seen.'

'Have you searched the shore?'

'No. The shore is well off my beat. I have enough to do with the lambs without hunting for grallochs. You could get your men to look. I had to come to the village for meal or I would not be here.'

'Yes, it's good of you to come. I might ride out that way later. Will you be there?'

'Yes. Somewhere on the hill.'

'Good. I will see you there.'

He returned to the sitting room, lifting his hat and coat off the stand in the hall.

'I have to go out.'

'In that weather?'

'There is poaching on Shiaba. I'm sure that MacGillivray has turned his attention to venison, though how he would kill a deer defeats me. It was him who stole the lambs, I'm convinced of that but have no proof, no evidence, and the people of Shiaba would never give evidence against him. To kill a deer he would need a gun and, if he has a gun, that is very worrying.'

'A danger to us?'

'Who knows? If his blood was up, he might be capable of anything.'

'He will have to be caught, John.'

'He will. Have no doubts.'

He had the horse saddled and was about to ride towards the village when he was stopped by the cattleman.

'You had better come and look at this, sir. One of the cows has cast her calf. Born dead before its time.'

'Where is she, Colin?'

'In the far away park, the one with the standing stone, sir.'

'Follow me.'

He wheeled the horse round and hurried down to the field. One of his best cows, bred with the new bull, was standing over her dead calf, licking it clean. He climbed the fence and crossed the field to examine the carcass. It was strangely dry, as if it had been dead inside her for some time. Colin caught up with him.

'Did she manage herself or did she need help?'

'I had to help her, sir. She was heaving for ages. Couldn't get it out.'

'And it was dead?'

'Dead for a while I would say.'

'I should have brought her in. We'll need to watch the others day and night. Could be a disease that will spread. We'd better bury the calf right away.'

'I'll go back and fetch a spade.'

Campbell ran his hand down the cow's back, trying to comfort her.

'Gently, maha. It's dead. Your wee calf's dead. All that heaving for nothing. I think we'll take you inside, eh? Keep an eye on you. Spoil you a bit.'

He rubbed the top of her tail, knowing they liked that, and walked away sadly.

Meeting the cattleman on the track, he told him to take the cow inside.

'Leave the burying for the moment. Put a rope on the calf and haul it to the bull-shed. She'll follow. Bury the calf after that. I'll come down and see her after I stable the horse.'

All thoughts of riding to Shiaba had been eclipsed by his concern for his livestock.

'The Lord hath given and the Lord taketh away. Blessed be the name of the Lord,' he said to himself.

When he returned to the house, Flora met him at the back door.

'You have a visitor, John. A man of the cloth. Donald McVean, the Free Church minister from Iona.'

'What will he want do you suppose?'

'He did not offer an explanation and I did not enquire. I have shown him into the study and offered him some tea which he declined. Had it been one of the crofters, I would have made an excuse for you and sent him away.'

'No matter. You were right to let him in, even if he has turned his back on the Church.'

'He is still a minister, a man of God.'

'True. I will see him.'

McVean rose as he entered the study, placing his tea on a side table.

'Mr Campbell.' He managed to offer the hint of a bow.

'Mr McVean.'

'I was telling your wife that my wife Susannah was born here.'

'Really?'

'Susannah MacLean. Forty years ago.'

'What a coincidence. She is well?'

'Indeed. She is expecting her eighth child.'

'I see. But what can I do for you, sir?'

'I have come to plead for the crofters. They tell me His Grace has raised the rents.'

'To a fair level. Comparing them with those of tenants elsewhere on the estate, His Grace's father was far too generous. It is a fertile island, Iona.'

'But not a good time with the failure of the potato.'

'The crofters have not suffered so badly, having some other crops. The cottars, the landless, the indolent, the worthless, those who relied on their potatoes, they have brought suffering on themselves and, in spite of that, His Grace has made every effort to assist them. He has provided meal, he has offered work, he has assisted emigration.'

'Indeed. I would not dispute that, but the Destitution Board has been equally generous and I believe the relief it has provided has come to an end, finished, a callous decision which will affect the whole population here. To raise the rents by a half at such a time will add to the hardship. The tenants will be forced to sell their cattle to avoid arrears and that will lead to arrears in the future.'

'We have made work available under the Drainage Act for all able-bodied men. I'm sure you would not argue with St Paul when he says "If any should not work, neither should he eat."'

'A pound of meal for eight hours work is not much better than slavery,' answered McVean, choosing to ignore the biblical reference.

'It is enough. Besides, there is work for the young men on the new railways in the south.'

'And, if they leave, who will work the land, sow the seed, harvest the crop? There are no easy solutions to this crisis but raising the rents is not one of them.'

'I will convey your concerns to His Grace but I cannot promise that you will receive a sympathetic response,' Campbell said, opening the door to indicate that the interview was concluded.

'Thank you, Mr Campbell. Please bear my plea in mind. To return your words from the Epistle of St Paul, perhaps I could remind you of Mathew Chapter 25: "Inasmuch as you have done it unto one of the least of these my brethren, ye have done it unto me." Good day to you.'

Campbell watched him through the window as he hurried away, tugging his hat down to shelter his neck from the sleet. He walked through to the sitting room to find Flora.

'I know what is troubling him,' he said. 'He is worried that he might lose half of his flock and therefore his living. They are all in that precarious position, the free church ministers. He may yet regret leaving the Church.'

'They are still Christian men.'

Since 1876 John Campbell had issued 80 families in the Ross of Mull with Summonses of Removal obtained from Tobermory Sheriff Court.

27

Catherine gradually defeated the children's initial antagonism by telling them tales which she had heard from her blind mother. She told them the tale of Fraoch of the Sharp Blades.

'There was once a powerful woman called Maeve who lived near Ardfenaig close to where I was born,' she spoke in an ethereal tone, 'and she had a beautiful daughter with pure white hands and fair hair. A young, handsome man called Fraoch came to the island and fell in love with Maeve's daughter. Maeve wanted him for himself and became ill with jealousy. Fraoch, being a kind young man, asked if there was anything that would help to heal her. There is an island near my home called Eilean Mhor where you can find beautiful red rowan berries but it was guarded by a terrible dragon. Maeve said the only cure for her illness was a handful of rowan berries from the island and asked him to fetch some for her.'

'But he would be killed,' interrupted John. 'Why did she want him killed?"

'She was so jealous that she would rather he was killed than see him marry her daughter. Maeve's daughter tried to help him by giving him a golden sword. He bravely swam out to the island, fought with the dragon and slew it but he died of his wounds.'

'She was a bad lady, Maeve.'

'She wanted him to herself so much that she would rather lose him than let her daughter have him. Jealousy can be a terrible thing.'

She was not used to precocious children who spoke without reservation. Her children were reserved, quiet, almost timid and she wondered why that was the case, what had she done to mould them in that way. Neither she nor Calum had been unduly firm with them or inflicted the harsh discipline she had seen in some families. Compared to the McBride children they were inhibited, shy. Yet she liked John. He was clever and had a fund of knowledge about his world which impressed her. He read books and could remember what he read. When he was dressed to walk out with Effie, he resembled a miniature of his father, with his hair slicked down, his collar starched, his breeches pressed and his shoes gleaming, and the resemblance amused her.

'Did your mother read these stories to you?' he asked.

'My mother is blind. She told me the stories.'

'She can't see? Anything? That must be horrible.'

'She can milk the cow, bake bannocks, gather seaweed from the shore for potatoes, cut corn with a hook and bind sheaves. Lots of things. She is quite happy really.'

'She must be a nice lady.'

She remembered how, between them, they had developed a code for colours—purple the scent of peat smoke, yellow the smell of gorse bloom, white the taste of salt for the herring, blue the sound of the sea and red the taste of blood. Black was the Factor Mor.

John's little brother Moses was very different, difficult to control, but full of energy and spirit, yet she liked him too. He was the one who had to stop and speak to the horses in the street, who went for rides on the coal cart and came home black with dust. He had little interest in reading and was often in trouble at school. She wondered how they would make their living in the end. John would follow his father no doubt and, she hoped, Moses would break away and travel the world.

And her Mary? What would become of her? She did not want her to return to the Ross, become a slave to the bitter land of Shiaba, or a servant to the likes of the Factor Mor or marry a man wed to his past. She wanted more for her—to be a teacher or a nurse, anything with a future. She had an inner strength, an unassailable resilience and a kindness which she never flaunted. Archie was the one who watched, who possessed a perception well beyond his years, who accepted whatever the world flung at him and bent with the storm. He would survive. In the meantime she would work so that they could thrive.

She began to take a pride in her tasks in the house, polishing the silver and glass till they gleamed, scrubbing the kitchen table till it blinded the eyes in the sunlight, ironing the tablecloths to leave the creases as sharp as a knife. Every fire grate was left spotless, every picture frame dusted, every candle trimmed and neat, and every rug beaten outside. She could make a perfect yeast loaf, an incomparable broth, butter whirls as delicate as a rose. The mistress praised her rose-water and her French toast. In spite of the long hours and endless work, she was content. Until the second Monday of her engagement.

When she carried the master's breakfast through to the dining room, he was not seated in his usual place, but standing at the window with his back to her. As she placed the tray on the table he turned to face her.

'Catherine, I have discovered that you were part of the mob in that riot. I find it difficult to believe, but my source is impeccable. Had you not denied it, I might have considered asking for an explanation, but your dishonesty, combined with your participation, leaves me no alternative but to dismiss you instantly. I have left your pay with Effie. Collect it as you go. Now please leave.'

She was so shocked that she did not try to argue but turned and left the room.

In the kitchen Effie held her finger to her lips to indicate that the children were not to know and passed her an envelope.

'Thanks, Effie. I'm going out for a moment. I'll be back soon.'

Lifting her shawl, she hurried out of the room so that the children did not see the tears in her eyes.

She stood in the street, trying to recover. Furious with herself for lying in the first place, but also at the injustice of her dismissal, she tugged her shawl round her shoulders and glared at a milkman who was watching her. McBride should have given her the opportunity to explain. That was unfair. As the anger subsided, it was replaced by worry. How would she support the children now? And she could not tell Sine the reason for her dismissal as she would blame Duncan and there was already tension between them.

Miserably she walked back towards their house.

When she arrived, none of the children were there and Duncan was sitting warming his hands at the lifeless fire.

'Where are the children?' she asked.

'At work. Are you alright, Catherine? You look feverish. There is cholera in the streets.'

'I'm well enough. The children, my two, are at work?'

'Yes. Sine took them all with her. You're home early.'

'I am dismissed. I was seen at the riot.'

'No! Someone is causing trouble. The meeting was a week ago.'

'No matter. Mr McBride dismissed me this morning. At least I have been paid but I will need to find another position.'

'You could join Sine in the mill.'

'Hardly. McBride would not have me.'

'I suppose not. Listen, there is a teacher in Oxford Street who needs help in the house. His wife passed away and he has children. A Chartist. A kind man. You could speak to him tonight.'

'A Chartist like the men at the riot? Is that going lead to more trouble?'

'No, no. He's not one of the "physical force" men. He's a thinker, a quiet person.'

'It is worth a try. I don't like the children, especially Archie, being in the mill.'

'They are perfectly safe. Our girls started when they were nine, as soon as the law allowed.'

'I'll speak to Sine.'

When Sine and the girls came home that night Catherine had a stew and fresh bannocks ready for them. Mary was transformed, her face glowing, her eyes bright, her energy restored.

'I'm working, mother,' she said, bounding across the room to embrace her. 'The foreman has taken me on. Sine is showing me.'

'That's wonderful, Mary, but it is dangerous work surely. And what about Archie?'

'He was helping too. Gathering cotton from under the machines.'

'But he's too young. He can't do that.'

'There are other children there. Aren't there, Sine?'

'Yes, Catherine. We all look after them.'

'It's against the law.'

'McBride would lose half of his workers, if they couldn't bring their weans.'

'And lose half his profit,' said Marion, removing her head-scarf and shaking it out in a cloud of dust.'

'Davie's funeral is tomorrow, Duncan,' Sine said, turning towards him. 'You had better stay at home. The constables are still rounding up people who were at the meeting and Bella heard them mention Davie's mate from the railways. No name. Just his mate.'

A silence froze the room, all of them looking at Duncan.

'I cannot miss the funeral. He would come to mine, if I was the one murdered.'

'You will end up in gaol yet,' Sine said, turning away and walking into the back room.

'Catherine has been dismissed,' Duncan announced, clearly keen to divert attention from his predicament. 'McBride dismissed her.'

Sine hurried back into the room.

'Is this true, Catherine?'

'Yes. He said that someone had told him that I was in the riot.'

'Who would do such a thing? Someone in the mill. It must be.'

'That woman McCulloch who was dismissed last week,' Marion said. 'She was always causing trouble. Poison she is. I'll go round and see her.'

'You will not!' Sine said in a tone that commanded obedience.

'I told Catherine to go round and see Eoin Lamont,' Duncan said quickly. 'I hear that he could be doing with help.'

'Yes,' said Sine. 'That is a good idea.'

'I've made a pot of stew. McBride gave me my wages so I bought some mutton and kale.'

'Stew!' shouted Archie. 'I love stew and I'm starving.'

Eoin was much younger than Catherine expected. He was in his shirt sleeves and clearly harassed when he opened the door.

'What is it?' he said.

'I'm sorry to disturb you, sir, but I was told you might appreciate some help in the house.'

'Who told you that?'

'Sine MacArthur from Main Street. She is my cousin.'

'Oh, Mrs MacArthur. Yes. Yes. Mrs MacArthur. Her people from Mull.'

'I am from the Ross too.'

'Yes. I can hear that. Your name is?'

'MacGillivray. Catherine MacGillivray. My mother is MacPhail.'

'Catherine. Yes. Yes. MacGillivray. Yes. My father was from Pennyghael. Come in, Catherine. I'm afraid we are in a state of chaos.'

He led her through to the kitchen where three small boys were fighting like fox cubs over a spinning top. They did not stop as she entered but continued to snatch and growl at each other She could barely see the far side of the room through the bitter smoke issuing from a pot on the stove.

'Behave, boys!' he commanded. 'Catherine is a sorceress like Medea and will turn you into toads, if you continue. I have burnt the broth, Catherine, as you can see. I had some school-work to correct and overlooked the broth.'

'It may be saved yet.'

'You think so?'

'If you have another pot, try tipping it into that without stirring it.'

'Ah yes. I will try that. I miss having a woman around.'

'I was about to ask you if you needed any help in the house.'

'Oh I see. I don't know. My wife did everything. Could you see to the broth for me? Boys! Please! If you are going to be gladiators, go into the other room. Maybe that's what I should do—send you to Sparta to be trained.'

'Have you another pot?'

'Oh yes, yes. Of course. It's in the sink.'

It was still lined with the scum of yesterday's meal. She scoured it roughly clean, carried it over to the stove and tipped the boiling broth into it. The bottom of the broth pot was badly burnt but she was sure that she had rescued the remainder. By this time the boys had fought their way through to the other room and the schoolmaster had collapsed into a chair at the table.

'Thank you,' he said. 'I don't know your name.'

'Catherine MacGillivray.'

'Oh yes. You told me. Thank you, Catherine. You are not from this foul city.'

'Argyll.'

'Oh yes, yes. The Duke. He who is keen to clean out his stables and dispose of what he sees as the refuse in the colonies. A benevolent autocrat—in his own eyes I'm sure.'

Catherine didn't know what to say, not understanding him. He seemed to be a kind man, clearly overwhelmed by his circumstances. Still youthful, with flaxen hair and blue eyes that seemed to look inward as if concentrating on affairs in his head. They gazed into the fire.

She waited for him to remember her presence. Eventually he looked round, seemingly shocked to see her.

'I'm sorry,' he said. 'I was lost in thought. You asked me if I needed help in the house and obviously I do, but I have to give it some consideration. I don't know how the boys would respond to another woman. They might think I was trying to replace their mother. Can you call back tomorrow? I know that seems ungrateful. I am most grateful for the offer, believe me. Very kind of you but I must think on it.'

'Thank you, sir. I will call again tomorrow. I will see myself out. Good night, sir.'

'Yes, yes. Good night, Catherine.'

She left him staring into the fire again, his eyes lost in sorrow. Thinking of his wife, she thought, with that expression of melancholy. Poor man and too young to be left without a companion.

28

Calum needed more powder. He had the calipers for making lead ball but there was barely enough powder in the horn to fire one shot. He decided that Oban would be a safer place to buy it than Tobermory and, although it might mean two days off the fishing, he would walk through Glenmore and use the Grasspoint ferry

He set off before dawn and headed east. Before he reached the glen at the head of Loch Scridain he was shocked to find people living in a tent made with an old sail. Leaving the road, he walked down to the tent and, from the gloom beneath the canvas, a woman's face peered out at him, a skull with a film of pale skin and lipless mouth. It wasn't so much the emaciated face that moved him but the expressionless eyes. He had seen more life in the eyes of a cod.

'Good day,' he said. 'This is a poor site for a tent. The ground is sodden.'

She said nothing and, as his vision became accustomed to the shadows in the tent, he saw that there were two half-naked children curled up together under a blanket.

'Where are you from?' he persisted.

'Tiroran. Turned out. Removed.'

'Where's your husband?'

'At the fishing in the east. They wouldn't wait till he came back.'

'They're all like that. The children look poorly.'

'They have the measles.'

'They should not be in a tent. Have you eaten?'

'The women in the hut gave me a handful of meal.'

He had a suspicion that her share had been given to the children.

'Can you walk at all?'

'We walked here but I can't walk now. I'm not sure that I can last till Archie comes back. Would you look after the children if I'm called?'

'It will not come to that. I will get you some meal and some fish. Will you wait here till I return?'

'I am not going anywhere.'

'I will come back tomorrow. What's your name?'

'Peggy. Peggy McNicol.'

He turned and walked towards Bunessan, horrified by the state of the woman and enraged by the injustice. She was close to death, alone with her children, abandoned. How could one human being do this to another and sleep at night? He would return to Bunessan and see if he could borrow a horse. Where was the Poor Board? Where were the stout men who filled the pews on the Sabbath? The Good Samaritans. It was not right that a mother should be reduced to a living skeleton.

He would ask MacQuarrie for the loan of a horse. He was a man with some kindness in his character. He had helped Catherine after all. Surely he would not refuse to help this poor creature.

He was right. MacQuarrie lent him his horse and his trap and gave him a bag of meal. He returned to Kinloch the following day.

'I will take you to Shiaba—to my house. My wife is in Glasgow so there is no-one there and I will find another place. You prepare the children and I will speak to your neighbour in the hut in case your man comes back from the fishing.'

When he returned she and the children were in the trap.

'This is kind of you.'

Those were the only words she spoke on the ride back to Shiaba. She did not sleep but sat with her head bowed, staring at her feet. Her shoes were split and her bare ankles black with peat. He decided not to venture into the dark place to which she had withdrawn by starting a conversation but held his peace, conscious, nevertheless, of her presence beside him and the children behind him.

When he reached Shiaba, he carried the two children and helped her into the house. The fire had been well smoored before he left, so he found some wood and a few pieces of peat and blew up the embers to a flame. He made a pot of broth with a fish tail and some porridge with the meal.

'See that the children are kept warm,' he said. 'I will be next door.'

The light was already dim when he left and walked round to Fergus to explain.

'If the Factor finds out, he will have you for sub-letting, Calum.'

'He wants me gone anyway.'

'And what will Catherine say?'

'I will not sleep there, John. The schoolhouse is empty. I'll go there.'

'Whose land was she on?'

'MacArthur's I think. He's the only one who would be so callous. I must return the horse to MacQuarrie. I will be back before dark.'

He abandoned the plan to fetch powder from Oban and spent his time fishing. More boats, most of them larger than his with four of a crew, were berthed in Bunessan and, finding other men fishing off Iona, he was forced to venture out into deeper, and more exposed, water. His small boat was not designed for the massive swell west of the island but he was determined to land enough fish to feed Peggy and her children and sell the rest to buy meal.

The children recovered and he watched Peggy gain strength and colour in her cheeks. As the life returned to her eyes and they looked at him, he realised how beautiful she was. No longer an invalid, a creature to be nursed back to health, an inanimate dependant, but an attractive woman whose presence might draw him out of the solitude to which he had become accustomed. The realisation came as a shock. He had not anticipated such a situation. Deeply moved by her suffering, he had treated her as he would have treated any poor creature, certainly not as a woman. He found himself thinking of her while he was at sea, remembering the expression in her dark eyes, the tenderness in her fingers as she washed the children, the sour scent of her unwashed clothes. They unsettled him, these thoughts, and he would dismiss them and haul roughly at his lines but they would return. He began to look forward to the walk home at night.

MacQuarrie stopped him one evening at the head of the pier.

'You've done well at the fishing, Calum.'

'I have by the Grace of God.'

'But there many more boats now and you don't have the fishing to yourself. You have competition.'

'I fish further out.'

'There is a great demand in the south for lobsters. Gallacher and MacDougall in Glasgow ship them to Liverpool and Dublin. There is money in it. Have you ever thought about trying your hand at that?'

'I know nothing about them.'

'You could learn. They're being caught in Skye, Easdale, Islay and Jura. I know a man who could show you, a fisherman from Gigha. If you don't start, someone else will.'

'Why are you telling me this?'

'I know you to be an honest, hard-working and compassionate man—a Good Samaritan, although you would not want people to know that. And you save to bring your family back from the city.'

'I am not saving much at the minute.'

'Too many demands on your time but lobsters might help.'

'I will think about it.'

'Do. God go with you, Calum.'

He walked away, leaving Calum standing with a string of pollock in his hand.

Peggy was sitting over the fire when he entered the house and the children were playing on the bed.

'I brought you some pollock.'

'I see that. Thank you.'

When she smiled her whole face seemed to shine with delight.

'Will I clean them for you?'

'No. I know how to clean a fish. Could you leave them on the table?'

He crossed the room and dropped them on the table.

'MacQuarrie, the merchant, was trying to persuade me to fish lobsters. He says there is money in it.'

'Yes. I would believe him. My father, before he died, had a few creels off Burg and saved us from starvation.'

'You know how to work creels, then?'

'Make them, mend them, bait them but not where to lay them. That's the skill, knowing where the lobsters are.'

Calum could not hide his astonishment.

'You think a woman is just an ornament?' she said.

'No, no. I'm very glad that you're here. You will need to teach me.

'It is the least I can do.'

No other boat left Bunessan that day. In the south-west wind the Sound of Iona in the ebb tide was whipped into a fury and it took him all morning to reach his old fishing ground.

The swell there was steadier than the chop in the Sound but still heaved the boat around, a long, heavy swell with breaking peaks and deep troughs. The sea bruise-black and malevolent, the clouds, like boulders, rolling across the sky. When he lowered the sail, the boat turned broadside to the wind and rocked dangerously, the gunwales dipping in the water. He had no sea-anchor to keep her head to the swell. He could see no way of paying out the lines so he hoisted the sail again, intending to head for home, but an immense wave lifted the boat high above the others. For a moment it hovered there on the peak but then it spun and the boom came crashing round, hitting him on the head. As the boat slid down into the trough, he fell to the deck and lay on the boards, blood seeping into the water sloshing around the bottom of the boat as it swung in the swell, the sail dipping into the sea.

29

Catherine thought it wise to delay calling at Lamont's house until late morning. When he answered her knock on the door, his shirt was hanging out over his trousers and his hair sprang from his head like a corn battle.

'Ah Catherine. I'm sorry, we are all at sixes and sevens. Could you come back later?'

'I called to find out if you wanted me to help in the house.'

'Yes, yes. Of course. How forgetful of me. Please come in.'

He led the way to the kitchen, his bare feet slapping on the floor. She could hear the boys in the bedroom, clearly mobbing and rioting.

'I would be delighted to have your assistance, Catherine. I'm sure you can see how urgently it is needed.'

'When would you like me to start?'

'Immediately if possible. I have no idea about these things. Do servants normally start on a Monday? This is Wednesday, is it not?'

'It is, and I can start when it suits you.'

'Well, let's start today then. It would be splendid if you could take the boys out for a walk. Some peace to see to my work would be a blessing. Usually I wait till they are asleep, but I find it difficult to see by candlelight. You could take them along the river. They love the cemetery for some reason. I'll dress them and you can relax—prepare yourself for the affray.'

He vanished into the bedroom to be greeted by howls of objection.

She cleared the breakfast table and washed the bowls, leaving the porridge pot to steep.

When the boys came through they were perfectly dressed for a walk, with boots, coats and peaked hats. Lamont was standing proudly behind them.

'I have instructed them to behave for you, to obey your orders and to respect passers-by.'

She had seen how obedient they were, but tried to conceal her apprehension.

'Do not worry,' he said. 'They normally behave outside.'

He opened the door and they tumbled out, stopping, however, in the street and, to her surprise, turning to wait for her. The oldest boy, Hector, six years old, seemed to be taking charge of the younger twins. Walking just ahead of her, they headed north to the river.

'Can we go and see the steamships?' Hector asked.

'The bridge is very busy. We will need to stay close together.'

'We will, We will. I promise.'

The twins came on either side of her and each took one of her hands, clearly a routine developed by their mother. She wondered what kind of person she had been and exactly when and how she had died. Lamont had not mentioned her death or even her name, perhaps too distressed to launch such a conversation. He was such an intelligent, warm and gentle person she could not imagine her as being very different. She would ask him about her one day when they were better acquainted. In the meantime she wanted to look after him, care for him as she would a helpless child.

She saw the smoke from one of the steamships as they approached Jamaica Street bridge, which swarmed with waggons, carriages, horses and pedestrians.

'We have to cross the road,' Hector said. 'I can't see the ships from here.'

'I know. We will have to keep close together and cross only when I say.'

She stood by the side of the road, waiting for a gap in the traffic, but it seemed to be endless.

'Mam just went across,' Hector said. 'She made them stop for her.'

'She must have been a brave lady.'

'Very brave. She's dead, you know.'

'Yes. I know. You must be very sad.'

'Not as sad as Pa. He cries a lot and calls for her. She's gone to the Lizzian Fields. She will be happy there.'

'I'm glad. Quick! There's a gap.'

They ran across the road and walked to the peak of the bridge.

'Please could you lift me up, Miss?'

She lifted him on to the parapet and held him close as they looked down the river. He smelt of soap and pipe smoke. She liked him. Uninhibited, yet polite, forthright, yet considerate, his character reflecting, she thought, the values of his father—and perhaps those of his mother. Hector was delighted but the twins, seeing his face, jumped up and down demanding to be lifted up.

'I'll have to put you down, Hector, and let Alexander and Anthony see the steamer too.'

She was surprised when he agreed, though his expression was chosen to indicate his displeasure.

The twins had to have their turn even if the steamer was well down the river.

As they walked back, she thought of Archie, crawling under the spinning machines, and Mary, delighted to be working in the mill with her cousins. A different life. At home, before the potatoes failed, she would have been outside in the clean air stacking peat or up at the summer grazings churning butter. A carriage thundered past and she gripped the hands of the twins a bit tighter.

When they returned Lamont welcomed the boys as if they had been away for a month.

'Did they behave, Catherine? I hope you behaved, you scoundrels.'

'They were very good.'

'We saw a steamer,' Hector said.

'Filthy contraptions. A clipper in full sail, now that is elegant and clean, a thing of beauty, don't you think, Catherine?'

'Yes. They don't send black smoke into the sky.'

The sharing of opinion seemed to please him.

'Do come in. I have put the broth on the stove.'

The boys threw off their coats and caps and ran through to the bedroom. She picked up the garments and hung them on a peg.

'I'm intending to take the boys to the museum after lunch. You would be most welcome to accompany us.'

'Should I not prepare the evening meal? Or wash their clothes?'

'No, no. All in good time. We will see to these things later. But perhaps you have visited the museum already and another visit would be tedious.'

'I have never been in a museum. I have lived all my life on the Ross.'

'Well then you must come. I insist. We will take a cab.'

At the entrance off the High Street she had to ask Lamont to sign the visitor's book for her but he accepted the request so easily that she did not feel embarrassed.

As they moved through to the anteroom she had to stop. Glancing into one of the mahogany cabinets, she saw a display of butterflies the beauty of which made her gasp. One with wings of vivid azure blue, another with spots exactly like eyes.

'I want to see the elephant,' Hector said.

'All in good time,' Lamont replied. 'We must allow our guest to savour the wonders of this establishment.'

'No, please,' she said. 'Let the children go where they wish.'

'They must learn to consider others.'

'I'm quite happy to follow them.'

'If you're sure.'

As they walked through the room she saw an extraordinary creature like a piglet with a long tail and protected with scales.

'An armadillo,' Lamont said, noticing her amazement. 'They curl themselves into a ball when threatened. The Indians eat them as a delicacy.'

They passed cabinets with beetles so large and strange that she squirmed at the thought of meeting them.

In the next room—the Saloon—she almost stopped again, surrounded by exotic birds with plumage as brilliant as sunsets. A paradise bird, delicate humming birds, a parakeet, an ibis, a white spoonbill. She wanted to stay there, to examine every bird, to learn their names, their country of origin, their habits. How could anyone have created the astonishing beauty and variety of these creatures?

To reach the basement where the elephant was they had to pass through the Hall of Anatomy where she saw displays of sliced kidneys, hearts, lungs, throats—everything to explain how the human body worked and all brilliantly coloured with red or white or blue to show the arteries and veins. There was even the head of an infant, the eyes so life-like that she stepped back.

'It's only a model,' Lamont said.

She was pleased to leave that room and follow the children down to the Elephant Room. When she saw the display she could understand why the boys were keen to go there.

In the centre of the room stood an elephant and its calf and, behind it, a zebra. The boys stood beneath the massive beast and stared with their mouths open, expressions of such wonder that she laughed.

'Now boys,' Lamont announced. 'There's something I want you to see.'

He led them across to some rather uninteresting stone slabs.

'You see the Roman numerals on these, Hector. When they were building Hadrian's wall, each legion was given a section of it to complete—just over three miles a section. Each legion made one of these slabs to show its section. The twelfth would show XII. Now here's a carving which I wanted you to see. This is Victory crowning a Roman horseman—you see the spear and shield—and, below him, two captives. Remember those lines from Tacitus about the great battle with Calgacus—maybe this was made to celebrate the victory.'

She could see that Hector was not impressed as his eyes kept wandering over to the South Sea war clubs on the wall.

'There's so much to see, Catherine. There's an art gallery upstairs with old masters like Titian, Rembrant, Murillo. You would love those. We must come back another day.'

'That would be wonderful. I could spend a week here and never weary.'

'Right. We will do that but now we must get back.'

She sat beside him in the carriage, listening to Hector telling his brothers about the narwhal and how people used to believe that its horn came from a unicorn. Like his father, she thought, serious and knowledgeable. The visit had increased her admiration for the teacher not only because of his intellect but also because of his relationship with his boys and the way he handled them.

When she returned home that night everyone was busy— Sine at the fire stirring a pot, Sarah making bannock dough on the table, Mary washing clothes and Duncan and Archie making a ship from a spindle. They all greeted her as if she had been to America. She went across to Sine to ask if she could help but, just as she spoke, Marion rushed in, breathless and shocked.

'Transportation!' she gasped. 'Eighteen years for Crossan and ten for five others.'

'How do you know this?' Sine asked.

'I went to the trial.'

'In the name of God, Marion! Do you think the constables would not be watching, noting the folk who were there?'

'There were too many. The court was bulging, heaving with onlookers.'

'What was the charge?' asked Duncan.

'Mobbing and rioting. Three others, Peter Keenan was one of them, got two years prison. Johnnie Johnston, that tall man in the mill, got two years, him and three others.'

'Johnnie from Govan Street? Has three wee girls?'

'Yes. There's word that they are still arresting people.'

'I said that you should never have gone to the Green,' Sine said. 'Stupid, stupid man! They'll come for you yet.'

30

Calum's boat came ashore on Ardalanish beach. A cattleman, seeing it drifting in the swell, its sail dragging in the water, hurried down to the shore and, finding what he thought was a body in the bottom of the boat, turned to run for help. He was stopped by a hoarse shout behind him. He helped Calum scramble over the side and up to MacIntyre's house where he eventually revived and was able to ride back over the hill to Shiaba on their mare.

Peggy cleaned the wound on his head and scolded him for going to sea in such weather.

'I must get a bigger boat.'

'To make sure you drown yourself.'

'It would be safer.'

He tried to sit still while she bathed his head but twitched with pain when she touched the wound.

'Sit still,' she said. 'Have you any sulphur?'

'No. Why would I have sulphur?'

'Have you tar, then—Russian tar?'

'There's some tar in the stall there.'

She dressed the wound tenderly with tar. As she came close to him, he could smell her sweat and the peat smoke in her clothes. He enjoyed the sensation of her body beside his. He wanted to place his arm round her waist but was afraid of her.

'You should rest,' she said. 'There could be harm inside your head.'

'I will sleep. Sleep is the best healer.'

'You may sleep here.'

He looked up at her, finding that her eyes issued the invitation.

'Thank you, but I will sleep in the schoolhouse.'

'As you wish.'

She did not seem to be offended.

He cut hazel rods as Peggy had instructed, the thickness of his finger, and carried them home. He had found thick twine and a board for her and they had burnt six holes, four at the corners and two half way along. He enjoyed working beside her and he felt that she liked his company. She showed him how to bend the rods to make three arches and force the ends into the holes. Weaving a net with the thick twine, she made a lobster creel, showing him how to bait it with mackerel.

'A good bait, mackerel. It flashes in the water. You will need to weight the creel with a heavy stone.'

He admired her dexterity and the confidence with which she worked but he was entranced by her dark eyes which met his so boldly. There was a challenge in them which he was afraid to explore. There was something wild about her, something untamed and unpredictable, like a creature of the sea or a sorceress. He thought she might cast spells or, having the evil eye, read all his thoughts and see his fate. The impression was enhanced by the long raven hair which, although unwashed, glistened as it slipped down over her breast.

'You will need a long line and corks to mark where you lay it.'

'I have plenty of line and will find corks. How do I know where to place the creel?'

'A reef or a rock, dark with kelp and edged with sand. Lay it on the edge of the kelp.'

'You have a fund of knowledge.'

'My father had. He had been all over the world—Greenland, Nova Scotia, Africa, South America. He sailed black slaves from Africa to Cartagena, whale oil from the Arctic to Glasgow, coal to Belfast. He had seen lands where the sun never sets and lands where it fries the soles of your feet. He would not wear shoes at home and his soles were like cow-hide. He wasn't faithful to my mother. He told me about his women before he died as if I was a priest and could forgive him. He named my girls Lucia and Miranda.'

'A real seaman then?'

'If I had been born a man, I would have followed him.'

'A handsome sailor.'

She smiled but did not respond, her former approach having been rejected.

'I must find a new bed of mussels for my lines,' he said. 'There are more men fishing now and all searching for bait.'

'I could bait your hooks.'

'The lines are too heavy to carry back to Shiaba and it would not do to have you work beside me at the pier.'

'Why not?'

'People would suspect me of betraying my wife.'

'You would not want them to think ill of you. That would never do.'

'What they think is of little importance to me.'

'Is that true? That your reputation does not matter? I think it does.'

He rose and pulled on his jacket.

'I'm going to speak to MacQuarrie about a bigger boat.'

He left the house, heading for the village.

Her image kept invading his thoughts as he walked. The raven hair, the white cleft of her breasts, the mesmerising eyes. And her invitation. There were moments when he regretted his decision, when the fantasy of lying with her excited him and overwhelmed his imagination. Yet his conscience reminded him of Catherine and his loyalty to her.

MacQuarrie was at the pier.

'Well, Calum. How are you? '

'I'm well, thank you. I want to speak with you.'

'I'm here.'

'Would you lend me the price of a new boat, a bigger boat?'

'You believe in coming straight to the point then. As it happens, I had been thinking of offering you a proposal. I was going to suggest a partnership. I will buy the boat and you could gradually buy my share.'

'Why would you do that?'

'I have faith in you. The Factor may be keen to get rid of you and, for all I know, he may have good reason to take action against you, but I know that you are good to the people in Shiaba and that you are a hard-working, intelligent man. The Ross would be poorer without you.'

Calum shuffled his feet awkwardly and looked down at the ground.

'What do you think?' MacQuarrie asked.

'I'm flattered. The Factor may have his way yet so perhaps your proposal would leave you with the boat, if I go to prison.'

'Prison? Why would you go to prison?'

Realising that the merchant would know nothing of his poaching, he tried to cover his mistake.

'John Campbell would dream up any story to have me arrested.'

'He would not tell lies. He is a godly man, Calum. He may be harsh in his dealings with the people but he is not corrupt.'

'A godly man would have compassion for the poor. To turn people out of their homes when they are starving and sick is not a godly act. God knows what is in his heart when he seeks the warrants but it is not charity and, if there is no charity, how can there be honesty? I don't trust the man.'

'I don't believe he's as evil as you think. He is employed as the Duke's Factor and carries out his duties as well as he can.'

'And enriches himself as he goes. Look at the land he has now and the cattle.'

'He is a man like the rest of us and will answer to his Creator for his faults and misdeeds.'

'I hope so.'

'You have not answered me about the proposal.'

'Of course I will accept it. It is a generous offer.'

'Good. I will order the boat. Where is yours by the way?'

'Ardalanish bay. They hauled her up above the high-water mark. We will float her on the high springs. The mast is cracked but I'll risk sailing her round.'

'You should have someone with you.'

'I will manage.'

'Oh, I'm sure you will.'

He smiled and walked away, leaving Calum to head for the shore for bait.

That evening, he carried one of the lines and a sack of mussels back to the house. She had said that she would bait his hooks so he decided to accept her offer.

'Well, what did MacQuarrie say?'

'He offered me a partnership in a bigger boat.'

'You don't look very pleased.'

'If I try to buy his share, bit by bit, I will have little left for myself.'

'Do you have to buy his share?'

'The boat will never be mine, if I don't.'

'Does that matter?'

'I suppose not.'

They knelt side by side by the fire, opening the shells and baiting the hooks, the children in bed behind them. It was not an easy task in the candlelight. Concentrating on the hooks, he did not look at her but felt her presence close to him and could see her fingers as she pressed the bait on to the sharp points. Long, supple fingers, ingrained with her life on the land, he was tempted to reach out and grasp them in his own but, knowing where it might lead, was afraid to launch into those dark, uncharted waters.

'Have you always lived at Tiroran?' he asked.

'I have never known anywhere else till we were turned out.'

'Is your man from the parish too?'

'No. He's from Skye. He is never at home.'

'He has obviously been at home twice anyway.'

She slapped his hand and he looked up to see her smiling.

'They are looking better,' he said, nodding towards the children.

'Thanks to you.'

He bent over the hooks again.

'Is your wife well?'

'I have heard that she is well and that the children have recovered.'

'She doesn't write to you?'

'She can't write.'

An image of Catherine, sitting where Peggy was sitting and listening to his stories, surfaced in his mind and he knew that she would be hurt, if she could see him at that minute. He should leave, he knew that too, but he longed to stay, to be with Peggy and see her dark eyes tempting him to stay all night. If he stayed, no-one would know but the children. Catherine would never discover the betrayal. He could leave before it was light. The fantasy of Peggy's naked body was bewitching. Yet it would be a betrayal, a transgression which he would have endure for the rest of his life, a scar on his mind. And people would hear. Everyone in the parish would stare at him and whisper of his treachery. The Factor would say that he always knew he was a blackguard, an untrustworthy wretch. In spite of that, he yearned for the feeling of her skin next to his. She would offer it. He was sure of that. The struggle in his mind showed in the sweat glistened on his brow.

31

In Calum's neighbour's house Lachlan, suddenly deteriorating, was struggling to breathe, grasping the air with his fingers and gasping hoarsely through his open mouth. Fergus sat beside him on the bed, smoothing his brow.

'You must go to Canada, Fergus,' he croaked. 'Leave Shiaba.'

'I will stay here.'

'I'll be leaving soon. Going to the house appointed for us all. Carry my head to a place in Kilvickeon. That's all I ask.'

'Nonsense, Father. You have ages yet.'

The tears on his cheeks showed how he lied. He fought to keep control of the torrent of grief that was threatening to overwhelm him. His father, the tall man who took his hand as a child when they searched for gull's eggs on the island, the man who could turn the land with his hand plough as fast as any horse, the man who wept at the birth of his grandson and lifted the child up to the rising sun as a symbol of new life, lay dying beside him. His wasted frame barely a shape under the blanket, his eyes searching the rafters for a gleam of light, his brow furrowed with a frown, he was already on his way.

'Promise me, Fergus,' he whispered.

'What?'

'Canada.'

'I promise—when the time comes.'

'There's no more laudanum,' Janet said.

'Calum might have some.'

'No, no. No more,' interrupted Lachlan. 'No more. Just stay.'

His breath became shallow and fast. He was not anxious or afraid but seemed to be content, the frown fading from his brow.

'Jessie,' he whispered—name of his wife.

'She's here, Father, waiting by the door. Waiting for you. She won't go without you, going to the shore, a walk along the white sand, holding hands as you did when you were young. Go with her. She is waiting.'

'Yes. Hands.' Fergus could just hear what he said.

A few missed breaths and the breathing stopped. Fergus's dam of grief burst as he wept, his body shaken with sorrow. Janet placed her arms round him and the children followed her. They stayed huddled together as Lachlan became cold and alabaster white.

'I will go and tell Calum,' Fergus said eventually. 'And all the others.'

'He may be at the schoolhouse. There is no hurry.'

'There's much to be done.'

He rose from the bed and left the house. He knocked on Calum's door, remembering that Peggy was there, and Calum answered.

Suddenly he found it impossible to speak the words, but Calum knew instantly what he had come to say. He reached out and placed his hands on his friend's shoulders.

'I'm very sorry, Fergus. Will you come in?'

'No thank you, I must tell the others.'

'I could do that for you.'

'No. I must do it myself.'

'If there is anything I can do, you have only to ask.'

'I know that, my friend. Thank you.'

He walked away, leaving Calum standing in the doorway.

The women came that night to wash Lachlan and lay him out, the men gathering outside the house. In the morning two of them left to dig the grave while Fergus insisted on walking to Bunessan to send word to the Free Church minister. As he returned he heard a horse behind him. Looking round, he saw it was the Factor so he stopped and waited for him.

'You are not welcome here,' he said when Campbell reached him.

'Whether I am welcome or not, I am here on His Grace's business to speak to Calum MacGillivray.'

'There has been a death in this township and you, as a God-fearing man, should respect that and allow us to bury our dead in peace.'

'Who has died?'

'My own father, Lachlan Campbell.'

The Factor removed his hat.

'I am truly sorry for your loss. These are hard times with so many deaths. I will call another time.'

He wheeled his horse around and rode back the way he had come. Surprised by the show of respect, John watched him disappear over the hill.

In Calum's house, Peggy ladled out porridge for children.

'I think it would be better if I did not attend,' she said, 'I'm a stranger here after all.'

Calum pulled his beard and frowned.

'I don't know. Fergus has been very civil to you and they all know you are here.'

He was worried about her taking part in the funeral. It might look as though she was replacing Catherine and the township would resent that. Yet he did want her to be with him as they carried Lachlan to Kilvickeon.

'I don't think anyone would object. You are not here by choice.'

'They will think we are lovers.'

He was tempted to reply that he wished they were and he could see the mischief in her eyes.

'They have known me all my life and would not suspect me of disloyalty. I expect Fergus will want me to carry the coffin so I would not be walking with you. I could ask Sarah Boyde who lives on her own to walk with you.'

'You would like me to be there?'

He was afraid that she would ask directly and hesitated to reply.

'Yes,' he said finally.

The procession left Shiaba the following day, the entire township, apart from those who were sick with the famine fever and those who were too weak to walk. A long, silent line, drawn from the twenty families, of people clearly afflicted by famine and the loss of one of their own. Lachlan's family first, behind four men carrying, on their shoulders, his remains on his door. Behind them the men and, at the back, the women, their heads covered in their shawls Not a word was spoken as they walked slowly up the hill towards the graveyard in the valley beyond.

At the summit they stopped to allow another four men to take over the burden of the bier.

As they descended, they were joined by people from Scoor and Saorphin and Assapol, the neighbouring townships. The ancient graveyard at the head of loch Assapol was soon overflowing with neighbours come to pay their respects to one of their people, the people whose gravestones, encrusted with lichen, bore the names of their ancestors. The roof beams of the church, sagging beneath the weight of sodden thatch, were green with moss and flakes of weathered stone covered the threshold. The service was held outside, the minister from Iona standing in the crumbling archway facing the loch.

Fergus was pleased to have Calum by his side and Janet on the other. He was worried that he might give way and wail in front of all his neighbours. He gripped Janet's hand so hard she winced and nudged his ribs.

When all were assembled the minister started the service. Fergus's eyes kept straying to the bier where his father lay shapeless under a rough blanket, telling himself that it was just a corpse, an empty vessel, that his soul was already in the sunlight of the new life. Yet, with every glance, his lips shivered and tears filled his eyes. He did not want him to leave, even though his last days had been dark with suffering.

When the minister chanted the first lines of the psalm and the mourners followed, he joined in:

> *I will lift mine eyes unto the hills from*
> *whence cometh my strength*

and found comfort in the multitude of voices surrounding him, as if they sang in harmony for him and his father, a mantle of kindness and humanity.

The sun shall not smite thee by day nor the
moon by night.

As they lowered Lachlan into the grave, he heard only the words,

....in sure and certain hope of resurrection
to eternal life...

and thought of his father, hand in hand with his mother in heaven.

Many of the mourners came to shake his hand and express their sorrow, as the crowd melted away, a gesture which made him feel cared for.

Calum found Peggy and walked back with her, conscious of some glances of disapproval but choosing to ignore them.

32

Having sat through some evenings with Lamont and watched how he taught his boys, it occurred to Catherine that Archie would benefit from his teaching and that she might learn to write and read properly. She had already succeeded in penetrating the mystery of words by watching Lamont with the children. She found that she could draw pictures—of trees, ships, birds or her house at home—and entertained the boys by starting a subject and asking them to guess what it was as she proceeded. Lamont admired her skill and encouraged her. Words, though, still frightened her. She would form the sound in her head, only to hear it corrected when one of the boys pronounced it. Maybe she and Archie could learn together.

'Do you think I could bring my son along?' she asked' 'He should learn to read and write in English.'

'Of course,' Lamont replied enthusiastically' 'I'm sure Hector would welcome the company of someone of his own age. You said he was the same age, didn't you?'

'Yes. He is very shy. Except apparently in the mill where he chats to the girls there.'

'He's far too young to be in the mill, Catherine. It's against the law. It must be extremely dangerous.'

'He likes it there with his sister and cousins, and he's proud of the small amount of money he gives me. Besides, I can't afford to send him to school.'

'I see. It's a dilemma. I think all schools should be free, but I don't see that opinion being very attractive to our government—but then it scarcely represents the mass of the people. Every citizen should have a vote as they did in ancient Rome. That would be democratic, truly democratic. Then universal free education would become a possibility. You would not have to pay.'

Catherine's expression must have betrayed her confusion, as he dropped the subject of franchise.

'Anyway, your Archie would be welcome at any time. It is the least I can do. Now boys, back to work. Twins, finish your drawing of the Roman soldier. Imagine those poor men building the Antonine Wall, far from home in a blizzard in a Scottish winter, their feet frozen in their sandals and their hands white with cold. Hector, you look over that piece from the Gallic Wars about Vercengetorix. After that, we will call it a day. I'll see Catherine to the door.'

She was not quite ready to leave but his demeanour suggested that he wanted to speak with her in the hall so she lifted her shawl and followed him.

'Please, do not be insulted by what I'm going to say, Catherine.'

He was so serious that she thought he was about to dismiss her.

'You have an extraordinary talent in your draughtsmanship. You must develop it. I have a friend who could help you. However—and please understand that I speak with the best of intentions—something tells me that you have difficulty with reading and writing.'

Far from feeling insulted, his comment brought a sense of relief, for she had longed to reveal her inadequacy.

'I did not go to school. Well, very rarely anyway.'

'If you will allow me, I would like to help.'

'I would be very, very happy.'

'Splendid. Let us say Sunday when the boys attend Chartist Sunday School.'

When she arrived home neither Mary nor Marion were there. Sine was cooking and Archie was at the table eating a bannock.

'Hello Sine. I bought a turnip on the way home. Where's Mary?'

'They have gone to a meeting.'

'No!'

She dropped the turnip on the table; it rolled across to Archie.

'Calm yourself. It's not like the last. No mob nor riot. A Chartist meeting in the City Hall.'

'Even so. It could be dangerous. Is Duncan with them?'

'No show without Punch. He can't keep his nose out of the nosebag.'

'You're not worried? I thought the constables were looking for him. He will be seen there surely.'

'He takes that risk, I suppose. He supports the Charter and likes to be there. How are things with poor Mr Lamont?'

'He's a kind man. I like him. He's happy to have Archie join his boys when they are at their schoolwork. It would help his education.'

'I don't want to go,' Archie said, pushing the turnip so that it thudded on the floor.

'It's after work. If you were at home in Shiaba, you would be going to school and your father would see that you went.'

'He's not here and he might be dead.'

'Archie!' both woman cried simultaneously.

'That's a terrible thing to say,' said Sine.

'You will be coming whether you like it or not, Archibald MacGillivray.'

'One of the girls will take you there,' said Sine.

Archie's pouting lips reminded her of a duck.

'You must learn to read and write,' she continued. 'Be something more than a cotton spinner—a clerk or shop assistant or even a teacher. You can't get far without reading and writing. Can you, Catherine?'

Catherine's pale cheeks coloured. Sine noticed and rescued her.

'Anyway, Archie, you might like his boys. Now, fetch the candles over. It is getting dark. And pick up the turnip.'

Some time later Catherine heard the girls on the stairs, chattering away like starlings. They breezed in, laughing and pushing one another. Catherine, although annoyed, could not help being pleased by the change in Mary, her vitality and the gleam in her eyes.

'Mother, Mother,' said Marion, 'it was so funny at the end. They did three cheers for the Queen, three cheers for the Irish martyrs—whoever they are—three cheers for Fergus O'Connor and then three groans for the Glasgow Press. Three groans!'

'The pusillanimous Glasgow Press,' Duncan added. 'The City Hall was overflowing, Sine. A huge meeting and completely orderly. In fact it could have been the General Assembly of the Kirk it was so orderly.'

'What was it about?' asked Catherine.

'Free Ireland is one thing.'

'Ireland? Where hundreds are dying of starvation. I don't understand.'

'They blame Trevelyan and the British government—more than a million dead. The Irish should govern themselves, they say. Repeal the Union. Repeal or revolution.'

'That's dangerous talk,' said Sine. 'I said you shouldn't go. There will be spies there. You will end up in the Bridewell.'

'They can't arrest us all, all the crowd at the City Hall.'

'You were at the riot as well, though. Anyway, sit in. I've made stew.'

There were only three chairs so the girls and Archie sat in the shadows with their backs against the wall as they ate.

'You've heard about Lizzie Kean from down the street, I suppose,' Sine said, looking through the candle flames at Duncan.

'I know she was charged.'

'Four months prison. They said she was seen stealing meal from Harper and Warnock's.'

'She has a family to feed.'

'And how will she feed them now?'

'And Michael Rodgers next door, sixty days. They're closing in. We'll hear the footsteps on the stair any day.'

'Nonsense, Sine. Don't be frightening the children.'

Catherine, although concentrating on the thin stew, glanced regularly at Mary, worrying about her presence in the riot. Someone must have seen her there. She should never have let her go with Marion, a girl a bit too forward for her own good. She worried about her influence on Mary. She had heard her talk about revolution and suffrage and the Charter and had seen her with a cigarette. She felt that she was losing her and resolved to spend some time with her on her own—difficult to achieve, as Marion had taken to sleeping with her upstairs.

The next afternoon with Lamont's boys at the table she asked about the Charter.

'Much of the time,' she said, 'I don't understand what they are talking about. I feel left out, stupid and I don't like to ask.'

She felt that she could talk to him, that he would not judge her or humiliate her. She trusted him.

'You're far from stupid, Catherine, and it's really very simple. The followers are nearly all working class, ordinary folk who do not have a vote when it comes to elections. They want all men, regardless of wealth, property or education, to have a vote.'

'But not women?'

He laughed.

'That would be too extreme, men's argument being that women would only vote for the most handsome candidate. A nonsense. Women in Sweden have had the vote for more than a century and the country has not disappeared beneath the waves and the Iroquois women in America chose their chiefs. Chartists, I'm afraid, are still mostly men.'

She admired his knowledge and eloquence.

'The MacArthur girls go to meetings.'

'Oh yes. Many women support the cause. I suppose they feel that it is a step in the right direction.'

'They take risks. What difference would it make to have the vote?'

'All the laws are made in Parliament by the MPs sitting there and they are elected by people allowed to vote. If only rich men, men owning property, have a vote, then only their own kind will become MPs and they will make laws to suit themselves. They can decide, for example, that it's acceptable for husbands to thrash their wives as long as the lash is no thicker than a finger. They can decide that young children of nine can work in mills and not attend school. They have a great deal of power. They make laws to suit capitalists, men who own mines and mills or vast estates like the Dukes of Sutherland and Argyll. If working people had a vote, I'm sure the nation's wealth would be shared more evenly.'

She liked to watch him talk. He was animated, passionate, when he spoke. She wanted him to carry on.

'The girls talk of 'moral force'. What do they mean by that?'

'There are those among the Chartists who believe in armed revolution as in Paris—physical force—and others, fortunately in the majority, who prefer to use persuasion to achieve their aims—they employ moral force.'

'You would use persuasion I think.'

'Indeed. I am not a man of violence. You should come to one of the meetings. They are very civilised as a rule.'

'I would like to do that. I would like to learn about these things.'

'We will arrange it then.'

She could see that he was really pleased at the prospect, as she was herself.

33

'Lord Clarendon is most agitated, Sir Charles. Fearing bloodshed in Ireland, he has sent his children to England. His nerves are said to be on the verge of collapse.'

Sir Charles sighed and turned away from the window where he had been remembering his holiday in France, the magnificent sweep of the Loire, the walnut trees by the river, the open markets with fresh apricots, the thunderous echo of the organ in Tours cathedral.

'Yes, I know, George.'

He had seen Clarendon's letter to the prime Minister.

> *No Tipperary landlord ever received more*
> *threatening notices than I do ... as to when*
> *and where I will be assassinated. I only go out*
> *in the carriage for a short walk in the Park*
> *which makes me nearly a State prisoner ... the*
> *life I lead is hardly endurable.*

Such whining was not very dignified, particularly from a Lord Lieutenant.

'I know, and Wellington seems to be agitating too but, in the face of this threat, what is needed is a calm, reasoned approach.'

'You don't think there will be revolution then? The Young Irelanders have sent representatives to Paris, seeking assistance, no doubt.'

'How can you have a revolution when the people are crippled with starvation and fever? As for France, George, we have pre-empted their approach. We spoke to Lamartine before they did .and threatened to close our Embassy. I think they will be disappointed. Anyway, Ireland is swarming with our troops and ships of the line.'

He sat at his desk, leaning back with his fingertips together as if in prayer, continuing to speak but in fact talking to himself.

'The Cabinet is certainly shaken by the revolutions in Europe—not only France but Venice, Sicily, Milan, Piedmont. Government after government. I can understand their unease but, behind the scenes, we have everything under control. The Irish will not be stirred into revolution by a few fanatics, and we are well prepared here in England.'

'The Chartists seem to have a mighty following—nation-wide, even in Scotland.'

George's intervention startled him, having almost forgotten his presence.

'Yes, the Chartists. The phoenix stirring in the ashes of recession. The bird itself, though, is not like the dragon in France. A tame version of the species, a peacock, strutting, displaying and screeching but really mere ornament. I'm not saying that we should ignore the movement, George, but most of the leadership is respectable and law-abiding. Besides it is awash with spies and informers. Never fear, all is in hand. We will root out the agitators. The new Treason Act is designed not only for Ireland but can apply her and in in Scotland. Listen to the terms:

"any person who, by open and advised
speaking, compassed the intimidation of the
Crown or of Parliament is made guilty of
felony"

and this means transportation for fourteen years or life. Pretty good deterrent, I would think.'

'Indeed, sir. Speaking of Scotland. I'm told that one of the Irish tried to raise volunteers in Scotland, but failed to recruit a decent number and scampered back to Ireland. Mind you, he did have four hundred names and there is this memorial sent to Lord Clarendon from a very well attended meeting in Glasgow City Hall. It is naturally predicting civil war in Ireland if the government fails to repeal the Union but—and here is the significant section—it says,

> *"if your Excellency and your Government determine to force the Irish people into an armed resistance, we tell you coolly, deliberately and firmly that all our sympathies will be with them—that we will not look tamely on the massacre of that people by British soldiers…".'*

'Bluster, George, hot air.'

'It continues, sir,

> *"They who seek to quench Irish liberty in blood may find a terrible retribution from quarters where they might least expect it.".'*

'Rhetoric. It is they who will suffer retribution, if they dare to move against the government. We are about to slice the head off the snake. We are suspending Habeas Corpus and plan to arrest the leaders, indeed anyone who might speak against the Crown or incite rebellion. We did have people at that meeting?'

'Several agents and informers, I believe.'

'Good. I imagine that they will have a list of names. I would like to see the list, if you can obtain a copy from the department. I am concerned that there may be an overlap between the Chartists and the Destitution Committee in Glasgow and intend to root out the troublemakers. The Treason Felony Act will apply there too.'

'I will see to that, sir.'

34

'We are going to leave, Calum. Things are no better here. The plague goes on and on and we have had another summons of removal. No doubt the Sheriff's men will be here soon. Anyway, without your help, we would have perished and would not have the strength to go now. I will never forget that. I came to thank you.'

Fergus stood in the doorway, glancing occasionally at Peggy, who was bent over the fire.

'You would do the same for me, Fergus.'

'I promised my father we would go.'

'If you gave your word, you must keep it. I'm truly sorry, though. You will be missed here. I expect there will be others of the same mind. Soon there will be no fires on the hearths of Shiaba—except mine.'

'You should come too, Calum. Neil MacGillivray and Catherine and their family are going, and James and Margaret MacGillivray with theirs, and Archie and the other James MacGillivray from Scoor. Twenty-nine children altogether. You should come. There is free land and no Factor to harass you. Our people are thriving there.'

Calum was about to express his view on the hardships of the new country but refrained, not wishing to cast a cloud of doubt over Fergus's decision.

'I'm doing well at the fishing now and MacQuarrie is helping me to buy a bigger boat. I will stay, if only to annoy the Factor.'

'If he gets the Sheriff's men, he will have you out one way or another. They'll bar the door and burn the roof. They'll get men from Oban, if they have to. You can't fight the law, Calum.'

'They may put me out, but, as soon as they've gone, I'll move back.'

'And they'll get you for breaking and entering. You'll end up in prison.'

'We will see. I'm not afraid of them and their threats.'

'And what about Catherine and the children?'

Calum was astonished, not anticipating the question, surprised that Fergus should be so bold in front of Peggy. Sitting at the table, he looked down at her but she was not embarrassed or upset, indeed she was smiling, waiting for him to answer.'

'She will be back, Fergus. I have almost enough saved now for her fare.'

'I'm glad. She is a kind woman and will do anything for the children.'

'She's a strong woman indeed.'

A long silence drove Fergus to announce his departure.

'I will go. Good night, Calum, and you Peggy.'

After he left, Peggy rose and joined Calum at the table.

'So,' she said. 'You are saving to bring her back.'

'Yes, but there's a bit to go yet.'

Her hand was on the table and he reached out to lay his on it.

'We have some time to ourselves still.'

John Campbell wrote to the Duke that summer:

> *The emigration of the year will be of the greatest benefit to the Estate, almost the whole of them being composed of the poorest and most worthless ...*

Calum walked to Fionnphort to see Fergus and his family as they left. The emigrant ships, anchored in the Sound, dwarfed the skiffs which carried the passengers out from the Ross. Behind them, he could see a crowd of people on the shore of Iona, dark figures on the white shell sand. He could not hear them, but he knew some of them would be weeping as many of the people around him were. Fergus was not facing the sea but had turned to look back up the road to Bunessan.

'My father lies in Kilvickeon, Calum, beside his wife and his father. Where will my head rest when the time comes? Though my head rests on the other side of the ocean, my heart will lie here. The pain of leaving is so terrible no words can be found to describe it. It is like a sabre through the heart. I will never see the Ross again. Those are hard words to say.'

'People have come back, Fergus.'

'We are leaving with nothing but the clothes we stand in. I don't think we will be back. There is one last thing I ask of you. Will you look after my father's grave?'

'You had no need to ask. I would have seen to it anyway.'

'Come, Fergus,' interrupted Janet. 'It is time to go.'

She embraced Calum silently, leaving her tears warm on his cheek, and walked away with her arms round the children.

'Will you look at that!' Fergus said, facing the road.

Calum turned to see on the skyline the figure of the Factor on his horse, watching the departure.

'Come to gloat,' Fergus said. 'God's curse on him.'

'Hurry, Fergus,' Janet called from the shore.

Fergus threw his arms round Calum.

'God go with you, Fergus.'

Again someone called out the first line of the psalm and, in harmony, others followed. Calum felt the grief of his friend's departure surging upward and, before it broke over him, he turned away and walked up the hill. Behind him, the mournful sound, heavy with grief, echoed across the Sound from the ships, the shore of Iona and the skiff in Fionnphort.

As he drew level with the Factor, his sorrow swung to anger.

'Well, Mr Campbell, you have come to rejoice in their suffering,' he dared to say.

The Factor looked down at him, his heavy brows drawn in a frown under his high hat.

'I have come to see them safely aboard without mishap, MacGillivray.'

'Having stripped them of everything they own.'

'To pay their passage and provide them with some money for their journey. You should have gone with your neighbours.'

'I will stay.'

'Whether you stay or not in His Grace's property is a decision for His Grace.'

'I will stay.'

Calum walked past.

'We will see,' he heard behind him.

A shipping agent wrote to the Duke later that year:

> The "Charlotte" and "Barlow" emigrants
> in Canada all passed free of disease at the
> quarantine station but many caught cholera
> on arrival at Hamilton where the disease was
> prevalent.

It was a long walk back to Bunessan past the mill at Ardfenaig where he could hear the great granite millstones grinding and smell the new meal. He was tempted to go down the driveway to see what kind of house the Factor lived in, but he did not want to see the man again that day so he carried on to the pier. There was no time before dark to check his lobster creels round at Erraid so he hoisted sail and, taking the short line, went out to catch mackerel for bait.

They were not difficult to catch. He liked the flash of silver deep in the water and the tug on the line. Elegant fish, stream-lined and swift, unlike the lazy pollock, he regretted having to kill them. They were so plentiful that he soon had a pailful and decided to take some home for Peggy and the children. Thinking of her reminded him of Fergus's question about Catherine, an enquiry designed to censure him and convey his disapproval of Peggy's presence in the house. No doubt they all felt that way, his neighbours, ruled by the strictures of their faith. He was not imprisoned in that way. He thought of himself as a free man with no-one or nothing between himself and his God, and even that entity was distant and indistinct, a figure in the mists of his imagination defined by the tales and conventions of his people. Because he was a free man, unfettered by their rules, he was entitled to follow his own path, which did not forbid a fulfilment of his desires. He absolved himself from what they might see as a 'sin of the flesh'.

When he had caught enough mackerel to bait the few creels which Peggy had finished, he sailed back to the pier. As he reached the village, he met Catherine's brother John, standing on the edge of a crowd at the meal store. He was struck by the change in his brother-in-law. He was always a sturdy man who was known for his military bearing, marching through the village to buy supplies for his mother. Under the flame of starvation, the figure had melted like wax and had become a bent, listless creature like the others. When Calum spoke, he raised his head slowly and, for a moment, stared at him without recognition.

'Well, John. How is your mother?'

'Calum. I see you have some fish.'

'Mackerel for the creels.'

'If they are on a string in your hand, they are not for bait.'

'I thought you were working for the Factor.'

'I was, till he bought in more men from Islay. We have nothing now.'

Calum handed him the fish which he grabbed hurriedly and turned away from the crowd.

'I hear you have a woman in the house.'

'I sleep in the school,' Calum answered, following him.

'Is that so? Very noble of you.'

'She was living in a tent with her sick children after being evicted. She is in my house till her husband comes back.'

'So she is married as well.'

'Yes. She is a good woman who did not deserve to die in a tent.'

'Indeed. I'm sure Catherine will approve of your kindness.'

'She would not think the evil thoughts that poison your mind anyway.'

'I have accused you of nothing.'

'No, but I can see it in your face and in the words you choose.'

'Thank you for the fish, Calum MacGillivray.'

They had reached the bridge at the end of the village and John left him to head for Ardtun.

35

John Campbell stood a head taller than the men around him at the cattle pens above Bunessan. He was concerned that there were so few dealers at the market and a profusion of poor, lean, beasts for sale, most of them in his own hands, having taken them from emigrants in part payment of their fare or from tenants to pay their rent. An unusual mixture of calves, stirks, breeding cows and heifers, their appearance was not improved by the rain and the mud in the pens. Campbell looked at their hollow flanks and listless eyes and knew that most of them would not be sold. They stood with their heads lowered, strangely silent, for the bellowing from the pens could normally be heard in the village. The sodden air was perfumed with pipe tobacco and cow dung.

'It's the Irish,' McClymont said, standing beside him and leaning on his stick. 'Loads of beasts coming over, good beasts, better than these half-starved creatures. If the trade continues, the market for your small Highlanders will be wiped out.'

A dealer from Ayrshire, he knew the trade better than anyone.

'These beasts will fatten up, though, on good land in the south,' said Campbell.

'Try convincing the arable men down there. I doubt if I could get ten shillings for the best of them.'

'I trust you'll give His Grace's tenants a fair price.'

'The last lot I took from Mull to Falkirk proved to be a catastrophe. I couldn't sell half of them, even to the knackers. Had to find grazing for them. Worst market for twenty years. Two pounds at best for two-year old heifers. Barely pays the ferry at Grass Point. I don't see any of your own beasts here. Too good are they?'

'They are a different class. I send them straight to Glasgow. No middle men.'

'Yes, I've seen them. Grand stock right enough. I would give you a good price.'

'No middle men, Mr McClymont.'

They were interrupted by a sheep man who had plainly come to see the Factor.

Campbell did not like the man, but he was the new tenant of Shiaba. He didn't wait for an introduction but planted his cromach in front of Campbell and, leaning on it, addressed him rudely.

'I thought I would find you here, Mr Campbell.'

The Factor nodded, rain dripping off the brim of his hat.

'There are still small tenants in Shiaba. I understood they were to be cleared.'

'Excuse us, Mr McClymont, while we deal with this matter.'

'Of course, Mr Campbell. We will speak later,'

McClymont turned away, leaving the Factor with the sheep man.

'His Grace's tenants in Shiaba have been issued with Summonses of Removal. There are procedures to be followed. I don't expect you to observe such inconveniences, but His Grace's affairs must be conducted properly.'

'Why can't you just get some men together, go into Shiaba, turn out the tenants, lock the doors and burn the roofs.'

'That is the kind of brutality which you might employ, but the young Duke would not welcome the publicity which would follow such a course.'

'It would get rid of them, though. They have no right to be there. Sheep-stealers, poachers, worthless, idle creatures.'

'You have evidence of the crimes? Individuals who can be apprehended?'

'No. I don't know which of them, but I'm sure you have ways to find out.'

'You have to have evidence, witnesses, something that will stand in law.'

'You are too lenient with them.'

'That is not the description they would use. They will be gone shortly, I assure you. Some have left already. Having issued summonses, the matter is in the hands of the Sheriff, I'm told that he intends to visit but he has many other removals to attend to on the island. You will have to be patient, a virtue which you should seek to acquire. Now, I have business to discuss with the few dealers who have managed to reach us in spite of the weather. Good day, Donald.'

He turned his back on the flockmaster and walked over to the group of dealers. He found the man coarse and impudent, but his complaint was justified. He would have to take action against the Shiaba people. They were an irritant like a tick in his armpit, an impediment to progress, relics of the past sitting on top of the best grazing in the Ross. They would have to be swept off the land.

As he rode back through Bunessan he met MacQuarrie outside the meal store.

'I hear that you are going into partnership with Calum MacGillivray in a venture with a bigger boat.'

'You don't miss much, Mr Campbell.'

'It is my business to know what is happening in His Grace's lands. Do you think that this is a wise move, considering his reputation?'

'And what reputation is that?'

'He is reputed to be a poacher and a thief.'

'I know him as a kind, hard-working and honest man. I take it that you have no evidence to support such allegations or he would be in the gaol by now.'

'You would be wise to remember that you are a tenant of His Grace too and that your tenancy depends upon my good will.'

'How could I forget, Mr Campbell? But I have never failed to pay my rent and, when I met His Grace with Dr Boyter here in the village, he seemed to be impressed by my management of the relief and the work undertaken on the Uisken road.'

'I dare say. But a word from me and his impression will change. You should forget this partnership with MacGillivray.'

'Thank you for your advice, Mr Campbell.'

The Factor kicked the flank of his horse and rode away.

That night he wrote to the Duke:

> *I have just finished with rent collection*
> *for the Ross which I am very sorry to say has*
> *been exceedingly bad, having only recovered*
> *£284.16.8. A number of crofters complain*
> *of not being able to dispose of their stock*
> *and others, who did sell, complain that some*
> *the dealers who purchased their cattle have*
> *proclaimed themselves bankrupt and others*
> *will pay only according to the price they*
> *get for them at Doune or Falkirk markets—*
> *and that is little more than half of the price*
> *they were purchased for here during the*
> *season. There is no such thing in this quarter*
> *as paying for cattle at the time they are*
> *purchased—it is all by promissory notes ...'*

He had travelled to Glasgow to see the Tyree emigrants safely aboard the *Charlotte*, accompanied by the Rev Farquharson who had seen fit to hold a short service before the ship sailed from the Broomielaw. The minister had chosen his text from Hebrews Chapter 6 about hope, urging them 'to flee for refuge to the hope set before them, even Jesus Christ, who is an abiding place from the wind and a covert from the tempest.'

Report in *The Witness* 1849 by a Canadian correspondent about the Mull and Tiree emigrants:

> *By the time they had reached Toronto*
> *they had suffered severely, many having*
> *died of cholera, but it was only at Hamilton*
> *that their sufferings reached a crisis. There*
> *the Canadian Government succour totally*
> *abandoned them. The emigrant sheds, already*
> *crowded with the miserable Irish, could afford*
> *no shelter. Huddled together on the wharfs*
> *or on the commons betwixt the bays and the*
> *city, old and young, they lay without shelter—*
> *exposed to the scorching beams of a Canadian*
> *summer sun and the cold damp dews of a*
> *Canadian night. On the first night 13, on the*
> *second 8, were seized with cholera—in all 18*
> *were sent to hospital.*

The correspondent raised funds and persuaded the city authorities to give £150 to help them to Fergus, forty-five miles away. They were conveyed by wagon to Fergus and one of the drivers reported that three people on his load died on the way and their bodies were thrown into holes by the wayside. All the drivers had similar reports.

> *The wretched remnant linger on at Fergus*
> *until the spring. They have not so much as an*
> *axe to penetrate the primaeval forests, no food*

nor a single necessary for life in the bush ...
.there is something terrible in their situation;
a cold cheerless winter is before them and ill
prepared are they for the heart-chilling frosts
of a Canadian winter.

The correspondent reports that more than one third of the emigrants died.

John Campbell wrote to the Duke:

I am glad to say that the accounts from the
emigrants are by no means so bad as might
be anticipated from the representations made.
I shall endeavour to ascertain the number of
deaths accurately which will not, I believe,
exceed a tithe of the number stated. The benefit
resulting from the emigration of last season
is very sensibly felt, there are not nearly the
number of poor applying for aid as in former
years.

36

It was almost dark when Calum walked down the hill towards Shiaba. In the east a full moon had risen above the silhouette of Beinn Cruachan and he could feel a frost on his face. A stag bellowed somewhere along the shore, the echo ringing over the sea. Blue smoke from the houses curled into the air, a sight he always found reassuring, a sign of warmth and continuity.

'You said you would bring fish,' Peggy said, as she saw him come in without any.

Once again he was struck by her beauty in the candlelight.

'I'm sorry. I gave them to Catherine's brother who is starving.'

'Never mind. I snared a rabbit.'

'A rabbit?' He laughed. 'Is there anything you can't do?'

She rose from the fire, lifted the candle, went over to the table and started to skin the rabbit.

'I'll do that,' he said, coming to stand beside her.

'I can skin a rabbit.'

She was close to him, and the sour scent of her body, mingled with peat smoke, drew him closer. He watched her fingers stripping off the skin, leaving the flesh shining in the dim light. He reached out and placed his arm round her waist.

'I will cut myself,' she said, coyly, keeping her eyes on the task.

'I will heal the wound.'

'So you're a surgeon as well. You could fetch some water, if you wish to help.'

'Anything for you,' said with a hint of sarcasm, concealing its sincerity.

Noticing that the children were watching, he released his arm, lifted a pail and left the room.

As he walked towards the burn, he imagined lying with her naked in the bed, the bones of her starved body beneath his, her lips against his. He tried to devise a way to remove the children from the room—have them sleeping in the beast's quarter behind the hessian, move them into Fergus's empty house—anything to leave him alone with Peggy. Yet there was an impediment to every plan. When he reached the burn he knelt down and washed his face in the cold water, thinking that it would cool the heat in his head. He wanted her desperately. The forbidden nature of his lust added to the turmoil as he fought to dismiss his conscience and convince himself that he was free to indulge his craving. Catherine had left him. She might never return. She never wrote. He filled the pail and returned to the house, the conflict unresolved.

'Did you go Bunessan for it?' she asked.

He smiled but offered no excuse.

'Fill the big pot and swing it over the fire.'

He obeyed and she came over beside him and slid the rabbit into the water.

'You did not tell me that Catherine had a brother here.'

The mention of the name jarred, interrupting the flow of his thoughts as he tried to find the words to test her compliance.

'A brother and a mother who is blind.'

'Does she not write to them?'

He wanted to get away from the conversation, steer it in another direction.

'She cannot write.'

'She could find a scribe surely.'

'I think she has turned her back on her life here.'

'She's not coming back?'

'She is making a new life for herself in the city.'

'You could join her there.'

'I will never leave Shiaba.'

He turned to look at her and found that she was smiling, her eyes bright with amusement.

'Stubborn,' she said, and left him to sit at the table.

He kept his back to her, pretending to peek into the pot.

'The house next door is empty,' he said.

'Poor Fergus. He did not want to leave.'

'We could sleep in there.'

'Why would we do that? There is no fire, the hearth is cold, the house is bare.'

'I can re-light the fire. Just you and me, I mean.'

'Without the children?'

His hopes rose.

'Yes.'

'No, Calum. I can't leave them on their own.'

Deflated, he tried to quell the anger that was simmering beneath his disappointment. At times she seemed to be flirting with him, encouraging him to test her, and yet, when he made an advance she retreated. He did not understand.

'They are all that I have. My man is not at the fishing. He is a convict. Sent to Australia for poaching.'

'For poaching?'

Calum spun round, horrified.

'And for threatening the constables with a firearm when they came for him.'

'That's a heavy sentence. Will he come back?'

'Some of them never come back. You know that.'

'Yes, I'm sorry. So you are on your own?'

'With my children. They are my life. I will do anything for them.'

'I'm really sorry, Peggy.'

He stood over her, lifted her face towards him with his fingers on her cheeks and kissed her on the lips—not with the passion he had felt earlier but with gentleness and sympathy. No longer a target of desire, but a fellow human being, a victim of injustice like his neighbour and all the other people driven from their homes.

As he picked his way through the rabbit stew, he thought of the sentence passed on her husband.

'What was he poaching?' he asked her, wiping his fingers on his trousers.

'A hind. He had no need to do it. He had money from the fishing. Just foolishness. He liked the thrill of it, going out with my father's musket, never thinking.'

'And he threatened the constable?'

'He pointed it at the man and it was neither primed nor loaded but the sheriff had none of that. Transportation. That's all he had in mind. He knew the laird.'

'Did you not want to go with him?'

'I had nothing. He paid a lawyer to defend him. How could I go?'

'Would you want to go now, if you had the fare?'

'I don't know, Calum. They say there is terrible disease on the ships and I wouldn't risk the children. And what would I do when I got there? Alone in a strange land. They might stop me seeing him. He might be dead. They don't tell you if they die out there.'

'There is work there for women.'

'As a harlot in the gold fields?'

'In service. There are big houses there too, people with money.'

'Are you trying to persuade me, trying to be rid of me?'

'No, no. I would like you to stay here. You must know that. I'm thinking of what is best for you and the children—and your man. It must have been dreadful for him to be taken away from you and shipped to the other side of the world on one of those filthy convict ships like a cattle beast. Do you still love him, Peggy?'

She placed her hand on his and looked at him with an expression which he thought might be pity.

'I don't know what it means, that word. If you mean, would I want to be with him for the rest of my life and bear him more children, the answer is yes. He is a kind man, however foolish.'

'You can get help with the fare. Two pounds is all you need—a pound for you and ten shillings each for the children.'

'That is a lot when you have nothing.'

'I'll see what can be done. I will speak to MacQuarrie.'

'You have been saving to bring Catherine back. I want none of that. Give me your word that you will use none of that.'

He rose from the table.

'I'm going to the schoolhouse.'

'You can stay here,' she said, still holding his hand.

Confusion brought a frown to his brow. He didn't understand. She seemed to be offering herself while, at the same time, hoping to be with her husband. Perhaps he was misreading her invitation. Perhaps she meant he could lie by the fire or with the children. On the other hand, perhaps she meant to lie with her, regardless of the children. He looked at her bewitching eyes and the lips that he had kissed earlier and longed to stay.

'What about the children?' he said.

'I will see to them.'

This was temptation indeed.

When they had eaten she ripped down the hessian from the beast's quarter and made a bed for the children by the fire.

'You will be warm here,' she told them.

She lay down on the bed, still fully clothed but clearly waiting for him to join her.

'They do not say much, the girls,' he said, nodding in their direction.

'They have barely spoken since their father was taken. I think they blame me for it.'

He looked down at them and found them staring at him with eyes so like their mother's he was disturbed by the similarity.

'They are very like you,' he said. 'Eyes like deer calves. Gentle.'

He stood in the middle of the room, trembling, torn between excitement and fear, frozen on the lip of a precipice, trying to shut out the consequences of stepping over the edge yet trying to convince himself that there was no cliff, that only ecstasy and fulfilment lay on the other side. The temptation was too much for him and, removing his jacket, he lay down beside her.

For a while he lay very still, staring at the rafters where the hens used to roost, and then he stretched out his arm above her head and she curled towards him. Just as he turned to kiss her, Lucia, the eldest, crawled up the bed and lay between them. He waited for Peggy to scold her and order her back to bed but, when he turned to look at her, Peggy was smiling, almost laughing.

'She does not need to speak,' she said.

The other one joined them.

Although he resented the intrusion and could not help showing his frustration by withdrawing his arm, he was relieved and enjoyed the sensation of Lucia's head on his chest.

She had not come to the bed to interfere, to protect her mother, but, like a small animal, had sought comfort and the warmth of another creature, trusting in its kindness. Her trust in him washed away all the resentment and irritation and, stroking her hair with one hand and holding Peggy's in the other, he slept peacefully.

37

Catherine, waiting impatiently for Archie and Mary to return from the mill, poked the embers of the fire until there was a slight glow, a flicker and then a flame, and put a few pieces of coal on the more promising corners. There was little heat from the grate, not enough to melt the frost on the window pane. Hearing footsteps on the stairs, she lifted her shawl to leave but it was not Mary. It was Sine, coughing roughly as usual and clearly distressed.

'You're home early,' Catherine said.

'Is Duncan back yet?'

'No.'

'They are arresting people all over the country. Anyone taking part in what they call illegal meetings. Where's that Chartist paper that Marion had? '

'I used it to light the fire. I'm sorry.'

'No, no. I'm relieved it's gone. Look. It's here in this paper. Chartist leaders arrested in Edinburgh. All their homes searched, their papers seized. They raided the place where that paper is printed—what's it called?—oh, yes, here—*The North British Express*—the one that Marion had. My God, Catherine, if they found that here. There's one of them charged with treason. You know what that means.'

Catherine watched Sine pace up and down the room, but was thinking of Lamont and worrying about his involvement in the movement.

'I wish he would come back, Catherine. Every time he goes out looking for work, I think he's seeing his friends in the spirit dealers and they're all involved. He's such a fool.'

'Maybe he's found work.'

'I don't think so. Thousands out of work and he's just one of them.'

Just then they heard someone running up the stairs. Sine's hands flew to her cheeks. The door was flung open and Marion almost fell into the room.

'Father,' she gasped. 'They've arrested father.'

'I knew it!' shouted Sine. 'Where? Where is he?'

'I don't know. Jim Taylor stopped me in the street to tell me.'

'I must go and find out. You look after things here, Marion, and don't leave the house.'

She rushed out.

'That's dreadful, Marion,' Catherine said. 'Are you sure?'

'Taylor was in the spirit dealers when the constables came in but ran out the back door.'

'I'm really sorry. Sit down and I'll make some tea. Where is Mary?'

'On her way. She stopped for a smoke. She won't be long.'

Catherine swung the kettle over the coals and gazed into the fire, worrying about Lamont. She had planned to take Archie over for lessons but felt that she shouldn't leave the house till Sine returned.

'You've heard about the arrests in Edinburgh, then. I see mother has read the paper.'

'Yes. She was telling me about them. It's like a war. So many. All over the country.'

'For nothing. Speaking against Her Majesty's Government. Possession of weapons of a destructive kind—a kitchen knife or a pair of cropping shears or a printing press. That's what they're really afraid of—the truth. People knowing the truth.'

Catherine poured two mugs of tea and sat opposite Marion as Mary arrived with Archie and Sarah.

'What's happened?' Mary asked, immediately sensing the anxiety in the room.

'Father has been arrested.'

Sarah ran to Marion and flung her arms around her.

'Why?' asked Mary.

'We don't know yet. Mother has gone to find him.'

Catherine was becoming increasingly anxious about Lamont, a worry which was gradually overcoming her concern for the MacArthurs. Finally, she let it win.

'I'm going round to Mr Lamont. I'm worried that he might be involved. Come, Archie. You can come, if you like, Mary.'

'No. I'll say with Sarah and Marion.'

Catherine hauled on her shawl and left with Archie behind her.

'Come in, come in,' Lamont said, opening the door.

Archie ran past to join the boys in their room.

'Duncan MacArthur has been arrested,' Catherine said,

'Come into the kitchen, Catherine.'

Touching her elbow, he led her through.

'I'm sorry to hear that. On what charge?'

'I don't know. They don't know where he is. Sine has gone to look for him. They are very upset.'

'Of course. Sit down, Catherine.'

'There are arrests all over the country. They have not been here?'

'No, no. I have been to meetings but I'm not what they would see as an activist. Not like James Smith in Greenock who was foolish enough to hand round home-made pikes to people in the town. I can see why they would arrest him.'

'I was worried that they might have come for you.'

'No. I'm just a poor teacher. Insignificant. Once you discover what charges they have laid on Duncan, let me know. Some of the charges they have used are so vacuous that they will never stand. I may be able to help.'

'Thank you, Eoin. It's a great comfort to have someone like yourself to turn to in this city. I'm so lost at times and I don't always understand what is happening around me.'

'You underestimate yourself, Catherine. You are an intelligent, resourceful, compassionate woman and have an inner strength of which you are completely unaware.'

'Flattery, Mr Lamont,' she said, her colour showing her embarrassment.

'But true. Look how quickly you have learned here. And Archie too. What a clever and diligent boy. A credit to you.'

'We have had a superb teacher.'

'Now who is using flattery? Come, I have something for you.'

He led her through to the front parlour, a room rarely used, as she could tell from the wave of cold air when he opened the door, and the smell of damp. There seemed to be books everywhere—on the chairs, on the table, in the bookshelves, some open, some piled. He lifted a small, leather-bound volume from the table and held it towards her.

'For you. A small gift. *The Rights of Man* by Tom Paine. In your native tongue, in Gaelic. Keep it safe. There was a time when you could be transported for possessing it and, who knows, the time may come again. Take it.'

'Why? I don't understand. There is no need—'

'Take it.'

She reached for it but he held on to it and, for a moment, she thought he was about to withdraw it. It lay there in both pair of hands as if it was a bond between them. In his eyes she saw a glimpse of his fondness for her, a flicker of yearning but it passed quickly as he released the book into her hands.

'I don't know what to say.'

'Say nothing, my dear. Read it and you will see the world in a different light. He believes that free education is the answer to a better society.'

'You're very kind. Thank you, Eoin. I will look after it. I have never owned a book.'

'Come. Our pupils await. Await is the wrong word, I think, judging by the rumpus next door.'

She went into the kitchen, clutching the book to her breast. She heard him clap his hands and bring his boys to order, his influence over them always astonishing her. He never used force or threats of violence.

When the children came through they all took their place at the table.

'I don't like writing on slates,' announced Hector. 'That's what we have to do in school.'

'When you are older you will write in exercise books and you will learn to write elegantly and fluently in copper-plate script. Have patience. Roman boys had to learn on wax tablets and they did not have books—not as we know them. Why, Hector? Why do you suppose they did not have books?'

'Were they too poor?'

'Rome was a wealthy nation. Could there be another reason?'

'I don't know.'

'They did not have paper. They made a kind of paper by crushing reeds—papyrus reeds—so it was very delicate. When they wrote on it, they rolled it into long scrolls. If you wanted to read, you had to hold the top with one hand and unroll it slowly as you read.'

'We don't have books,' said Archie, to Catherine's surprise.

'They are expensive, Archie,' Lamont replied. 'If it is a choice between food and books, we must choose food to survive.'

Catherine admired the way Lamont dealt with the children, listening intently to what they said and answering with respect. She wished that she had his knowledge, that store of information about the world so that she could answer questions with confidence. Words were the answer and words had to have meanings, pictures in her head to be recalled when she saw the shape on the page, each shape a picture. She was determined to learn so that she could read as easily as her teacher and speak with the kind of authority he possessed.

'I will,' she announced, immediately startled by the sound of her voice.

The children stared at her, but Lamont smiled kindly.

'Yes, you will.'

He seemed to know what was in her mind. He was nodding as if to encourage her resolve.

'You will. I'm absolutely certain of that.'

They were interrupted by a knock on the front door.

Lamont rose.

'Hector, read that translation of Tacitus. Twins see to your reading with Catherine.'

He left the room, but she could hear the conversation at the door.

'I thought you should know, Mr Lamont,' the caller said, 'that there is cholera next door.'

'I thought it was all on the north side of the river.'

'It was. There are fifteen cases in the Gorbals and one death so far. Two thousand cases in the city, nearly half of them dead.'

'Hector took the woman some soup the other day. She looked so frail and under-nourished.'

'You will have to watch him. It is desperately infectious.'

'I will, I will. Yes, yes. I will. Thank you for letting me know, doctor.'

She heard the front door closing but he did not return immediately. She imagined him standing in the hall, his brow creased with worry, trying to absorb the news and decide how to deal with the crisis.

'Can I speak to you a moment, Catherine?' he said from the door, indicating that she should follow him into the parlour.

He closed the door as she followed him into the room.

'I expect you heard most of that,' he said. 'I'm worried about the boys, particularly because Hector has had contact with the woman, but I'm also concerned about Archie and yourself. I think we will have to curtail the lessons for a while. There is too much of a risk. It is a dreadful disease and highly infectious. We don't know where it comes from, how it's transmitted or how to cure it.'

'Like the rot in the potatoes.'

'Indeed.'

'I could still come and help in the house. I really want to help.'

'No, Catherine, but thank you for the offer. You must look after your own and your cousins. If it gets into the mill where they work, God knows how many will perish.'

'What will you do? How will you manage?'

'I managed before and will manage again but it will not be same without you, Catherine. You have brought a breath of spring to the winter which has gripped this household since my wife passed away. You must promise to return when it is safe to do so.'

'Of course. I give you my word. But I'm perfectly willing to continue just now.'

'No, no. I will not put you at risk. I'll give you two weeks' wages and see what happens after that. Come, we must see to the boys.'

38

Calum rose at dawn, hauled on his boots and left Peggy and the girls sleeping. It was a clear, still morning with the ghost of half-moon hanging in a blue sky. A new creel rubbed against his thigh as he walked towards the village. He had to speak to Donald Shaw about a supply of corks and the arrangements for marketing the lobsters and he was trying to decide whether to ask MacQuarrie about a passage to Australia for Peggy. If he once broached the subject, he would be bound to help her emigrate. He was sure that it was best for her and the children and yet he wanted her to stay. It was not enough to lie next to her, fully clothed and harassed by small children who burrowed like moles into the space between them. He wanted to feel her skin next to his and the taste of her mouth on his lips. He kept imagining it and planning ways to accomplish it. At times the fantasy was so vivid that it made him tremble and gasp for air. On other occasions he scolded himself for thinking such things. She was not his. He had no right to lie with her. The conflict was wearing, sapping his energy, bleeding him like leeches, poisoning his memories of Catherine and his children.

Shaw reminded him of a sack of oats, squat, legless, stiff with a small head like a bladder and tight black hair. There was something alien about him, as if he had been born in a distant land as yet unknown to explorers. Indeed, some superstitious people in the Ross, nudging their neighbours in the ribs, whispered that he had not been born at all. Others claimed that his real father had been a Spanish seaman wrecked on the Torran rocks. Calum never felt comfortable when the small blue eyes examined him.

'Can you get me some corks?' he asked him.

'If you have money to pay for them.'

'And more rope.'

'Is this for your creels?'

'Yes. Tell me about the lobsters. Will you buy them?'

'You will have to build a crate to keep them in the sea till you have a few. I won't buy them in ones and twos and I won't take small ones but I'll give you a good price. They are selling well in the south.'

'Fair enough.'

'Have you some ready?'

'No. I have a couple of creels set.'

'Where?'

'Off the rocks near Kintra.'

'Take me out and I'll show you where to set creels.'

'Why would you do that?'

'Because I'm as keen as you are to get lobsters and big crabs and I know more about the ways of these creatures than you do.'

So Calum reluctantly agreed to take him out.

Shaw showed him where to set the creels at the edge of the wrack and to think of how the tide runs around the reefs. When they had set the creels, they turned for home.

When they reached Bunessan, MacQuarrie was supervising a team of men extending the pier.

'Can I have a word with you, Calum?' he said as they climbed out of the boat.

Calum looked round at Shaw.

'You carry on,' he said. 'I will see to the lobsters.'

Calum walked up to the head of the pier with MacQuarrie.

'Peggy and her girls are at my house,' said MacQuarrie. 'Yes, I thought that would surprise you. She came to ask me about Australia, and I think I can arrange a passage for her. In the meantime, she will be living in the hut behind our house.'

Calum was too shocked to speak, the sudden storm in his head preventing any cohesion of thought that would lead to a sentence. Images tumbled over each other like a swell thundering on a reef, swirling, breaking, ebbing. He tried to grasp one of them to make sense of it, but they slid away as another crashed on top of it. Her hair on his shoulder, the white cleft of her breasts, her fingers gutting a rabbit, her laughter, her gaunt face in the tent, her invitation, her amusement when the girls joined them in the bed, his erotic fantasies and devious ambitions.

'It is not right that she should live with you,' MacQuarrie continued.

'It is no business of yours.'

'It is. I offered you the partnership because you claimed that you were saving to bring Catherine home. I helped her to leave and I know how the leaving tore at her heart. I saw her eyes full of tears and her fingers flutter with grief. I wanted to help her to come back. Peggy's man, the father of her girls, is in Australia. She has told me why, and she should be with him.'

'So this is your idea? That she should live here.'

'She asked me to find her somewhere to stay.'

Calum turned his back on MacQuarrie and stared out to sea, his hopes of lying with Peggy splintered. He remembered the invitation in her eyes, the seductive smile, the alluring touch of her fingers and could not reconcile the memories with her latest decision. He did not understand.

'I must speak with her.'

'Of course. No-one would wish to prevent that. Remember, though, what is best for her.'

He turned back to face MacQuarrie.

'I will decide what is best for her. She is in the shed now?'

'She's in the kitchen with my wife.'

Calum walked away but he passed the house and headed back to Shiaba. He could not confront Peggy if she were not alone. His confusion changed to fury as he climbed the hill out of the village. MacQuarrie had thwarted his plans, interfered with his schemes. He had no right to do that. He lifted a stone and, flinging it towards the village, cursed the man. He started to run, sprinting faster and faster, thinking that the pain in his legs and his lungs would relieve the rage and its heat in his head. When he reached Assapol he had to stop, breathless and exhausted, his chest burning. He sat on a rock and wept, his wails echoing over the loch. As the anger and grief subsided, his head began to clear. MacQuarrie was right. Peggy should be with her man and Catherine should be with him. All those fantasies were foolish nonsense, dreams of a desire of which he felt ashamed, embarrassed. He cringed when he remembered them. He had betrayed the woman who had loved him, the woman who had endured his selfishness and obstinacy and still loved him. He realised that he had almost thrown it away, all the years of sharing hardship and happiness. So close to the precipice. So foolish.

He stood and turned towards Shiaba, walking at a normal pace. He resolved to resume his mission of saving to bring Catherine home. That would become the priority. Yet he would not neglect his neighbours in Shiaba. They were good people, always grateful for the food he brought back, admiring and respecting him for his kindness and the risks that he took. Now he felt ashamed of the deception. They did not know of his betrayal, his lust and his scheming. Somehow he had to make up for that, redeem himself in his own mind.

As he reached the top of the hill above Shiaba, he met two families, the MacIntyres and the MacKinnons, their belongings in cart, clearly leaving the township.

'Where are you going, Duncan?' he asked.

'Fionnphort and then Glasgow. We have had enough. The Sheriff's men were here again today, a great crowd of them, and barred the doors. The children were terrified, the way they shouted and pushed us out. I know we could open the doors but what is there here for us now? The Factor will not rest till he sees the place empty and we are slowly dying of hunger anyway. You have been good to us, Calum, but we can't go on.'

'I understand. I will miss you all. Shiaba is slowly becoming a graveyard, houses like tombstones filled only with memories, silent and smokeless.'

'You will stay?'

'I will stay till they carry me to Kilvickeon.'

'God be with you, then. We must hurry.'

'And you, Duncan, and with you all.'

When he reached his house, there was still a thin plume of smoke from the roof but he found the door barred and nailed shut. He kicked the bar away and barged the door open. The room was empty, with not a sign of Peggy and her girls. Nothing to suggest that she had been there except two finished creels in the corner. On the table, however, there was a letter, addressed to John Shaw in Shiaba. Intrigued, he unfolded it, the seal being broken already, and was shocked by the news from the township of King in Canada.

I have to inform you that all the emigrants
got very favourable passage at sea—but I

*am sorry to say that a great number of them
suffered after the arrival at Toronto—Fergus
Campbell and his wife died and their children
are with Neil MacGillivray and the other Neil
MacGillivray who left Shiaba and his wife
and daughter and his youngest bearn—Robert
Campbell who left Shiaba died after taking
cold water (being too hot with fever) ...*

Calum collapsed into a chair, let the letter slip from his fingers and sat with his head in his hands.

39

When Catherine returned to the house Sine was sitting at the table, holding a mug of tea in both hands.

'Have you found Duncan?'

'No. The constables are not helpful. Looking at me as if I was the criminal.'

'Even the Highland men?'

'Even them. They seem to catch the infection of disdain when they enrol.'

'Talking of infections, I was going to tell you the woman next door to Mr Lamont has cholera.'

'My God! He will need to stay away from her, then—and his boys.'

'Hector took her soup.'

'He did what? Oh Catherine, that was really foolish. He may be infected now.'

'He didn't know then. Mr Lamont has told me not to come round.'

'He's right. I don't want it and I don't want any of us to have it. It's a dreadful sickness. You're dead within a day, if you get it.'

'I heard the doctor say there were fifteen cases in the Gorbals.'

'Good God! I thought they were all north of the river.'

'If I'm not to be with Mr Lamont, maybe I could help you find Duncan.'

'Thanks. That's good of you but you don't know the city. You could cook for us, though. That would allow me to search.'

'Mr Lamont gave me wages, so I'll go out and buy some butcher meat.'

She was about to leave when she heard the girls on the stairs and Marion burst into the room, followed Sarah, Mary and Archie.

'The power loom weavers are on strike,' she announced.

'Christ Jesus, will it never end? One affliction after another.'

'McBride's bound to lay us off. He sells yarn to them.'

'I know. I had worked that out. It may be a day or two before he does anything.'

'Six big works on strike, Mother, maybe four thousand workers. Started, they say, in Smith, Hamilton and MacLeary.'

'You seem pleased about it.'

'I am. They're mostly women. I want them to win, take back some of the profits earned by their sweat.'

'That's right,' said Mary. 'The owners grow fat while we grow thin.'

'And how are we supposed to eat?'

Mary's intervention worried Catherine. She did not want her to become involved.

'If McBride lays you off,' Sine continued, 'no-one in the house will be working. Not a penny coming in.'

'Maybe I could find work in one of the big houses,' Catherine said.

'We'll wait and see what McBride does.'

'I'll go out and get the butcher's meat for us.'

'And what about the cholera out there?'

'What cholera?' asked Marion.

'There's cholera in the village.'

'I'll take the risk,' Catherine said, lifting her shawl. 'You can go and look for Duncan, Sine.'

'I'll come with you, Mother,' Marion said.

'And me,' added Sarah.

'No. You wait with Mary and Archie. Someone has to be here in case there is word of him or in case he comes back.'

Catherine left the room and went down the stairs. A cold, sulphurous fog had settled above the houses like a blanket resting on columns of smoke from the forest of chimneys. Looking up, she wondered if the cholera floated in that black cloud, descending in the droplets that fell on her face. No-one could explain its origins or how it passed so easily from one person to another. Approaching people in the street, she stepped into the road to avoid them, imagining that any one of them might infect her. The butcher's house was easily identified by the hens hanging by their claws outside the door, small beads of blood on their beaks and their feathers ruffled. Inside, the carcass of a wedder hung from a hook on the ceiling, its ribs glistening inside their cage, and a haunch lay on the single table. The place smelt of entrails and blood. The butcher laid his cleaver on the table as she stepped forward.

'What can I do for you, mistress?'

She noticed that his fingers were like the sausages on the shelf behind him.

'Mutton flank. Do you have mutton flank?'

'I have indeed, if you'll give me a minute to bone it out. You're a stranger here. From the Highlands, I think, by your voice.'

'From Mull. I'm staying with my cousins, the MacArthurs.'

'Ah yes. Sine. A good woman. I hear there is fearful hunger on Mull and disease.'

'Yes, and many have died. That's why I came here with the children.'

'It may be no better here. There are thousands with no work.'

He had turned his back to her to bone out the flank with a knife big enough to kill an ox.

'I was working as a domestic till the cholera came next door but I'm hoping to find another job of the same kind.'

'Yes. There's a chance of that, right enough. I hear Sine's man is in trouble.'

'Bad news travels quickly in this village. We don't know where he is.'

'He should never have been seduced by these agitators, these Chartists, poisoning the minds of ordinary folk with their nonsense.'

She was tempted to argue but decided that it was better that he did not know her views.

'If they spent their time raising funds for the poor in the Highlands, I would have more respect for them. I raised twenty pounds for the Highland Fund.'

'That was good of you.'

'That day of the riot, I signed on as a constable. I saw Duncan there and saw him and his daughter ridden down by the cavalry. He wasn't involved in the looting and violence but he shouldn't have been there at all.'

A woman came into the shop behind Catherine so she said nothing and didn't look round to examine her.

The butcher finished preparing the flank and rolled it in newspaper.

'That will be two shillings, mistress. I hope you find him.'

'I hope so too.'

'Catherine?' the woman behind her asked suddenly.

She turned to find Effie from MacBride's standing with a basket.

'Effie! It's good to see you. How are you?'

'I'm well. Worn out with her children, but still able to escape on my day off. How are you? The mistress asks after you often. You made quite an impression on her.'

'Really?'

'Oh yes. She was raging with him for dismissing you. There was a right royal row.'

'Really? Do you think they would have me back?'

'I'm sure she would. I don't know about him, though. She never found a replacement. Lots of women applied, mostly poor, starving creatures off the street, but she didn't like any of them. I could ask if you like.'

'Yes. Would you? I would be very grateful. How are the children?'

'As precocious as ever. Spoiled. Ruined.'

'Clever, though. I liked them.'

'They talk about you—the woman who told them stories.'

'Tell them I have lots more. I must hurry back, Effie. I will call at the door one day.'

'Do that. It would be good to see you.'

She left and returned to the house.

She sliced the flank for stew and made some bannocks so that there would be a meal for Sine and Marion when they returned. They were clearly exhausted when they did come back, Sine coughing so harshly that she choked.

'Did you find him?'

'No. They all deny that they have him.'

'The butcher saw him at the riot—and you Marion.'

'Oh God!'

'But he says that Duncan was not involved in the looting and violence.'

'Truly? Do you think he would swear to that?'

'I don't know. He was one of the constables.'

'Could you ask him? I have had words with him about the Charter.'

'I will ask.'

40

Three men met in an elegant room of the Freemasons' Tavern in Great Queen Street in Covent Garden. Sir Charles had invited his old friend Sir John McNeill and Sir Thomas Murdoch to meet him to discuss the intractable problem of destitution in the Scottish Highlands and Islands.

He rose from the comfortable leather chair in which he had been dreaming of France to greet his guests.

'Ah John, good to see you, and you Tom. Do sit down. I have ordered some tea, or would you prefer something stronger?'

'No thank you, Charles. Tea would be very welcome,' answered McNeill.

Murdoch nodded his agreement.

As they settled in their armchairs, Sir Charles looked across at Sir John, envying, not for the first time, his handsome appearance.

'I'm pleased you could come, gentlemen. I have had something on my mind which I would like to discuss with you. I've been considering the formation of a new organisation, an organisation to encourage emigration to Australia. I know that your Commission, Tom, already offers generous support to potential emigrants from Britain as a whole, but this would direct its attention specifically to the Highlands. I'm aware the idea has been floated before and attempted on a limited scale but I have in mind a much more powerful body with some real power and energy.'

'I hope you're not suggesting that my Commission is inadequate in some way?' asked Murdoch.

'No, no, Tom. Certainly not. This organisation would focus on the Highlands, raising funds to help the natives. Now, I know that the Highland Relief Fund already exists to deal with destitution, but also that its members have never been comfortable in employing funds raised to prevent starvation used instead to promote emigration. I think some of the radicals feel that they would be seen to be encouraging evictions.'

'Do they have a point there?' asked Murdoch.

'Certainly not,' replied Sir John. 'Evictions are the result of arrears of rent.'

'And imprudent proprietors who slip into debt helping their tenants—MacLeod, for instance,' added Trevelyan. 'But let us not be distracted. Here is the point. The goldfields in Australia have seduced so many of the farm labourers and shepherds into leaving the farms that the flockmasters cannot harvest their wool. This has serious implications for our Yorkshire mills. If we can replace the labour force on Australian sheep farms with emigrant Highlanders, we will save the Yorkshire mills.'

'Yes indeed,' said Sir John, brightening with enthusiasm, 'and the Highlanders are born stocksmen,'

'Also I believe that most of these Highlanders will be Protestant, which would balance the flood of poor Catholic Irish to the colony, thus ensuring that Australia does not become a Catholic ghetto. I would not use that argument in public, of course.'

'A splendid plan, Sir Charles,' said Murdoch. 'A way of strengthening the Empire. I'm sure Her Majesty would lend her name to it.'

'Well let's discuss whom we can approach. First financial backers.'

'I would suggest Thomas Baring.,' said Murdoch. 'Rich as Croesus.'

'But he backed us with the Slave Compensation Scheme. Still, I will write to him and to Baron Rothschild.'

'Bank of England? W.G. Prescott?' suggested Sir John.

'Yes indeed. I can see the bones of a committee forming here. We need some men of the cloth and a sprinkling of aristocrats.'

'It might be useful to include the Australian Agricultural Company. It has the Directors of the East India Company on its Board, all of whom you will know, Sir John, and a score of MPs,' offered Murdoch.

'Splendid. I find myself becoming quite excited, gentlemen,' said Sir Charles.

'Perhaps Prince Albert would act as a patron.'

'Yes. Both he and Her Majesty have that romantic affection for the Highlands. I will approach the Palace.'

Sir Charles clapped his hands for service.

'Enough, gentlemen. We have the skeleton. We will put flesh on it later. I think it should be called the Highlands and Islands Emigration Society so that it sounds like a charitable enterprise. We must give the impression that it is independent, although we will exercise control. Now, let us have some tea and even some cakes.'

'How is Hannah, Charles?' Sir John asked as a servant poured the tea.

'Well, thank you. In fact, I'm going round to the market to buy some flowers for her. Would you care to come? And you, Tom?'

'I have never visited the market. I would be delighted, Charles.'

'I will have to decline the invitation unfortunately, Sir Charles. I have to chair a meeting of the Commissioners. Should I mention the scheme?'

'I think not, Tom. Let us advance a little yet.'

Having finished their tea, the three rose and left the building, Sir Thomas heading for Westminster.

Sir Charles and Sir John walked round to the north end of the market where the flowers were shown. In King Street a line of wagons, having delivered their goods just after dawn, were filling the roadway.

'Isn't that a wonderful perfume?' said Sir Charles. 'It is quite intoxicating.'

The sweet scent of flowers pervaded the space beneath the roof. Roses, geraniums, violets, fuschia, lilac, heartsease, all freshly cut, created a blaze of colour.

'Reminds me of India,' said Sir John, lifting a rose to hold beneath his nose.

Sir Charles bought a bunch of the roses and they turned east into the main hall where there were stalls of strawberries, peaches, raspberries and plums. The hall was unpleasantly crowded and they found themselves jostled by strangers of all classes. Sir John knocked against a woman with a tower of baskets on her head and received a rosary of swearing. Young boys, their bare feet black with mud and their shirts torn, flitted beneath the stands, watching for a chance to steal. One of them bobbed up in front of Sir Charles, lifting a peach from the stall. Sir Charles gripped him by the collar.

'What are you doing?'

'Buying a peach, sir.'

'Show me your money.'

The boy dropped the peach and did not reply.

'You have none, do you?'

The child shook his head.

'It's for my sister, sir. She has nothing to eat.'

'Oh? And where is this sister of yours?'

'Over there, selling cress.'

Sir Charles walked across the hall, keeping hold of the boy, to a girl holding out a tray of water cress.

'Is this your brother?'

'Yes, sir. Would you like some fresh cress for the table? Just picked this morning.'

The girl, he noticed, had scarcely the strength to carry the tray, her pale, gaunt face as close to being a skull as possible in someone still alive.

'He's been stealing.'

'He's always stealing. I knew he'd get caught but we have to eat somehow.'

'Are your parents here?'

'My Ma is sick at home but my Da is in King Street.'

'Let's go and find them, then.'

'If I leave here, I will sell nothing.'

'I will buy the whole tray. Now come. You lead the way.'

She set down the tray and walked towards King Street.

They found the father begging in the street.

'Is this your son?' asked Sir Charles.

'That is my son, sir.'

'He's a thief.'

'He may have been stealing but he is not a thief. Not by nature. He is honest by nature.'

'Semantics. He was stealing and I should hand him over to the law.'

'We have nothing, sir. Nothing to eat. My daughter sells a little cress that she gathers in a freezing stream. My son steals fruit and I am reduced to begging.'

'You're Scotch, I think?'

'Yes, though I'm far from my native land.'

'What part of Scotland?'

'The island of Tiree.'

'Tiree! Why are you in London?'

'They stopped the relief, sir. I was working on the railway in the South and we heard that the people at home were starving so we went back to see they were safe.'

'You left your work?'

'For an easier life at home?' said Sir John.

'It is not easier to turn the land with a spade or carry kelp from the shore, to harvest corn with a hook or dig potatoes with a fork. We work from dawn till the sun sets to feed our families and to pay our rent. Not an easier life, sir.'

Sir John did not answer but did look slightly chastened.

'When we went home, the Duke's men refused us meal. Said we did not qualify so I took my family and came back to the railway but there was no work. I am not afraid of work, sir. An Englishman told me there was any amount of work in London. I should not have listened to him.'

'You could leave and go to Australia,' said Sir Charles.

'I don't have the fare and my wife is sick.'

'If you had the fare, would you go?'

'To leave your native land where your forefathers are buried, never to see it again, is like having your heart cut out.'

'You have left it already,'

'But I could walk back. I could still go home.'

'There is plenty of work in Australia, work on the farms. Not in Factories or on railroads but work that would suit you. You could have a new life with your family. You would not have to beg in the streets there.'

'A new life in Canada was promised to the people who left on the *Charlotte* and *Barlow* and most of them are in their graves under the snow.'

'You did not answer my question, If you had the fare, would you go?'

The man looked at him suspiciously.

'If I had enough for the fare to Australia, I would call a doctor to my wife.'

'And if she was cured?'

'I would go home.'

'I despair,' Sir Charles said to Sir John, 'but I'm convinced that many will go, given the incentive.'

He turned back to the Highlander.

'Did the Duke not provide work for you?'

'The Duke does not want the likes of us on his land. He would sweep us into the sea, if he could. We had no lease. Cottars, we are called. We could make a living till the potatoes failed.'

'Perhaps there were too many of you, a surplus population depending on potatoes, and some had to leave. In the end, those who remain may have a better life.'

'The rest of us dead of starvation or scattered over the earth like sweepings from a barn. We were not so worthless when they needed men for their army or navy. They have short memories, sir. My father died with the 91st in Africa two years since.'

'I'm sorry to hear that. If you remain here for the rest of the day, I will send my servant to see what can be done to assist you and your wife and, in the meantime, you will take your boy in hand and see that he refrains from stealing. I should really hand him over to the constables.'

'Thank you, sir. I will do what I can.'

Sir Charles and Sir John threaded their way through the crowds toward the entrance.

'You know, John, the Scotch are so much more civilised than the Irish. We need to catch them before they leave home, before they descend to that level of destitution. I don't understand their intransigence, their resistance to emigration and the prospect of a better life. It doesn't make sense. I tell you, John, five hundred years hence a few aristocratic families of the great Australian Republic will boast of being able to trace their ancestors in the records of the Highlands and Islands Emigration Society.'

Sir John laughed as they parted company on the Strand, Sir Charles heading back to the Treasury.

When Sir Charles reached his office, he found George uncharacteristically distressed.

'Dreadful news, Sir Charles. Sir John's brother and his wife and two daughters have been drowned.'

'Good God! I have just been speaking to him and he didn't know. How could this have happened?'

'They were on the steamer *Orion* on their way from Liverpool to Glasgow when the ship ran at full speed into rocks off Port Patrick during the night. The impact apparently tore the hull open and it sank within minutes. Sixty drowned.'

'This is ghastly news, George. Anne and the girls. Are you sure?'

'By telegraph. It will be in the newspapers tomorrow.'

'Call me a carriage immediately. I must go round to John. Oh, and there is another task but it can wait.'

'Very good, sir. Please pass my sincere condolences to Sir John.'

41

Calum called on Peggy early in the morning. For some time he stood outside the door, gazing over the bay towards Ardtun. A pair of oyster catchers strutted along the tide-edge, prodding the seaweed for food. They mate for life, he thought. Maybe they had been sent as a sign, a reminder of his marriage. He still wanted to speak to Peggy but couldn't decide what to say. He started to walk away, stopped for a moment and then came back and knocked.

'Well, Calum,' she said as she opened the door, smiling and clearly pleased to see him.

'I came to say that I think you did right in moving here.'

'As I lay in the darkness beside you, I thought of the convicts in Australia toiling in the blazing sun with the chains tearing the skin off their ankles and I knew that I should be there with my husband. It was yourself who planted the notion.'

'I will miss you by the fireside.'

'You will have your Catherine back one day, I'm sure of that and, while I'm waiting for word of a ship, I will make more creels for you if you bring me the wood.'

'You don't need to do that.'

'You took us in when we might have perished. It is one way of repaying your kindness.'

'It was the least I could do. If you could make the creels, I would be very grateful.'

'It would speed Catherine's return to you.'

'Indeed. Thank you.'

'I think Mr MacQuarrie wishes to speak to you. He is in the house.'

'What does he want?'

'I don't know. He said to tell you, if you called. Go now. I must see to the girls. Don't forget the wood.'

She turned back into the house and shut the door.

He stood for a moment, pleased that he had a reason to call again, then walked round to the house. MacQuarrie was just about to leave for the Uisken road.

'Ah, Calum. I was hoping to see you.'

'Peggy told me.'

'I'm glad she has decided to join her man in Australia. She may not be able to see him very often, but her presence will ensure that he does not despair. Despair kills many of them I fear.'

'Yes, she is right to go. Of course she is. She has offered to make creels for me while she waits.'

'That's good of her. I wanted to tell you that there is a slight problem connected with the boat.'

'What's that?'

'The Factor has threatened me with eviction if I help you. Not directly. He is too sly to make a threat openly. He chooses his words cautiously. He hints, but it is there nonetheless.'

'He has no right to do that.'

'I have no intention of reneging on our agreement, Calum, or of cancelling the order, but I think you should know the extent of his ill will towards you.'

Calum laughed.

'I'm well aware of his malice but I'm not afraid of him.'

'David and Goliath again. Beware, he has the power of the Duke behind him and the law.'

'David had only a sling.'

'All the same. Be careful. You may yet suffer from his spite. Now I must go. When this road is finished, your fish will reach the markets in half the time. God go with you.'

He walked away up the hill towards Uisken.

Calum's fists clenched as the full force of his fury erupted within him. Without any hesitation he set off west towards Ardfenaig. The walk might have given his anger time to dissipate but it solidified into purpose as he rehearsed what he intended to say, gathering his words like sling stones, selecting the sharpest ones to hurl at his enemy. The risk and the consequences of such an attack never appeared on the horizon of his planning.

He walked past the mill and the gate lodge and down the long drive to the Factor's house. Undeterred by the size of the house or the expanse of the gardens, he knocked on the front door. He did not recognise the maid who answered it.

'Is Mr Campbell in?'

'Have you an appointment?' she asked.

'No.'

'Who shall I say is calling?'

He knew by her speech that she was from Islay.

'Calum MacGillivray from Shiaba.'

'Just a moment, please.'

She shut the door. When it opened again the tall figure of the Factor filled the doorway. Because of the steps, he towered over Calum, glaring down at him.

'Yes, MacGillivray. What can I do for you? You have a nerve coming to my door like this.'

'You have been threatening Mr MacQuarrie.'

'I don't make threats. That is a very serious accusation.'

'You have been attempting to interfere in a private arrangement between him and myself.'

'I know nothing of such an arrangement.'

'You know that Mr MacQuarrie is helping me to buy a bigger boat so that I can make a living by fishing. I have every reason to believe that the Duke would approve of my efforts. Indeed, I'm sure that he would disapprove of any attempt to prevent me fishing.'

'His Grace has little time to consider such trivial matters. He gives me the power and authority to deal with them. I am his representative here and have the power to terminate the tenancy of any troublesome tenants.'

'You said that you didn't make threats, Mr Campbell, so I will take what you have just said as a statement of fact. Nothing more. The times are changing. The newspapers from the south have suddenly become interested in the plight of the people here, they are listening to what we have to say, we have a voice and, if it was printed that the Duke's Factor tried to prevent a poor fisherman from making a living, I'm sure His Grace would not be too pleased to have such a stain on his reputation.'

'You are threatening me, MacGillivray. How dare you!'

'I am not afraid of you, Mr Campbell. My people were here long before you were born and will be here long after they carry your head to its grave. No-one here will mourn your departure when you go to meet your maker and account for the misery you have inflicted on the poor people of the Ross. Good day to you.'

Calum turned and walked away up the drive, leaving the Factor aghast in the doorway.

He did not regret what he had said but he was worried, knowing that Campbell could have him evicted and could ensure that he found no employment in the area. He could even bring a charge of poaching against him, calling the herd as a witness and instructing the sheriff to find him guilty. He might have to join Peggy's husband in Australia. Still, he was pleased with himself for confronting the tyrant. David challenging Goliath.

As he passed a hazel coppice, still on the Factor's land, he left the road and cut some rods for his creels, delighted to be able to strip something from his adversary. Carrying them back to the village, he dropped the bundle outside Peggy's hut, and headed back to the pier. For the time being he would concentrate on line fishing until he had enough lobster creels to warrant spending time on them.

That night he wrote a letter to Catherine.

> *Dearest Catherine, I am writing to let you know that I am doing well at the fishing and am saving to bring you all home soon. I have started fishing for lobsters as there is good money in them. MacQuarrie the merchant is helping me to buy a bigger boat so I will have to take on men as crew. I will ask your brother if he wants to sail with me.*
>
> *Two more families have left Shiaba after being harassed by the Factor and the Sheriff's*

men. It is sad to see the houses empty and no smoke from the roofs and sheep grazing round the doors. The line of starving people at the grain store does not get any less so I am sure that more people will leave the country.

I am missing you every night when I sit on my own by the fire and think of the times we cut the corn together and watched the sun go down behind the hill. I think of you with Mary, our first-born, at your breast and the way you looked down on her with such loving in your eyes. I think of your smile when I said I loved you for the first time. Come back to me soon, Catherine, I am only half a man without you.

Your loving husband, Calum

42

Catherine came down the stairs in the early morning to find Sine kneeling beside the box bed.

'What is it, Sine?'

'Sarah is sick with the flux. Look at her clothes, all soaked with sweat.'

Catherine came beside her and looked down, recognising the stench. Sarah's face was as pale as ivory and glistening with a film of cold sweat. The veins shone blue on her forehead.

'I have sent Marion for the doctor, but I fear it's cholera. God, I wish Duncan was here. He would know what to do.'

'Still no word?'

'Not a whisper.'

'Have you plenty of water?'

'No. I have used what we had.'

'I'll send Mary for more and for some cloths from the rag lady.'

She called up the stairs to Mary and sent her for water.

Sarah squirmed as a sudden spasm of pain shot through her bowels. Her face crumpled like paper and her jaw quivered.

'It's alright, Sarah,' Sine said, mopping her brow with a damp cloth. 'The doctor will be here soon. The man who fixed Marion's leg.'

Mary struggled up the stairs with two pails of water and placed them by the fire.

'I'll go back for the cloths. I couldn't manage them and the water.'

Catherine filled a pot with water and swung it over the fire.

'I have none of the African's remedy left.'

'I hope Buchanan will have something—laudanum or something.'

'How did she get the sickness? Is it in the mill?'

'I don't think so. It's in the Gorbals, though, but she has been nowhere near the ones who are sick.'

They heard footsteps on the stair and the doctor hurried in with Marion.

'Cholera,' he announced. 'I can tell by her appearance and the perfume. How many live here?'

'Myself and the girls, one of them on the bed here, and Catherine and her two children but they sleep upstairs. My husband is usually here but is away just now.'

'You have a room upstairs?'

'Yes.'

'Everyone except yourself and the patient must move upstairs immediately.'

'What? All of them?'

'All except you. You have already had contact with the patient and will probably be infected anyway. I will give her some laudanum to help the pain and the spasms but there is no cure. We can help her through the disease but, in the end, is up to her, her resilience, her strength.'

'No cure?'

'To be honest, no. There are all kinds of remedies suggested by our well-dressed witch doctors—bleeding with leeches, calomel, castor oil, prayer—but the truth is that we don't know and we don't know for sure how the sickness travels. Some think that it is by bad air, the stink of the middens, the sewers in the street, the filth in the abattoirs, but I'm sure it is by contact. That's why the others should move upstairs. Now, what is this one's name?'

'Sarah.'

'Sarah, have you had contact with anyone with cholera?'

She did not answer as another spasm shook her.

'I'm sure she hasn't,' Sine said. 'There's no sickness in the mill that I know of. It is here in the Gorbals, though.'

'Yes. The butcher down the street is very ill.'

Catherine gasped.

The doctor opened his bag and lifted out a bottle of laudanum and a spoon.

'Can you raise Sarah's head so that I can give her some of this.'

Catherine wondered if she should mention her visit to the butcher. Perhaps the sickness was on the meat and would infect everyone in the house. She imagined the bodies lying on the floor in their own filth, dying of fever, and then she remembered that the butcher was the witness who could save Duncan from prison. There seemed to be no end to their troubles.

'Now,' said the doctor, pointing at Catherine, 'you will live upstairs with your children and the other girl. Stay away from this room. Mrs MacArthur will have to live here with Sarah till the fever passes—if it passes. I will leave the bottle here. Give her ten drops every four hours and plenty of water—iced water if you can get it. Try to keep her clean and warm. I will return tomorrow.'

He shut his bag and left.

'I don't want to leave you on your own,' Catherine said.

'Best to do what he says. Take some hot coal on a shovel upstairs for your fire. And a pot of water.'

Mary returned with an armful of cloths.

'We have to move upstairs,' Catherine said. 'Leave the cloths.'

Mary dropped the cloths and Marion lifted a shovel and carried some smoking coals upstairs.

'What about Duncan?' asked Catherine. 'Should I try to find him?'

'No, but Marion can. She knows where to look. Thank you all the same.'

'I'll make you some tea.'

She lifted a pail of water and carried it upstairs. When she opened the door, the room was thick with coal smoke. She could barely see the fire.

'The chimney must be blocked,' Marion said. 'Not completely for there is some smoke going away. Maybe it will clear. If father was here, he would drop a big stone down the flue.'

'We'll just have to suffer it. I was about to make some tea.'

'The fire is alright. It will boil a pot. Hand me the pail and I'll see to it. You sit down.'

As she waited for the water to boil, Catherine thought about her predicament. She wanted desperately to move out with Mary and Archie, find other lodgings, escape from the sickness, but that would be disloyal. Sine needed her help. She wished that Calum could be there. He always had a solution. Yet, if he were to arrive, he might catch the cholera. She couldn't turn to Lamont for advice. He would not welcome a visit, particularly as she had contact with the sickness. And McBride. O God. She could not go there either. She felt trapped, enclosed in a net which was drawing tighter day by day.

She found it difficult to steady herself as she tottered down the stairs in her bare feet with a candle in one hand and a bowl in the other and, when she reached the door, she could not press the latch. She had to lay down the bowl and open the door. The room was in darkness so she carried the candle to the table and returned for the bowl.

'I have brought you some broth, Sine.'

Sine did not answer. Perhaps she had the sickness. She was sitting on the floor by the bed, her head resting on her arm which was draped across Sarah's legs. A wet cloth was slipping from her other hand.

'Sine!'

She woke, startled.

'Jesus, Catherine, you frightened me.'

'I've brought you some broth. How is she?'

'No better. Worse, in fact. She shivers and yet runs with sweat and she breathes as if she had run from the Green. Leave the broth on the table. Thanks, Catherine.'

'I will come back later. You should get some sleep.'

'I will. She's very sick. Is she going—?'

'She's doing well,' Catherine interrupted. 'She'll come through. You will see.'

'I wish Duncan was here.'

'Marion will find him. She will go out when it's light. I can take a turn here, if you would like to sleep.'

'No, Catherine. You heard what Buchanan said. I may have the sickness already. I don't want you to have it too. You go back to bed. I'll stay with Sarah.'

'Don't forget the broth. And the candle,' she said as she left the room.

Upstairs she poked the fire till a flame flickered from the embers. Behind her, the three children were asleep in the bed, Mary in Marion's arms. She glanced at the window but there was no sign of light. Turning away from the fire, she sat at the table. Above her the black webs quivered in the faint heat from the candle. She did not intend to sleep but, within ten minutes, her head was in her arms across the table.

Marion was standing beside her when she woke, her shawl over her head.

'I'm going to look for my Da.'

'Wait and I'll make you some porridge.'

'I've had a bit of cheese and a cut of bannock. I'll be fine, thanks.'

Mary hurriedly slid out of bed.

'I'll come with you, Marion.'

'No,' said Catherine. 'I might need you here.'

'I want some fresh air, Mother. I can't bear being shut in here all the time. The place is full of smoke and the smell of the midden at the back makes me feel sick.'

'You didn't smell so sweet yourself at one time. Oh well, go then. Take some cheese with you.'

'Can I go too?' asked Archie from the bed.

'No. Certainly not.'

As the girls left, she swung over a pot to make porridge but remembered the meal was downstairs.

'You wait here, Archie. I'm going down for meal.'

She was relieved to find that Sine had taken a chair to the bed and was sitting more comfortably beside Sarah.

'How is she?'

'Burning. I've tried to get her to take water but she will only have a sip at a time I've cleaned her as best I can.'

'I really want to help. You can't do it all on your own.'

'I can. I will. You don't come near, Catherine. You have children upstairs. I don't want them to catch it.'

'If there's anything I can do, just ask. I'm making some porridge so I'll take some down to you. You never ate your broth.'

'I forgot. I'm sorry.'

'I'll pour it back in the pot. I came down for some meal.'

Just as she lifted the bag, Doctor Buchanan knocked and came in without waiting for a reply.

'How is she this morning?'

'No better.'

'Let me see.'

He bent over Sarah as Sine moved out of his way.

'Extremely high fever,' he said, 'and heart racing. Not good, I'm afraid. Not good at all. Has she had water?'

'Only sips.'

'She must have liquids. That's essential. Listen, send someone over to the Saltmarket for some ice. I know it's the Sabbath but there should be someone there. Put some ice on her tongue. Keep giving the laudanum. It's not a cure but it helps the cramps and the pain. I will call again tonight.'

He rose and left them without a farewell.

'He doesn't sound very hopeful,' Sine said.

'Maybe the ice will help. I'll go and get it. I wish I hadn't let Mary go. Archie can sit at the door here.'

43

The roar of the wind woke Calum after midnight. Worried about the boat, he rolled out of bed and hauled on his boots. He knew there was going to be a storm, but there was something menacing about this gale, the way it persisted, never abating for a moment, an uninterrupted bellowing, a monstrous bull battering the walls and goring the roof. He tried to light a candle from the fire but the flame blew out. He staggered across the room in the dark and opened the door. The wind blew him against the wall. He could hear the thunder of the swell on the Torran rocks and taste salt spray on his tongue. The wind was uncannily warm and the night sky far from dark so he could see the sea below crashing on the rocks, tall plumes of spray whipped away by the gale. He had to see to the boat. The creels, he knew, would be wasted.

He had to lean far forward to make any headway against the storm and even then he was often blown backwards. Strips of white grass were plastered on to his face and bunches of loose heather rolled past and vanished into the night. When he reached the top of the hill above Shiaba, the full force of the wind flung him to the ground. He wondered if he would ever reach Bunessan. Struggling to his feet, he carried on, sometimes having to lean his knuckles on the ground. As he passed Assapol he heard a loud crack as one of the trees fell across the road ahead of him. Had he been a few yards further on, he would have been crushed. He remembered his own roof and cursed himself for not checking the ropes.

When he reached the village he was relieved to see the silhouette of the boats against the pier. One of them had broken free and was wrecked on the Ardtun shore, its broken mast swaying in the wind as it rocked in the swell. There was some shelter from the high ground as he struggled round to the pier, worried that the wreck might be his and knowing that MacQuarrie was relying on the sale of the boat to help pay for the new one. If his boat was wrecked, he would be left with nothing. He was sure that no other boat had come in after him and his would be most exposed to the storm. As he turned the corner the road was almost blocked by the top of a corn stack, virtually intact but gradually being stripped as the flail of the wind thrashed it clean. Someone at the top of the hill would wake to find their last hope of survival stolen by the storm.

He reached the pier to find that his boat was safe but the two creels that he had left on the bank waiting for ropes had been blown away. He thought of the creels set out by Kintra, reckoning that he would lose them, that the storm would fling them on to rocks. Then he remembered the creels stacked outside Peggy's door. He would have to check on them. First, though, he had to be sure his boat was properly tied. The pier was relatively sheltered from the south-west but the boats were still being tossed about. He climbed down, relieved to find that the mooring ropes were secure. The boat, however, moored between two others, was rocking violently against them, the top strake being badly damaged by the movement. There was nothing he could do but hang fenders over the side, so he climbed out and headed back to the village.

Passing Peggy's hut he checked the creels and found that they were sheltered from the storm. He was tempted to knock on the door but resisted the notion as it was still the middle of the night and he might frighten her. In any case he was keen to return to Shiaba in case the gale damaged his roof.

By the next morning the storm had passed but there was still a massive swell running out at sea. He decided not to sail that day and visited every family in Shiaba to ensure that they had not suffered in the storm. The only house damaged was Fergus Campbell's where the gale had blown open the door and, lifting the roof, had smashed the timbers. The broken roof had caved in and lay in a heap between the walls. Some of the younger men had left for work on the Uisken road but, in every house, the gaunt faces, tattered clothes and skeletal children reminded him of his good fortune. Famine, he thought, like a voracious spider, still sucked the juices out of its victims,

He decided that he should visit Catherine's mother as her house lay directly in the path of the storm. He did not relish the prospect of her antagonism and invective but he felt that Catherine would blame him if any harm had come to the old lady. He smoored the fire and set off.

'Christ Almighty, Mima! What are you doing?'

The blind lady was struggling to lift John's sodden mattress out of the house.

'It's yourself, Calum MacGillivray. About time too.'

'Sit down, Mima. Let me take that.'

He took it from her as she felt her way to the chair and sat.

Calum was shocked that the storm had swept the high tide into the house. Weed and debris from the sea was strewn across the floor and the hens were scratching among it for grubs. A byre brush lay at the door where the old woman had swept out the water.

'Where's John,' he asked.

'It was rumoured that the blacksmith had some whisky so he went to investigate yesterday and has not been back since. He is not good with whisky. It does not take much. Last time he was so bad he proposed to me.'

'You should be flattered.'

'He would have proposed to a billy goat the state he was in.'

'I will take this out and come back. I see the fire's out. Is there kindling?'

'In the barn, I think. The tide has taken the peat stack. I went round and it's gone but there might be an old peat or two in the barn.'

'I will look. You sit there.'

'Where else would I go? To London to see the Queen?'

He dragged the mattress outside and laid it on a rock to dry. Finding some dry wood and an armful of peats in the barn, he returned and, sweeping the slime of wet ash off the hearth, set the fire.

'Have you a match at all?'

'On the kist. Tear some newspaper off the wall and use that.'

He did what she said and lit the fire.

'If Catherine was here,' she said, 'she would make some tea.'

'Would she now? I suppose that's a polite way of asking me to do it.'

'What else would you be doing, a good-for-nothing like you?'

He lifted a pot and flung out the salt water.

'You can't even make your own creels.'

He looked up quickly. How does she know that? he asked himself. John. It must be John. He must have heard in the village. Gossip. He wondered what else they were saying, whispering poison in each other's ears.

'I had a letter from Catherine,' she said. 'Written by herself.'

'She can't write.'

'She can now and beautiful writing too, MacQuarrie tells me.'

'MacQuarrie was here? '

'Oh yes and brings me a pinch of meal too.'

He wondered what MacQuarrie would have revealed to her.

'Have you any tea?'

'In the kist. At the bottom, seeing there's no meal. In a tin so it should be dry.'

The pot boiled and he made tea for her. He was keen to ask her about the letter but did not want to give her the pleasure of refusing to say.

'I will go and buy meal for you and make some gruel.'

'MacQuarrie will bring meal.'

'And will he cook it too? I'll be back.'

Furious with himself for allowing her to irritate him, he left the house. So Catherine could write. How had that happened? Her accomplishment annoyed him. He knew that he should be pleased, but the fact that she had achieved it without his help stung like a nettle. He felt guilty too. He should have paid the schoolmaster to teach her. He should have encouraged her but somehow it didn't seem important at the time. He wondered what other skills she might be learning in the city. Maybe she was making a new life for herself. Maybe she would never come back. He had to find out, go to Glasgow before it happened. Yet he had not saved enough for the fares.

In the village he met John, who looked more sickly and feeble than ever.

'Here, take this to your mother. Three pounds of meal. And you will need a new mattress to sleep on.'

'Why? There's nothing wrong with the one I have.'

'While you were carousing last night the storm blew the tide into your house. Go home and see for yourself.'

He walked away, relieved that he had not asked John to crew for him.

The next day he untangled his boat from the others and set sail to investigate his creels. There was still a long swell but the wind had dropped. Gulls were feeding on an animal carcass off the point. There was no sign of his creels off Kintra. He sailed along close to the rocks, hoping to see the corks or a length of line, but there was nothing but a smashed oar. He sailed on to the back of Erraid, a small island off Mull, where he had set two new creels and was astonished to find a smack wrecked on the rocks, a vast hole in its planks and its keel broken in two. He took the boat in as close as he could, searching for survivors or bodies in the water, but could see none. That puzzled him. Perhaps they were in the wreck. He landed the boat in a safe place, tied it to a rock and scrambled across the rocks to peer into the wreck. There were no bodies but there were barrels and bales, casks and long sacks. Some of the bales had spilled out on to the rocks, one of them split to reveal the contents. He crawled across to find that they were bales of feathers. Intrigued, he pulled out a handful, wondering why feathers were included in the cargo. Perhaps they were valuable.

He examined the casks and discovered they were full of golden oil—gull oil, he reckoned. He had heard that the people of St Kilda paid their rent in feathers and fulmar oil so they must be valuable. Yet a powerful man like their landlord, MacLeod of MacLeod, would surely use a steam boat to transport his goods to market. It was a mystery. Maybe the Factor was creaming off some of the rent and these were stolen goods so, if he took them, he would be stealing goods that were stolen anyway. That seemed like something of a justification. He decided to help himself to the cargo. He guessed that the big barrels held salt fish and were too heavy to handle so he would take the lighter ones. He climbed up to the top of the rocks where he had a good view of the surrounding land and the sea. There was no sign of anyone.

Grinning with excitement, he started to load the bales and the casks on to his boat, guessing that the casks of oil would be more valuable than the feathers. It was heavy work, scrambling across the rocks, backwards and forwards, but soon his boat was loaded. This treasure might be his salvation. It might pay for Catherine's fare. Yet he would have to leave the wreck as soon as he could, knowing that legally he had no right to its cargo, so he released the bow rope, jumped in and set sail. Then he had to decide where to go.

It would have to be Glasgow. Having neither money nor food for the journey, he would have to put into Oban in the hope of selling a keg of oil so he set sail eastward. He was worried that someone there might question his load but there was no choice.

When he reached the town, he covered the load with the jib and went ashore. Walking among the folk by the pier, he saw a man whom he had seen buying lobsters in Tobermory. Tall and as lean as it was possible to be without being blown away, he was inside a fisherman's jersey and under a cap, the peak of which shone with fish scales. Calum asked him if he would like to buy a keg of fulmar oil.

'And what would I do with fulmar oil?'

'It would improve your complexion for a start.'

'My wife is very happy with it as it is.'

'It would improve her eyesight, then.'

'God, you're an insolent creature! How much would you want for this snake oil?'

Calum snatched a figure out of his imagination.

'Four pounds. Only.'

'Away with you! Four pounds! Is it the oil they anoint Kings with? Four pounds indeed.'

'Three pounds and ten shillings, then.'

'Three pounds. Not a shilling more, boy.'

Calum spat on his palm and they shook hands.

'For your information,' said the fisherman, 'the going price for fulmar oil is twelve shillings a gallon. I could tell you were guessing.'

They walked down to the boat and Calum managed to heave a cask unto the pier, delighted to have some money. Having bought some bread and cheese, he spent the night on the boat wrapped in the jib.

Very early the following morning he set sail for Glasgow. It was a long journey and he had no knowledge of the reefs which could tear his boat apart. He had heard of a whirlpool north of Jura which, it was said, could swamp a small boat. When he was a child his grandfather had told him that it held a dreadful monster which would swallow any boat that dared to sail near its vortex and consume the sailors. One of the old man's stories, he knew, but still a hazard. However, there was a half-moon so the tides would not fierce enough to stir the whirlpool into a fury.

There was a canal at Crinan but he had little money and was uncertain of the dues. Besides, he had no idea how to navigate a canal or work the lock gates. He had to sail south and round the Mull of Kintyre, which had a reputation for treacherous currents and violent squalls.

As the wind and tide were behind him, he passed the point of Jura four hours later, but there he met a flood tide which slowed his progress so he did not reach Gigha till after sundown. Just south of the island he noticed the masts of several ships at anchor and, assuming it was a safe anchorage, spent the night there, listening to the chorus of seabirds on the stack on Cara, the small island in the south.

During the night he felt the movement of the boat change and woke to find the wind had swung to the south-west. That worried him as he had still to navigate the dangerous tides round the Mull of Kintyre and he wondered if he should wait until the wind eased. He waited until daylight and noticed that none of the larger vessels had made any attempt to set sail. Yet he was anxious to reach Glasgow and dispose of his cargo so he decided to take the risk and hoisted sail.

By beating against the wind, he reached the cliffs of Machrahanish in the late morning but, as he approached the Mull, the wind increased and the boat dipped dangerously with each squall, the sea lapping at the gunwales. He decided to head far out into the open sea so that he could have the wind behind him as he rounded the point. It was a risk as the swell out there was breaking and uneven. The bow slapped down with a thud in every trough. He glanced down into the dark water and imagined himself floundering in the freezing depths as the boat sank but quickly dismissed the thought. The fear lingered, though, as the wind flung his small craft around like driftwood.

He saw the floating log in the trough ahead but was not quick enough at the tiller to avoid it. The bow crashed down on the timber and he knew by the crack that it had broken a plank. Water poured in. He had to leave the tiller and the main sheet and scramble up to the leak. The boat spun broadside on the swell and started swinging dangerously, the boom dipping in the sea. He tore off his jacket and tried to plug the leak. The fear turned to terror as the boat began to fill.

44

In January 1850, the third year of the famine, John Campbell wrote to the Duke from Ardfenaig:

> The destitution is far greater here than in Tyree. I have heard this day of two instances of females fainting for want of food, one of them a woman who formerly got wool to spin and only returned a part of it in yarn and I gave order to MacQuarrie that such persons were to get no meal. I have however in case of accident told MacQuarrie to give a little meal in the most urgent cases.
>
> I am forwarding a list of tenants and cottars warned of removal, 78 on Tyree and 48 in Ross and Iona. As you can see they are mainly for arrears but nine for selling whisky and eleven for neglecting to build their fences within the time stated. One is for unruly conduct on the farm and another for giving home to a bad character.

In June he wrote again:

> It is impossible to describe the state of destitution both here and Tyree and, although I am using my utmost endeavours to ascertain the real state and relieve extreme cases, I dread very much—independent of all I can do—some may fall victim at least insofar

*as losing their health and falling burden on
the parish. Many of the crofters have not
wherewith to sew the land which will tell
severely next year.*

That month he saw 241 'souls' leave on the emigrant ships
Conrad and *Cumbria* for Montreal, 74 from Mull and 167 from
Tiree, at a cost to the Duke of £786.

As harvest approached many of the younger, more able
men and women from the larger crofts left the Ross to work
in the cornfields of the South, the men to reap with sickle and
scythe, the women to bind the sheaves.

John Campbell told the Duke that 'they are off in shoals to
the harvest in the South' but for those who remained prospects
were bleak. Potatoes once again turned to slime and he warned
that 'the people will be as ill off this year as ever.'

By December he had to write:

*I am sorry to say that the state of the poor
is bad enough. This will I think be the worst
year they have had yet, the committee funds
being apparently at an end and all their little
means exhausted. I have daily applications
for food but I distinctly tell them that not
one pound of meal is in future to be given to
anyone able to work unless he or she work
for it first and, unless they work, they must
starve, having had the offer to emigrate. Those
not taking advantage of it have no further
claim upon proprietors for relief. The number
employed are as yet but between 45 and 50. I*

have agreed to give some tiles for the drains
to the larger tenants and they are to employ
their cottars at working the drains at their own
expense. At the last meeting of the Parochial
Board I kept a great many off the roll who
could knit, considering it would be preferable
to promote habits of industry than increase
pauperism.

7th Dec. Letter from the Home Office to MacLeod of MacLeod in Skye:

> *Sir George Grey is not aware of the*
> *existence of any sufficient ground to justify*
> *the expectation, which you state prevails*
> *extensively, of assistance from Government ...*
> *it is not in Sir George Grey's power to hold out*
> *any hope that the population, which for the*
> *last several years has been largely assisted by*
> *charitable description, can now be maintained*
> *by grants of public money.*

When Calum sailed into Greenock, the smell of sugar
mills and the smoke of the foundries drifted across the water.
After the fresh air of the open sea, they were quite unpleasant.
The harbour was busy with ships of all descriptions, from tall,
square-masted sugar ships to small fishing boats like his. He
found a space on one of the quays, tied up, and walked up the
wharf towards the warehouses. He was fortunate in finding
a firm, Stewart and Shannon, which imported fish oil from
Newfoundland and asked to speak to the manager.

When he emerged, Calum was not impressed, a stout man whose waistcoat buttons strained to contain his paunch and little porcine eyes which studied him suspiciously. Calum imagined him with a cigar between his teeth and a glass of port in his delicate fingers.

'I have fifteen kegs of fulmar oil and was told that you might be interested in buying it.'

'Where would a fisherman like you get hold of a cargo of fulmar oil?'

'A fisherman like me, an honest man, can pay for it and I hope to find an honest man who will give me a fair price, when I sell it'.

'I would need to send a man to see it, but I'll offer you thirty pounds.'

'The going price for fulmar oil is twelve shillings a gallon. Fifteen kegs would come to forty-five pounds.'

'You're well informed, fisherman. I'll come down myself and see it.'

They walked down to the quay, where the manager agreed to the price and bought the feathers for fourteen pounds. Calum was delighted. A new life lay ahead.

45

'Calum!' Catherine gasped. 'What are you doing here?'

She almost tripped as she came down the stairs and he stepped in from the street below her.

'That's hardly a welcome.'

She was tempted to rush down and fling her arms round him and yet she hesitated, feeling awkward in his presence, as if they had become strangers,

'Are you going to invite me in?'

'Sarah has cholera. She's in there.'

'My God and you are still here? What about the children?'

'We live upstairs.'

'In the same house? Where's Sine and Duncan?'

'Sine is in the room there with Sarah. She's looking after her. We don't know where Duncan is, but we think he might be in gaol.'

'This is terrible, Catherine. We must leave with the children.'

'No. I'll stay and help Sine.'

He did not reply immediately, clearly shocked by the vehemence of her refusal.

'The sickness may be in us anyway. There's no point now. Do you want to come in?'

'Of course I do.'

'Well, come upstairs.'

She turned and climbed back to her room, listening to him following. Crossing to the fire, she swung a pot over the fire, keeping her back to him.

'I'll make some tea,' she said.

She guessed he was still standing at the door, so she turned to face him.

'This is a grim place you're living in. It smells like a midden.'

He was standing at the door, looking around the room with an expression of distaste.

'There's a midden at the back and some of the smell is likely the flux from the room downstairs. We have a roof over our heads and these are kind people. How did you get here? I thought you were saving for the fare.'

'My own boat.'

'You sailed here?'

'And I nearly drowned off Kintyre. I hit a log and it cracked a plank. I managed to plug the leak but had to put into Campbeltown to mend the plank. Had to spend two nights there. Then sailed up the Clyde and tied up the boat above the bridge. I have more than enough for the fare and plenty besides. There's good money in lobsters.'

'Oh yes, lobsters. I suppose you need creels for them.'

She watched him turn away and look out of the window. She let him squirm. She knew about the woman who made his creels but was not going to say so. Let him worry. Let him try to guess whether she had heard about his woman.

'It is good to see you, Catherine,' he said finally. 'I have been missing you.'

He did not move, though. He didn't cross the room to take her hands or try to hold her. She took that as a sign of his guilt, an indication that something had passed between him and this woman. He did step forward but sat at the table.

'I want you to come home, you and the children.'

'I am not leaving yet. When Sarah is better perhaps, and the house is clear of the sickness, but I know how things are in the Ross—the hunger, the disease, the endless battle to survive. Why would I go back there when there is work here?'

'Work? What kind of work?'

'I was working for a teacher, helping in his house. Mary works in the mill with Marion and Archie too.'

'Mary in a mill? What kind of mill?'

'Cotton spinning with machines worked by steam. A huge mill—McBride's—with more than two hundred workers, mostly women, and they are well paid.'

'That's dangerous work surely—dirty and dangerous. And Archie too? What can he do in the mill?

'He goes under the machines and sweeps up loose cotton. He gets paid for it.'

'For God's sake, Catherine, that's terrible. Under machines that could slice the top off his head and no-one would notice.'

'The girls look after him. Would you like some tea?'

'I would, thank you.'

A silence settled between them, Catherine finding his interference irritating. They were managing well until the cholera struck. She poured some tea and carried it across to the table. As she came close to him she noticed how healthy he looked, tanned and vigorous. She wanted to pass her fingers through his hair as she used to, but she resisted the temptation, wondering if he was tainted by intimacy with the woman. Yet she was not sure. She had no proof of anything untoward in their relationship.

'This teacher you worked for, has no wife to help in the house?'

'His wife is dead and he has three boys. He has no idea how to run a household.'

'He must be clever, though, if he's a teacher.'

'He is, very clever. He could write a hundred books with the things he knows—about Roman soldiers, about plants, about animals, about anatomy, about democracy. He's a Chartist but not a supporter of physical force.'

'Is he a God-fearing man? Does he attend the kirk?'

'No.'

'He'll be too clever for that, I suppose. Is he a young man?'

'Younger than us and quite handsome.'

Sensing his jealousy, she decided to rattle a stick in the wasp's nest.

'Are you in love with him?'

'I don't know. I admire him. He's kind, he's wise, honest, he loves his boys without spoiling them. He has taught me to read and write and he was teaching Archie before the cholera.'

Again he lapsed into silence, staring at a knot in the table.

Eventually he placed his arm around her waist and pulled her against him.

'Oh, Catherine I have missed you so much,'

He looked up at her, his eyes pleading for a response.

'And I have missed you, Calum MacGillivray. When Sarah took ill, I longed for you to be here. I thought that, if I was sick and my life nearing its end, I would want you there beside me, holding my hand.'

'I hope it never comes to that. That's why I think you should come home. You would be safer there.'

'I will not leave Sine at such a time. Not only is she seeing to Sarah but she has lost Duncan.'

'You said he might be in prison. Why?'

'He was at a meeting that turned into a riot. Windows were smashed, guns stolen, bread and meal carried away. The cavalry was called in. Duncan was there with Marion. Hundreds were arrested and some transported. We heard they might be looking for Duncan and, because he has not come home, we think he might have been arrested.'

'He should never have been there.'

'He thought it was to be a Chartist meeting, a peaceful affair.'

'Maybe something else has happened. Have they asked the police?'

'Marion has been round the stations but they all deny holding him.'

'I could help her. Many of the police are Gaels and might speak to someone with their own tongue.'

'Marion has Gaelic.'

'I meant a man with Gaelic.'

'Yes. I suppose you're right. Yes. That would be kind of you.'

She squeezed his shoulder, remembering how she had loved him, how he had lifted her into his house in Shiaba, made a daisy chain as her crown, a necklace of agates polished by the sea, a cradle for their firstborn. Surely he would not have lain with another, betrayed her in such a way. Had he not adored her all those years? And yet her mother was so sure of his adultery. She was torn between love and fury, the explosive amalgam swirling in her head, and she wanted to ask him directly but was afraid he might lie.

'Would you do that for them?' she said. 'Sine would be so grateful.'

There was a thunder of footsteps on the stairs and the children burst into the room.

Catherine stepped away from him as he stood.

'Father!' Archie shouted, ran across and hugged him.

Mary's hands covered her mouth as her eyes filled with tears. She stood, weeping silently.

'Are you not pleased to see me?' he asked her eventually.

She crossed the room and joined her brother, both with their arms round him.

Catherine watched the trio as they stood for some time in silent embrace. There was a glint from a tear in the corner of Calum's eye, a hint of an emotion which made her question her suspicions of betrayal. Yet, she warned herself, he could hold such affection for his children and still deceive her.

'You have grown, Mary,' he said, 'and you look well—underneath the dust. And you have grown too Archie. Look at you.'

He stood back, admiring them, with a hand on their shoulders.

'We thought you might be dead, Father,' Mary said. 'It was so long before we heard. It was awful.'

'It was the same for me, mo ghraidh.'

'How did you get here, though? We didn't know you were coming.'

'I started to run in Shiaba and didn't stop running till I reached Glasgow, through Glen Mor, past the Priest's Stone, past the three lochs, past Torness, down to Grass Point, over the sea, through Oban, over Loch Awe, past the Duke's palace, through Dumbarton and down to Glasgow. Running and running without stopping just to see you. The soles of my shoes are worn through.'

Archie looked down to see and Calum laughed at him.

'Seriously, Father, how did you get here?'

'I own a boat now and I sailed from the Sound of Iona to the Clyde.'

'A boat of your own?' said Archie. 'Is it here? Can we see it?'

'It's near the bridge. Yes, I'll take you to see it.'

Finally, he noticed Marion, who had taken of her headscarf and was shaking out her hair.

'Well, Marion. Were it not for the hair like a sunset in summer I would not have known you.'

'Not a sunset but a tangle of knots, a curse, a gift from my Ma.'

'How is she? Is she downstairs? That's terrible news about Sarah. I'm so sorry.'

'I must take some tea down,' announced Catherine, crossing to the fire to find the teapot.

'Is it safe?' asked Calum. 'If you go in with Sarah, will you not catch the sickness too and bring it up here?'

'I've been with Sine from the start. I could stay down there, if you like, if you think it better. You can see to the children now you're here.'

'No, no. Carry on as you were. I want to see you.'

Catherine carried the tea downstairs.

Sine was bent over the bed, bathing Sarah's forehead.

'Calum is here,' Catherine said, laying the tea on the table.

'Can you fetch me some warm water? I need to wash her.'

'Have some tea first and I'll fetch water. Has she had her laudanum?'

Sine uncoiled herself painfully, having been too long in the same position, and shuffled across to sit at the table.

'She had her medicine. What did you say about Calum?'

'He is here.'

'Good God. Why? What's happened?'

'He wants to take me back.'

'You should go.'

'No. I will stay and help. The truth is I'm not sure that I want to go.'

'Catherine! Why not? The Ross is a safer place. It's your home.'

'There's sickness there too. Different but just as deadly. People are dying of starvation, hordes of them at the meal stores crying for food. I can get work here and the children when the cholera is past.'

'If you don't die of it first.'

'It's not that anyway. My mother tells me that Calum has had a woman in the house.'

'Oh, Catherine. I'm sorry. Will it be true, though? You know what she's like, your mother.'

'God knows. I just don't feel inclined to go back. Afraid to find the truth one way or the other.'

'You could ask him.'

'I will one day. This is not the time. I'll go and fetch the water.'

She rose and left the room.

Upstairs she found Calum gutting a salmon.

'Where on earth did that come from?'

'I bought it. I thought you would need something extra.'

'It must have been twenty shillings or more.'

'More. If you enjoy it, it will be worth every penny.'

Such extravagance, she thought, but said nothing. He must have money right enough.

She emptied some boiling water into a pot, added some cold and returned to Sine who had stripped the bedclothes and Sarah's underclothes. Sarah lay shivering, her legs and lower body exposed.

'I don't know what to do,' Sine said. 'It is just running out of her, yellow, almost white and the mattress is sodden.'

'Just leave me alone,' Sarah croaked, her voice hoarse and harsh.

'I'll clean her and get clean cloth under her at least. Twenty years ago we had this and many came through it. The doctor gave them salt water and sugar.'

'Sugar? Calum can get some sugar. He seems to have money. I'll ask him and you need more cloths anyway. It's worth a try.'

She opened the door and shouted up the stairs.

'Calum! Will you come down here?'

He appeared in the doorway above, his hands shining with fish scales.

'Could you go out and get some sugar for Sarah and call at the rag lady's for more cloths? Mary can go with you to show you where to go.'

'When I've finished the fish I'll go.'

She returned to help Sine roll Sarah on her side and fit a clean cloth beneath her.

46

Calum did not sleep well. The thin blanket did not really insulate him from the floor so he woke stiff and still tired. The others were asleep, all the children on the bed and Catherine on the floor by the fire. He was disappointed, and a little annoyed, that she chose to sleep so far from him. He rolled off the blanket and sat at the table, not wanting to disturb Catherine by raking the fire. She had her back to him but he could remember her face as she slept, the way she would smile sometimes, her lips slightly parted. He wanted to lay his hand on her hair, feel her warmth beneath his fingers, but he was unsure of her reaction.

Moving quietly, he left the room and went out into the street. It was empty, apart from the midden man wheeling a stinking cart towards the river, its wheels rattling on the cobbles. He was about to walk in the opposite direction when Marion appeared at the door, a pail in her hand.

'I'm sorry,' he said. 'Did I wake you?'

'No. I was awake. I saw you leave. I'm going for water. I like to go early. There's a queue sometimes and I hate standing around. Good for gossip, though.'

'I'll come with you. Carry the pail.'

They walked down to the tap, which had been left dripping.

'Are you not afraid of the cholera?' he asked. 'Sarah must have shared your bed.'

'There's no point in worrying. You either have it or you don't. No-one knows how it happens. Maybe in the cotton from America. Maybe we will all get it. God knows.'

When the pail was full, he lifted it and turned back towards the house.

'Will you help me find my Da? I'm really worried about him.'

'Of course I will. What about your work, though? Will you not be missed?'

'Mary offered to take my place, if I had to look for him.'

'Do you think the police have him?'

'I don't know. That's the awful thing. Not knowing. He could have been attacked. He could have been killed. It happens. Just last week a man was murdered in the street and no-one knows why.'

'I'm sure he will be alright. Maybe he fell in with friends and had a little too much whisky.'

'He has no money for whisky.'

'We will look for him after we have eaten.'

Marion followed him up the stairs but stopped at Sine's door to speak to her mother.

'How is she?' he heard her ask.

'Weaker by the hour. There's nothing of her.'

'Has she had the ice?'

'All the time. Sucks it all the time.'

'That's good then. The doctor said to give her ice. I'm going to look for Da.'

'Good. Could you make some porridge before you go?'

'I will.'

Everyone was up when he entered the room and Catherine was at the fire stirring a pot. He carried the pail over to her.

'We went for water.'

'Good. We'll need more, though.'

'I'll do that.'

He placed his hand on her shoulder. She did not shake it off or pull away. That was encouraging. He squeezed gently and sat down.

'Ma said I was to make porridge,' Marion said.

'I'm seeing to it,' Catherine replied.

After they had eaten, Calum and Marion left to search for Duncan.

As they passed over the Clyde, Calum pointed out his boat with some pride.

'It's not very big. Did you sail it all the way from Mull?'

'It's big enough for one man and it would surprise you how much it can carry. I'm buying a bigger one when I go back.'

He looked down the river at the mass of ships west of the bridge—barques, steamships, paddle-steamers, schooners—remembering how his boat with its precious load had almost been capsized by the wake of a paddle-steamer.

'Yes,' he murmured to himself. 'A bigger one would be safer.'

'What did you say?'

'Nothing. I was talking to myself.'

'You can be locked away for that.'

He laughed. She was a bright girl and he was pleased to be with her.

'Take me to the stations you have not visited.'

'There is one off the High Street but cholera is everywhere there. Hundreds have died. I didn't want to go there.'

'That may be the very one, though. Show me where it is then you can come back to the Green and I'll meet you there.'

She directed him into one of the streets off the Saltmarket where he was appalled by the filth in the gutters, the dark narrow vennels with the houses almost touching, the stench and the lack of fresh air. It felt as if he was breathing sickness and fever, as if the thick oppressive air belonged to them. Destitution at home never led to conditions like these. At least there was clean air and light.

He found the house in Albion Street which served as a police station and walked in to be met by a constable so much taller than himself that he had to step backward to see his face.

A top hat and the row of shining buttons on his tunic added to his height.

'What can I do for you, sir?' he asked.

Calum answered him in Gaelic.

'I'm looking for my cousin from the Gorbals. He has not been home for a couple of days. I wonder if you might have come across him.'

'Has been missing before?'

'No. Never. It's not like him.'

'What's his name, this cousin of yours?'

'MacArthur. Duncan MacArthur.'

'From Argyll likely. And by your queer Gaelic you're from Mull yourself.'

'I am and Duncan's people were from the Ross too.'

'You will know John Campbell, the Factor, then?'

Calum was about to launch into a scurrilous portrait of his adversary when it occurred to him that the constable, being a figure of authority, might be related.

'Yes, I know Mr Campbell. He's from Islay I think.'

'Indeed he is. His wife is Islay too, from Mulindra. Her people are neighbours of mine.'

'She runs a soup kitchen from Ardfenaig for the poor of the parish.'

'That would be like her. They lived at Ardmore. An honest, God-fearing, hard-working man, John Campbell.'

'As is my cousin. He was working on the new railway, not a job for the faint-hearted as you know, out in the blizzards in winter and the scorching sun in summer. They were laid off a few weeks ago and now he is missing.'

'Duncan MacArthur, you say. I will have a look in the ledger.'

He stooped over the ledger, running a thick finger down the names and turning the pages until it stopped at one of the entries.

'Aha. Here he is. Main Street, Gorbals. Mobbing and rioting.'

'It can't be the same man. He would never be involved in rioting, a quiet gentle soul with a daughter dying of cholera.'

'He was not like that when we took him in. I remember now. Battling like a Russian bear and swearing like a soldier.'

'Driven to distraction by the prospect of not seeing his daughter before she died.'

'You have a way with words, my friend. You should be an advocate. He was working on the railway, was he? And his family are from the Ross?'

'A Gael like yourself.'

'As it happens, I have not submitted a report to the Fiscal and the only witness to his presence at the riot is a rogue.'

'He went to the Green thinking it was to be a peaceful meeting and was not involved in breaking windows or looting or disorder of that kind.'

'So he claimed. He said his daughter was ridden down by the cavalry.'

'That was the other girl.'

'I see. I will hand him over to you, if he promises to avoid these meetings and stay on his own side of the river. Wait there.'

He left the desk and disappeared towards the cells. When Duncan emerged, Calum was shocked by his appearance. One eye was almost closed with black bruising and a lower lip swollen and cut but he managed to smile when he saw him.

'Calum! In the name of God, what are you doing here?'

'I came all the way from Bunessan to rescue some stupid man from the consequences of his folly.'

'I'm glad you came. I thought I was for the gaol.'

'If I ever see you this side of the river or at a Chartist meeting,' said the constable, 'you will be in the gaol quicker than a ferret after a rabbit. Go and behave yourself. I hope your girl recovers.'

'Why? What's wrong with her?'

'I'll explain. Just come with me, Duncan. Marion's waiting on the Green. Thank you, constable. I can tell people now that I have met a good policeman.'

'Go for God's sake!' roared the big man.

Calum took Duncan by the arm and led him out into the street.

'What's this about my girl? Which girl? What's the matter?'

'I'm afraid Sarah has cholera.'

'Jesus Christ Almighty! How did that happen? When?'

'When you were in the cells.'

'Is Sine alright? And Marion?'

'Yes. So far.'

'And why are you here?'

'I'll tell you on the way and you can tell me how you come to have your face re-arranged. Let's get out of this place. The stench is unbearable.'

They met Marion on the Green and returned to the house. Mary and Archie had already left for the mill.

'Ma's in with Sarah,' Marion told her father at the door. 'We are all living upstairs, trying to avoid the sickness.'

'I'll go in anyway. I have to see Sarah.'

'It's a risk, Da. I don't want you to get it.'

'I've got to see her.'

'She's very sick, not able to speak. Poor Mother's worn out looking after her and I'm worried she catches it too.'

'Maybe I can help.'

'Maybe you can. I'll need to get back to work. Thanks, Calum, for all your help. We might never have found him without you.'

She kissed her father on the cheek and hurried away.

'I'm frightened to go in, Calum, afraid to find her dying. I couldn't stand that. It would break my heart. I should be strong for Sine, not break down in front of her.'

'Sine is a powerful woman, stronger than any of us, but she'll be mighty relieved to see you. She was desperately worried. She'll be glad of your help.'

'Right then. I'll go.'

47

Catherine heard Calum enter the room behind her as she stirred a pot of stew over the fire. They were alone together and she felt uncomfortable about it.

'We found him,' he said.

'Well done. Sine will be so relieved. Where was he?'

She turned round to find him sitting at the table.

'The cells in Albion Street.'

'And they let him go?'

'The constable was from Islay. He knew John Campbell's wife.'

'Good God!. I hope you didn't air your views.'

'I said nothing. I managed to hold my tongue.'

'For once. That was a feat.'

'If I had spoken the truth, Duncan would still be in the cells.'

'Yes, you're right. You did well, Calum.'

An achievement indeed and she admired him for it, knowing how difficult it would be for him to conceal his aversion to Campbell. In spite of his success, he looked quite despondent, staring at the table as if he was trying to find the words for something unrelated.

'Where is he now?'

'With Sine I think. Is she going to live, Sarah?'

'God knows. I doubt it. It would be a miracle if she does.'

'Terrible. Would you not think about coming home out of here? You would be safer, you and the children.'

'No. I told you. I'm staying here with Sine. I've heard you have company anyway.'

She saw the blow striking. He jerked back in his seat with his mouth open and his eyes wide with horror. His reaction spoke to her of betrayal.

'I found a poor woman living in a tent by the roadside with her children behind her. Evicted and starving, her face so thin you could see her skull. As near death as she could be and still living. I took her into the house and fed her children. What else could I do? Pass by like a Pharisee and let her die? '

'A good Samaritan.'

'You would have done the same. I slept in the schoolhouse.'

His hurry to include that detail was suspicious. She was tempted to ask if he was in the schoolhouse every night and whether he spent the evening by the fireside with her, but she waited for him to tell the truth, whatever it might be.

'Her husband was transported to Australia for poaching and she is waiting to join him.'

'Why did she not follow him immediately?'

'She had not the means. MacQuarrie is helping her now.'

'A kind man, MacQuarrie. He was good to me.'

'Yes. He is helping me to buy a bigger boat and he gives meal to your mother.'

'She told me.'

'She says you can write well now.'

'Yes, and read easily.'

'That's wonderful.'

'Yes, thanks to Mr Lamont. A clever man, a classical scholar. He took me to a museum and gave me a book. I would be working for him yet were it not for the cholera in the house next to his and I hope he will have me back when the sickness passes.'

'What? You intend to stay here?'

'Is there a reason why I should leave?'

'You're my wife. And I want you to come home.'

'Did you remember you had a wife when you took your woman in?'

'All the time. Every minute of the day I remembered.'

'May God forgive you, Calum MacGillivray. If liars burn in hell, you will be joining them.'

'It's true.' He rose from the table, crossed the room and took her hands in his. 'I swear.'

She looked into his eyes, searching for confirmation, hoping that they had not changed, but there was something different, just the faintest flicker, a shadow of something concealed.

'I love you, Catherine. I really want you to come home.'

'I know but I'm staying to help Sine. Marion may get ill and Duncan. It's been said it runs in families.'

He dropped her hands and turned away.

'I have to go back. I need to keep fishing, saving for the new boat, so that we have a better life when you come home.'

'I know.'

'I don't want to go without you.'

But she wanted to stay, not only for Sine and her family but for her own sake. The thought of returning to that remote township, ruined now by hunger, eviction and emigration seemed like walking alone into a prison. She wanted to see Lamont again, to read more, to learn about the world. His knowledge amazed her and the way his mind moved so easily from one fascinating piece to another without affectation or pride. She wanted knowledge like that. She wanted to fill her mind with it, master it like he did. She had become aware of how limited her life was, how stunted, like a sapling seeded on a bare rock. Transplant it to fertile soil and it would surely thrive.

She was about to answer when she heard footsteps on the stairs and the girls came in, shaking the dust off their headscarves, followed by Archie who was covered in white dust like a miller.

'McBride has laid us off, scores of us,' Marion announced. 'I knew he would.'

'All very well for the power loom hands to go on strike,' Mary added, 'but they sweep us along with them whether we like it or not.'

'They have a right to strike,' Marion said.

'All three of you?' asked Catherine.

'Us and all the younger ones.'

'That means no-one in the house is working. No money coming in. Nothing. I know about strikes and what they do to families.'

She stared at Calum but he avoided her glare as Duncan came up the stairs and he turned to look at him. His eyes were rimmed red and his lashes still wet.

'I think she's dying,' he murmured.

Calum moved across the floor to clutch his arm.

'Nonsense,' Catherine said. 'She would have died before this. There's not much of her but what there is as strong as iron. She will come through.'

'I hope you're right, Catherine. What are you girls doing here? I thought you went to work, Marion.'

'McBride has laid us off.'

'Why? I thought he was doing well.'

'The power loom weavers are on strike and he can't pass on his yarn.'

'For God's sake. What a time to strike when there's thousands looking for work and the city is swarming with Irish.'

'We should all strike work, every mill, every mine, every iron works. All act together and the masters will have to listen, pay a decent wage,'

'That'll never happen. Anyway, what are we going to do? We have to live. A prisoner in the cells told me there's work in the slaughterhouse. I can try there.'

'If anyone hears of cholera in the house,' said Catherine, 'they will never give us work. None of us.'

'I won't say,' said Marion.

'That would be a lie, the same thing at any rate.'

'I'll try the big houses. They won't suffer from the strikes. Surely they will be needing servants.'

'I'll come with you,' Mary said.

'And both of you will lie about Sarah?'

"What else can we do, Mother? We have to eat.'

Catherine wanted to forbid Mary from taking such a course, but she knew it was true. They had to eat. She could call on Mrs McBride and plead for work but she could not bring herself to deceive the woman. And what if she carried the cholera to one of the children? She would never forgive herself if one of them perished because of her deception, so she said nothing.

'I will leave you money for food,' Calum said. 'Enough for all of you for a few days anyway. I have go back to Mull and return to the fishing. I don't want to leave but there is little choice. I would sooner you came with me, Catherine, but I can see that Sine needs you more than I do. And you, Mary, will you come back?'

Catherine saw Mary glance at Marion.

'No, Father. There is nothing for me there. I want to stay with Marion. I'm sorry.'

'Don't be sorry. You must do what you think is best. You are old enough now.'

Catherine could see that he was hurt by her decision and felt sorry for him. She knew that Archie would stay with her. Calum guessed it too as he did not ask him.

Early next morning, while the cloud over the city was stained by the blaze of the iron furnace, Catherine walked with Calum towards the river. A cold east wind cut through her shawl and numbed her lips but she knew that it would speed his journey down the river. She took his hand as she walked.

'It was good of you to give us money. I know you were saving it for the boat.'

'I was saving it to bring you back.'

She did not reply, wanting to avoid that discussion, so they walked on in silence.

'What is her name?' she asked suddenly.

'Who?'

'This woman you took into your house.'

'Peggy McNicol.'

'You lay with her, didn't you? I can tell. There is something eating you inside.'

He stopped to face her, taking both her hands in his.

'Here's the truth of it, Catherine. I lay in the same bed fully clothed with her children between us. One night, and she left the next day.'

'She left, fearing what might have happened, I think, had the children not been there. And what would have happened, Calum? Don't tell me you were not tempted.'

'I don't know. That's the truth. I don't know what came over me.'

'Lust, Calum. That's what came over you. It's the serpent that lies coiled in all men.'

'I was glad when she left.'

'I'm sure you were. She removed the temptation.'

'I love you, though. I don't want anyone else.'

'I'm not sure you know what that word means, surprising given your way with words, but you will have time to think on it now—if you don't take another woman in.'

'Will you come back to me?'

'I don't know. When trust is broken, like a glass it is hard to mend. Go back to your fishing and make a life for yourself.'

'A life without you is not worth living. Please say you will come back.'

'I can't promise that but I'm not saying that I won't. I'm glad you told me. That is the first step. Now I have to think about it, try to untangle the mass of feelings in my heart. It's broken, Calum. You broke my heart.'

'I am so sorry, Catherine. If I had the time over again, it would never have happened.'

She watched the tears slide down his face and knew that he meant it.

They walked to the river where he kissed her hands and was about to kiss her lips when she stepped back slightly, enough to indicate that there should be no embrace. He climbed down into the boat, hoisted sail and cast off.

She watched the wind fill the sail and the boat slide into the middle of the river, its wake rippling behind it. When he reached the bridge, he turned and waved. The boat seemed so small and insignificant beside the immense ships further down the river. She watched till he was out of sight, wondering if she would see him again. She leaned on the parapet of the bridge and stared into the thick, brown water, a flood of dark despair bringing tears to her eyes.

'Are you alright, missus?' a passing seaman asked.

Startled, she turned to face him, suddenly aware of tears cooling on her cheeks.

'Yes, thank you. I'm fine.'

'I thought you might be goin' to jump, the look on your face.'

'No, no. I was watching the gulls. Thank you for asking, though.'

'No trouble. Look after yourself.' He walked on towards the docks.

48

Calum was glad to be sailing out of the city and into the countryside west of Anderston. Salmon fishermen were already hauling their nets on the south bank and, on the north bank, a flight of doves swirled round a dovecot beside the mansion at Stobcross. It was a relief to move past green fields instead of the dull grey streets and the smoke of the city. There was freedom to move, to breathe without the constant taste of sulphur, although the following wind still carried traces of the black smoke from the funnels of the steamers. He passed a barge carrying a diving bell and shivered as he thought of the men trapped inside it far below the surface with their picks and shovels. That's what he felt like in the city, trapped like the divers. Instead, he was sitting with one hand on the tiller, the other gripping the main sheet, with the wind filling the sail and driving his boat towards the open sea.

He was glad that he had told Catherine about Peggy. Although there was a risk now that she might not return to him, he no longer felt the burden of deceit, the constant fear of discovery. It was in her hands. She had changed, becoming stronger, more defiant. That worried him, wondering if the transformation could be due to the teacher. He was jealous of her admiration of him yet he was sure it had not led to any intimacy. She was not the kind of person to betray him or anyone else. Loyalty was part of her creed. Still, there was little he could do if, hypnotised by his intellect, she chose to stay. He had to wait. His aim now was to save enough to buy the new boat and to offer her and the children a better life. Lure her back.

He decided that, this time, he would use the Crinan Canal. He had money to pay dues and did not want to risk the sail round the Mull. Only an east wind would help him on that course and that could not be trusted. Sailing south-west down the firth, he reached the island of Bute as the light was beginning to fade and anchored in Rothesay for the night. The following day, after rounding Garroch Head, a warm south-west wind filled the sail and set the boat speeding up Loch Fyne. He was able to sit back and enjoy the soft roll beneath him and the whistle of the bow through the swell. Reaching Ardrishaig by noon, he put into the basin to wait for his turn in the first lock.

The horseman on the towpath was not pleased when Calum declined the offer of a tow and chose to row between the locks. On the long, level stretch north of Ardrishaig he was given a tow by a small steamboat so he could sit back and watch the countryside passing. By watching other boatmen he learnt how to work the locks and was soon in the Crinan basin on the west side and on his way home.

When he reached Bunessan he went straight to MacQuarrie's house.

'Well, Calum MacGillivray. We thought you must have drowned but there were no reports of shipwrecks such as yours. Where have you been?'

'Glasgow to see my wife.'

'I'm pleased about that. She is well? And the child—Mary?'

'All well. Mary has recovered.'

'They did not come back with you?'

'They will be coming shortly. The open boat was not the best way for them.'

'No, of course not.'

'Is Peggy still here?'

'No. She left for Australia while you were away. She left you a pile of creels as high as the house."

'That was kind of her. I have some money for you for the boat.'

He handed him three five-pound notes.

'Good heavens, Calum! Your lobsters must be made of gold.'

The thought of gold lobsters made him laugh.

'I have more set aside. I will need crew and new lines. The men in Kintyre use long lines with floats. I want to try that.'

'Yes, I have heard that is better.'

'It is worth a try anyway. I need some meal to take out to Shiaba.'

'More have left Shiaba, Calum, while you were away. The Factor rode out with men from Tobermory, drove them out of their homes and boarded the doors. I believe some went back as soon as he left but two families had suffered enough and left for Glasgow. Come round to the store and I will give you some meal.'

Calum carried the bag of meal on his shoulder as he walked out to Shiaba. At the top of the hill looking down on to the township, he stopped and sat on a stone. The sun was setting over the Uisken hills behind him, lighting the crow-coloured clouds blood red. In the still air the first hint of a slight frost cooled the sweat on his brow. Thin columns of peat smoke rose from some of the houses. He counted six. Half of the families had left, their doors barred, their hearthstones cold. The school lay empty, the stones of the small mill silent. They would never be used again. He was sure of that. When the last family left, the sodden roofs, untended, would soon fall in, the lintels crack, the empty rigs grow grass. The people, scattered over the earth, would try desperately to remember the scent of freshly sickled corn, the thwack of flails, the glint of sun on open sea. Far from Kilvickeon, their graves would lie under the blazing sun of New

South Wales or in the frozen wastes of Owen Sound. He realised that he too would have to leave, that Catherine, having tasted a different life in the city, would never settle here and, more than anything, he wanted her to come back to him.

He lifted the bag of meal and walked down to the houses. The fire was out. For the first time since his father built the house the hearthstone was cold. He broke some kindling from the cow stall and lit some straw beneath it. When he went outside to look for some peat, he found none. Clearly his neighbours, thinking that he was not going to return, had used them. He would have to burn the rest of the cow stall and bits of wood in the house. Fetching water from the burn, he boiled it and made some porridge. There were no candles so he sat and ate by the light of the fire.

Staring into the flames, he formed a plan. He would fish every day till the new boat arrived, setting creels for lobsters and crabs and using his lines for cod and ling, and save as much money as he could. When the new boat came, he would hire two men, and make new long lines such as he had seen off Campbeltown. He would get a carpenter to make a new bed and furniture for the house for Catherine's return and buy a cow in-calf for milk and seed oats for the rigs and promise Catherine that they would move as soon as she wanted to leave Shiaba. The Factor, no doubt, would see it as surrender. As he would himself, but Catherine was more important than his pride.

He looked around the house. There was indeed little left to show that they had lived there. A spade and caschrom in the corner with a flail lying on the ground. In the shadows the bed with a soiled chaff mattress and coarse blankets. A table with candle burns, a chair with a cracked back, the heavy meal kist and an oil lamp with a broken glass. All that remained of their life. It was when he saw the hand-mill that his loneliness and the emptiness struck him. He remembered her small fist gripping the handle as she turned the stone and her jaw set with the effort. She sang through her clenched teeth, always the same song. He had made a plan for her return but still could not be sure that she would come.

Having eaten, he went outside and stood against the wall, gazing over the sea. A full moon lit the shore and the distant peaks of Jura in sepulchral light. A curlew called over on the point, its melancholy twin notes echoing across the Sound. He remembered his friends waiting on the shore at Fionnphort for the ship to take them to Canada and their dreadful fate in the new country. The sea that had given him hope had carried them to their deaths.

49

Catherine returned to the house and looked in on Sine, whom she found stretched out on the floor, utterly exhausted. Sarah still lay with her face to the wall, her knees drawn up and her dark hair tangled like a heron's nest. Catherine took a decision.

'Sine,' she said, shaking her shoulder.

She did not wake the first time and Catherine had to shake her more firmly. When she did open her eyes, she stared round the room, trying to orientate herself.

'Go upstairs, Sine. Go up and get a decent sleep in the bed. I will stay with Sarah.'

'No, no. I'll manage.'

'You'll drive yourself till you drop and you'll be of no use to anyone. Go.'

Sine struggled to sit up, brushing her hair back so that she could see.

'How is she, Sine?'

'The same, but I think the flux is less.'

'Good. I think she's going to win.'

'She asked for ice this morning.'

'That's wonderful. Now go and get some sleep.'

Sine stood, shivering, for a moment and then headed for the door.

'Is Calum away?'

'Yes. He sailed this morning.'

'I hope he'll reach home safely. He's been so kind. A good man, Catherine. Not many like him. He did not need to help us in that way.'

'Not many like him indeed. Go. Go and sleep.'

Sine left the room and Catherine pulled the chair over to the bed, noticing that the ice in the bowl had almost melted. She would have to get more. She thought about washing Sarah but she seemed to be sleeping peacefully so decided it was best to leave her. She sat back in the chair and wondered how they were going to survive and what she could do to help. There were so many people unemployed and the streets were full of poor Irish, begging for food and sleeping in the closes. She could ask Mrs McBride but would have to conceal Sarah's sickness and that was a risk as Effie would have heard. She could plead with Mr Lamont but returning to his house might endanger the boys. She would have to visit the big houses, knocking on doors and pleading for employment like hundreds of other women. She was imagining herself standing in the rain on the steps of a mansion, begging for work, when the door opened and Marion came in, carrying a letter.

'A letter addressed to you,' Marion said. 'You must have a secret lover. Beautiful writing, copperplate. Look at the twirls and tails.'

Catherine held it in her hand, frowning as she studied the writing which was indeed elegant and neat. No-one she knew had a hand like that. Alexander in Shiaba could write neatly but not with such a flourish. Besides, very few people knew where she was staying. Mr Baillie perhaps but why would he trouble himself to write to her? His African servant? Or MacQuarrie with bad news of her mother? She did not imagine that he would write like that.

'Are you not going to open it?' Marion asked.

She broke the seal and opened it out.

Dear Catherine, I hope this finds you well and that none of your relatives or friends have been infected by this dreadful disease. After you left I was overwhelmed with a sense of guilt, having turned you away in such a peremptory manner. I have since heard that the mill is laying off hundreds and must assume that your relatives will be among those declared redundant. I can imagine the distress this must inflict on the household and particularly yourself.

I have, therefore, taken steps to compensate for your loss of employment with me and, recalling the wonder and amazement in your eyes when we visited the Museum, have approached the curator, who is a personal friend, to see if you could obtain a position with the Museum. He replied that

he would be happy to provide you with work
cleaning the premises, menial work I know and
not generously remunerative, but it may give
you some respite in these terrible times.

If you would be interested, do call at the
Museum and take this letter with you.

I hope, when this plague has passed,
that you will resume your position here. Both
myself and the boys miss your presence in the
house. The place is very dull without you.

Yours faithfully, Eoin Lamont.

'Who is it from?' asked Marion.

'Mr Lamont.'

'Mr Lamont! And what does it say? Don't keep me in suspense. Has he asked you to marry him?'

'No, Marion. Nothing like that. He has found me work in the Museum.'

'The Museum! What kind of work?'

'Cleaning I think.'

'The Museum?' A hoarse voice from the bed startled them.

Sarah rolled over and looked at them, her eyes brighter than they had been for days.

Marion rushed over and took her hands.

'Sarah! You look so much better.'

'Ice. Can I have some ice?'

Catherine rose and poured some loose ice and water into a mug and handed it to Marion.

'Where's Ma?'

'I sent her for a sleep upstairs,' Catherine answered.

Marion held up Sarah's head and helped to drink.

'Are you going to see the man at the Museum?' Marion asked.

'Yes, I think so. He may not pay well but it will be better than nothing.'

Catherine stopped on the bridge, gazing down the river where she had watched Calum disappear earlier. A loud flock of gulls were quarrelling over the floating carcass of a dog, one of them balancing precariously on its back. A seaman rowing past in a small dinghy stopped to fling a piece of coal at it, which caused the whole flock to rise screeching into the air. The carcass reminded her of Calum and the dangers of the journey north. His craft looked so small beside the sailing ships. She imagined it in a storm, swamped in a massive swell and Calum's body floating in the tide, gulls swooping to feast on his eyes. She shook her head to dismiss the vision and walked away.

She was nervous entering the museum, there being several gentlemen in the anteroom. She wondered if she should sign the visitor's book. She was not really a visitor, being there on business, so she pretended to be interested in the butterflies. Carefully and slowly she read the title of Papillo Menelaus, repeating it to herself until she could say it fluently. When the room cleared, she went over and signed the book, pleased with her new skill. In the saloon she saw a gentleman locking one of the cabinets and, guessing that he might be a member of staff, approached him quickly.

'Mr Lamont asked me to speak to the curator and to hand him this letter.'

'I'm sorry, I don't know Mr Lamont and the curator is very busy.'

'Could you give him a message for me? Tell him that a friend of Mr Lamont is here and would like to speak to him. I will wait here.'

'Very well. but you may have a long wait.'

She was astonished by her own impudence. Having Mr Lamont as a friend and being able to sign the book gave her a new confidence. She felt in charge of what was happening, no longer a puppet in the hands of people superior to herself. When the member of staff returned, she was examining the sea fan on the mantlepiece.

'This is from the India Ocean?' she asked, having read the information.

'Yes, ma'am. Mr Fullerton will see you now. He's in the gallery. Do you know where to go?'

'Yes, thank you. I have been here before.'

She swept through the saloon and up the grand staircase, passing the stuffed birds and animals. She recognised the eider duck, remembering its plaintiff call across the sea at home, the otter and the seal. As she entered the gallery she had to stop, transfixed by the colours on the walls around her—vast landscapes, bright seascapes, portraits of people and animals.

'I see you are admiring our Wouverman—Hunting the Stag.'

'I'm sorry, sir. They have taken my breath away, these pictures.'

'They are a magnificent collection. I believe you are a friend of Eoin Lamont. He comes here often and brings the children. A tragedy about his wife. So young. Still, the boys seem to have taken it in their stride. Now, I believe you have a letter for me.'

She handed it to him and he read it carefully.

'Well, Catherine. Eoin seems to think very highly of you. As it happens, we could do with an extra cleaner. You do realise that the work would be in the evenings or very early mornings?'

'Yes, sir. I thought that it would not be through the day.'

'I have a couple of women who see to the floors, washing and mopping the tiles and polishing the wooden floors, so your duties would be cleaning and dusting all the cabinets and exhibits—an endless task you will be pleased to hear.'

'I would be happy to work in any way required of me.'

'You're not from the city I can hear.'

'The island of Mull, sir. The Ross of Mull.'

'The Duke's kingdom. Your English is very clear.'

'The schoolmaster in Shiaba taught me to speak English.'

'He did well. Good. Come here tomorrow night at six and someone will show you what to do. Five shillings a week is the normal rate. Is that acceptable?'

'Indeed it is. Most generous.'

'Good. Till then, I wish you good night.'

'Thank you, sir. Thank you very much.'

On her way back she stopped on the bridge again. She was delighted that she had found work, particularly in such an exciting place, and yet accepting it meant that she could not return to Mr Lamont., except for an occasional visit. She would have to see him anyway to thank him for his reference. That would be the excuse, for she really wanted to spend more time in his company, to listen to him reading to the boys, to watch his eyes fired with passion as he taught, to feel close to him, part of his world.

It was almost dark and the gas lights, one after another, were blinking into life on the river. Behind her, carriages and carts still rattled across the bridge but fewer people hurried past. She wondered where Calum would sleep that night and realised that she never asked him about his journey down. Perhaps he slept on the boat—or did he put ashore and beg a night's sleep in a barn? She wondered if she would ever return to Mull. Her life was changing, new paths were opening out before her, exciting, promising, illuminating. She wanted Calum to share the adventures, to be beside her as she travelled. Stubborn, wilful, rash he might be but he could be kind, imaginative, child-like and loving. Probably he had betrayed her, in his heart if not in his actions. She tried to decide whether she could forgive him but a final answer eluded her. There were times when she longed to feel him close to her, to hear him laugh, to see him smile, but there were other moments when she imagined him with the other woman and found the thought of his touch repulsive. She wanted to suppress these visions, to cut them out of her memory, obliterate them so that they no longer troubled her mind but they persisted and surfaced every time she thought about him. Perhaps, she told herself, they would fade with time and her love for him would overwhelm them.

Historical note

The letters from Emigrants, the Petition of the Shiaba people to the Duke and accompanying letter from Neil MacDonald are from original documents, as are most of the letters from John Campbell. The excerpts from the Press are also from contemporary newspapers.

ACKNOWLEDGEMENTS

First, I must remember the late Donnie Cameron with whom I gathered sheep through the ruins of Shiaba. Had we not met, I might never have seen that extraordinary settlement and been moved by the sorrow in its stones. I would like to thank Sir Tom Devine for taking the risk of employing me to search in the Duke of Argyll's archive in Inveraray where I discovered the original letters and petition of the Shiaba people. I must pay tribute to the Ross of Mull Historical Society for its help and to its founder, the late James McKeand, and to James Hunter, whose 'Making of the Crofting Commmunity' inspired my fascination with Highland history. Thanks too to Skipper Alison Chadwick whose advice on sailing was invaluable. 'Shiaba' was originally staged as a play and I would like to thank all those young actors in Argyll Youth Theatre for bringing the words to life. My daughter, Erin Jordan, spent hours reading the MS and spotting all the repetitions, omissions and other mistakes, an indispensable ally. The book would never have happened without the team at Sparsile – Lesley Afrossman, who saw that the project had some potential and was brave enough to take it to print, Alex Winpenny, whose sensitive editing and imagination gave it colour and shape and Stephen whose meticulous proofing polished the text.